P9-CAO-923

COLOR OF
JUSTICE

Dear Reader:

How often do siblings become separated only to later reunite? Growing up in different circumstances and surroundings, they can find themselves not sharing anything in common.

J. Leon Pridgen II's sophomore novel is a tale of two half-brothers who live such an existence. James Pruitt, who was raised by his grandparents, connects with his older brother, Warren Johnson, twenty-seven years later in an unlikely situation. James is now a prosecuting attorney and Warren is on Death Row, charged with murder. James is forced to race against time to save his sibling's life.

The legal justice system is the backdrop of the novel that takes place in the South: Charlotte, N.C., where the author's debut novel, *Hidden Secrets, Hidden Lives*, is also based.

Follow the process of the legal system while readers trail one brother's mission to rescue his older brother as the talented author weaves a story of family and crime. He reflects on the notion that our environment can shape who we are.

As always, thanks for the support shown to the Strebor Books family. We appreciate the love. For more information on our titles, please visit www.zanestore.com and you can find me on my personal website: www.eroticanoir.com. You can also join my online social network at www.planetzane.org.

Blessings,

Zane

Zane
Publisher
Strebor Books International
www.simonandschuster.com/streborbooks

Also by J. Leon Pridgen II
Hidden Secrets, Hidden Lives

ZANE PRESENTS

J. LEON PRIDGEN II

COLOR OF JUSTICE

SBI
STREBOR BOOKS
NEW YORK LONDON TORONTO SYDNEY

SBI

Strebor Books
P.O. Box 6505
Largo, MD 20792
http://www.streborbooks.com

ISBN 978-1-59309-326-6
ISBN 978-1-4391-9885-8 (e-book)
LCCN 2011928045

First Strebor Books trade paperback edition November 2011

Cover design: www.mariondesigns.com
Cover photograph: © Keith Saunders/Marion Designs

10 9 8 7 6 5 4 3 2 1

Manufactured in the United States of America

For information regarding special discounts for bulk purchases,
please contact Simon & Schuster Special Sales at 1-866-506-1949
or business@simonandschuster.com

The Simon & Schuster Speakers Bureau can bring authors to your
live event. For more information or to book an event, contact the
Simon & Schuster Speakers Bureau at 1-866-248-3049 or visit our
website at www.simonspeakers.com.

For Souls of the Falsely Accused,
Wrongfully Convicted
and Unjustly put to DEATH

ACKNOWLEDGMENTS

Color of Justice is a work of fiction. The characters and incidents that transpire are of the author's imagination. Any references to real people or locations are used to give the novel a sense of authenticity and introduce the audience to the city of Charlotte—the home of the 2012 Democratic National Convention.

Thank you, father, for the words that you have given me. Forgive me for the translation and interpretation of them; I'm still a little stubborn. Know that He is not through working with me yet.

To all that have supported, wanted to support, and will support my debut novel, *Hidden Secrets, Hidden Lives*, I want to express my sincerest gratitude to you. In a time when discretionary dollars are a tougher invest in wants versus needs; I am humbled by your support. Thank you and happy reading.

To my Literary Agent and my friend, Sara Camilli, you are a godsend to me. For your endless support, I thank you. Several years ago you read a self-published novel that was raw and needed to be refined. In spite of its shortcomings, you took a chance on it and its writer.

Between these pages are that work. Let's keep it rolling!

To Strebor Books, an amazing home to so many fantastic and talented writers. I have found myself having to put their works down so that I can pick up a pen to create another. Please keep the words and titles coming!

To my brother, Tim, you have always been and continue to be my hero. A big brother protects you and kicks you in the pants when it is necessary. Thank you for that. My sisters, Stephanie and Barbara; my aunts Mae, Jacque and Edythe; my uncles, Jerry, Ulysses, Bill, Sonny, Donald "Duck," Leon and Freddy; nephews, Timmy and Antoine; nieces, Bria, Mariah and Brionna, in-laws, Sidney "June," George "Amp" and Mike, my second mother, Margaret, and my cousins Richard, Terry S, Thomas, Ricky, Renee, Sheldon and friends, your presence in my life no matter how long or brief constantly shapes, shifts and molds me. I am a better man because of you. I apologize in advance to any and all names that I have missed and here is a quick shout out to a few of my friends that are my brothers and sisters—Terry, Tammy, André, Shaunese, Rainaldo, Nadine, Steve H., Steph and Jay.

While I have taken a moment to mention my Aunt Jacque and Aunt Edythe, I would like to take an extra moment to thank them for their presence in my life. They have always been important forces in my life because we are family. They are my father's sisters who viewed my mother as if she was their own blood sister. When my mother passed on, and although I was grown, they have stepped up as my own surrogate mothers. My only regret is that the time I spend in the presence of my aunts does not last forever.

To my queen mother, Mamie Sue Mitchell Pridgen, and father, Timothy Garfield Pridgen, Jr., without whom, there would be no me. I spend time with them daily and they are treasured moments. Thank you for the great gift of life that you have given me. My mother's love continues to sustain me during times of want and plenty. From her I know what the term "unconditional love" means. Pop, in my last book, I said, "know that I am making peace with it; some days are better than others but I am getting to it," I am a lot further down that road, there are some bumps every now and then but I have gotten around the curve. God rest your souls, be at peace, I love you both.

To my wife, Gail, you are my Queen. My mother told me that one day I would meet a young lady that would love me, respect my dreams, support me and lift me up when the world would say stay down. The first time you came to Fayetteville and met her, she smiled and nodded at me. That was a wrap, then my big brother came in and within five seconds of his introduction to you, he asked, "So, you're marrying my little brother?" Apparently they knew before I admitted it myself. Thank you for accepting me as I am. With you I have transformed from a young man into a man, husband and a father. You are my rock and the foundation of our family. I will never be able to thank you enough for your support and for the two special gifts that we call children. Leondra, my princess, and Leon Jr., a king in the making, are the best of whatever I will be. I place great expectations on you because I can't wait to see the man and woman you become. Always remember that a diamond is not formed without pressure. I love you three so deeply that it stirs my soul; the mere thought of you brings tears of joy to my heart and it beats with anticipation of the next moments we will share. Gail, you are amazing and make this all possible. Thank you for taking the time to listen to my Northern accent! Baby, it has not changed!!!

1

I always loved this feeling. The nervous energy that starts on the inside. That moment of anticipation, when you know you're on the verge of completing your mission and execution determines success or failure. There was an adrenaline rush I had become accustomed to playing college football at Eastern State University, but this was one of the few times I experienced that rush as a prosecutor.

I have prosecuted a number of cases. They were cake-walks; usually of the open-and-shut variety. I'd worked on several high-profile cases, but that was primarily doing research or as second chair. This was the first time the reins had been turned over to me completely. At twenty-seven years of age, I was being touted as the sharpest and most aggressive young federal prosecutor the city of Charlotte had ever known. I would not fail. I would not disappoint. It was time to execute!

Judge Henry Walters was presiding. He was nearing the end of his legal career and according to his detractors, losing control of his mental faculties. When I looked at him, that's not what I saw. I saw a man who had fought for my civil rights, who helped defend the Wilmington

Ten. This was the man who would regularly drive to Greensboro in the mid-seventies to have lunch at Woolworth's lunch counter with his "black" friends. I had an immense amount of respect for the man.

"Your closing argument, Mr. Pruitt," Judge Walters said.

Judge Walters had clarity in his voice and sharpness in his eyes that I had not seen him display over the last month. I sensed his adrenaline was flowing also.

I nodded my head, took a deep breath and rose to my feet. I looked at the defendant and his table of lawyers to my left. There sat Paul Hughes, a baldheaded and thick-bearded, heavy-set African American in his forties. For all intents and purposes, he looked like he could be a fun-loving, joke-telling uncle. But this man would take a life just as easily as he'd take his next breath. Trust me, he had the rap sheet to prove it. I then looked at his defense attorneys; both wore dark gray Brooks Brothers suits and starched shirts. The only way to tell these guys apart were their different color ties. I thought to myself, *Let's roll up our sleeves and knuckle up, boys. This is the last round and I'm about to unload.*

I took my time and walked to the center of the courtroom. The only sound was that of my shoes clicking across the wooden floor. When I reached the center, I turned to face the jury. I made eye contact with as many of the jurors as I could. They were waiting for me to ease their minds and tell them it was okay to send Mr. Paul Hughes to prison for twenty years to life. I would.

"The law for me has always been black and white; no gray area. It is either right or wrong. No in-between. Crack cocaine is illegal. No one has the right to produce and distribute this vile substance that is so vicious that it destroys the very souls of our communities. I wouldn't do it, you wouldn't do it, but Paul Hughes would." That momentary pause gave everyone the opportunity to look at Hughes. "One of my responsibilities is to ensure that if someone does break the law, they pay for their crimes against our society." I gave my captive audience some time to let this sink in. Slowly, I continued, "You and I are here to ensure that the defendant, Paul 'Major' Hughes— a.k.a. Major Player—pays for his crimes. You've heard testimony from one of his lieutenants and a number of his minions. We have provided evidence from the records of his felonious organization. These records attest to the gross of four-and-a-half million dollars in the sale of cocaine, here in Charlotte. I'd say that was major for a major player. He played his game and he got caught. Now it's time for you to play, to get into the game, and shut him down." With that, I took my seat.

I was in the zone. In my view, the case was a slam-dunk. No amount of double talk or diversionary tactics would be able to sway this jury. It didn't matter how much money Hughes threw at his lawyer; they couldn't change what was about to happen. They were here to buy down Hughes' time and pick up their check. If they had just mailed in their closing argument, it would have had the same effect as what they were going to be laying out for the jury.

I watched Hughes' lead attorney get up, go to the jury, and make his feeble plea to them. By the time I'd decided to pay attention to his closing, he was done. He was done? Wait a minute. Weren't they going to roll up their sleeves? Weren't they going to knuckle up? They had just conceded the victory to me. It was no fun beating someone when they just laid down. This definitely wasn't the monumental battle that I had hoped for. I was disappointed and almost became angry that they hadn't offered more of a challenge. That is, until I looked at Paul Hughes.

Hughes sat there as if he didn't have a care in the world. He was trying to convey to the judge and jury that he was an innocent victim of a conspiracy. He was not. He was a predator. He had wreaked havoc on countless people's lives. From drug dealers, to drug users, to innocent victims, lives had been lost and forever changed. The lives of sons, daughters, brothers, sisters, mothers and fathers had been destroyed. What did Hughes care about any of these lives? Nothing; not one thing. He had afforded himself all the things that go along with this lifestyle. Money, cars, women, clothes. In other words, all the flash. The Panther and Bobcat games, concerts and clubs; if it was happening, Hughes was in the middle of it. To hell with Hughes; if his attorneys were willing to send him to the slaughterhouse, I would oblige them. Now I would get to introduce his slick ass to the flip side of that flash.

"Ladies and gentlemen of the jury, this concludes the closing arguments," Judge Walters said. "Bailiff, please show the jury out. The court is in recess until the jury returns with a verdict."

It was 3:17 p.m. I knew that if the jury didn't reach a decision by 4:30, we would be back here again tomorrow. I picked up my three-year-old briefcase and put my file on Hughes inside. I couldn't stand the look of this briefcase. It was a gift from my parents when I finished law school. It was a great briefcase; it just wasn't worn enough yet. It didn't afford me with the look of someone who'd grappled with the law for twenty years. My friend Chuck Mays asked me if I had ever seen Johnnie Cochran's briefcase. He said it smelled of new leather every time he cracked it open. Now how Chuck had acquired that knowledge, I'd never know. Chuck had a knack for finding out things that others simply could not. His point was well taken, but I still liked the idea of a well-worn briefcase. It'd always been a part of my romanticism with the law.

I left the courtroom and decided to go get some air. It was mid-April. In Charlotte, North Carolina, that meant the temperature was already pushing eighty degrees. Not hot though; the winter cool was still in the air and the humidity was still a month and a half away.

"James!" A voice stopped me as I headed for the elevator. "What's happening?" I knew it was none other than Jason Baines.

Jason was a fellow prosecutor whose concentration was primarily corporate fraud and embezzlement. But he tried to keep up with all the disciplines, and usually did.

"Jason, what up?"

"Dude, I'm hanging."

Jason was from San Diego. He was thirty-six and had never totally given up the surfer attitude. A wife and three kids had brought him to Charlotte nine years ago.

"What's going on with Hughes in there? Got a verdict?"

Jason always wanted first dibs on every case. "Not yet. We just finished our closing statement; we're in recess."

"How'd it go?" There was a bit of apprehension in his voice. He knew it was my first time flying solo.

I wouldn't look him in the eyes. I looked down and shook my head. Jason started to extend his hand to my shoulder as if to say, *Tough luck, kid.*

I smirked at him. "I was good. I was very good." We both laughed.

"Dude, I thought you were getting ready to tell me you flaked."

Usually when other people weren't around, we would kick slang to one another. He'd throw me a little of his and I would send him some back.

"Nah, cuz, I'm handlin' mine," I said as we got on the elevator. "Where are you headed?"

"Across the street to the office; then home. What about you? I know you're not leaving.

"Catch some fresh air. Kill some time until four-thirty; then I'm out."

Once we reached the ground floor, we exited the elevator and walked out of the building. We were hit with the smell of dogwood trees and a cool Carolina breeze. You couldn't replace that smell, but it also meant there was only about a week or two left before the heavy pollination began, and for me that would indicate allergy season.

"You going to the gym tonight?" Jason said.

At thirty-six, Jason was in better shape than most of the twenty-five-year-olds I knew.

"Not tonight. I've got to take care of some other business."

"Denise does the five-thirty and six o'clock news."

"So?" I said. I knew Jason well enough to know this was a set- up question.

"You're trying to leave at four-thirty."

"And?" Typical of a prosecutor, already looking to incriminate me.

"Not meeting Denise; trying to leave early. Catching a little side action?" Jason asked, with a wink and a grin.

"Jason, you know that's not me. Now maybe you being married as long as you have, with all those kids, maybe *you* could use a little side action."

"Side action? Hell, I could just use some action." We laughed. We'd developed a solid working relationship and a pretty good friendship over the last two-and-a-half years. Denise and I had shared quite a few dinners with Jason, Beverly and the kids.

"If you're going by your house before you go to the gym, you'd better get moving," I said.

"Yeah, the kids will have me saddled up with a rope in my mouth riding me around the house like a show pony."

"Bet you wish it was Beverly."

"Man, I wish. Dude, I'm gone."

He was definitely all California. I sat down on a bench and watched Jason cross the street. He often jokingly complained about his wife and kids, but he did enjoy the role of family man. Those kids, Jack, Shane and Rachel, could really wear you down. There was definitely different parenting skills employed in his white household than the one I'd grown up in. Jason's kids at nine, six and four had opinions of their own and veto power. The only opinions I'd had were the ones my father told me I could have. My mother had given me the power to be told what to do. Jason's kids had time out. I'd had time to pull myself together before I got knocked out. My parents were great; they still are. I just understood very early on that there were rules in our house, and severe consequences for breaking those rules. But I had no kids. Maybe the rules had changed.

To pass the time, I started to read the *Charlotte Observer.* There was an article about Warren Johnson that caught my attention. Johnson was a death row inmate on short time. Before I could read it, my cell phone started to vibrate. The text message read *"deliberations over."* Three fifty-nine p.m. and it was already time to go back to court. Forty-two minutes into deliberations and the jury was finished. I folded the paper under my arm, secured my briefcase and rushed back into the building and straight to the elevators. I pushed the button for the elevator, but it wouldn't come fast enough. I was only going to the third floor, so I turned to the stairs and bolted up, taking the steps two and three at a time. That adrenaline rush was back. On the third floor, I stopped to straighten my suit and tie and compose myself. This might have been the first case I was prosecuting on my own, but I had to behave as if I'd been here a hundred times before. I took a deep breath and opened the stairwell door to the third floor.

I headed straight for the courtroom, where the press had already gathered. I was definitely playing with the big boys now.

"Mr. Pruitt, why do you think the jury has reached a decision so quickly?"

"Will they convict?" The barrage of questions had begun.

"No comment," I quickly answered, without breaking stride. I went into the courtroom and to my table. Some members of the media had already taken their seats. They were waiting to see what would be left of Hughes. The courtroom wasn't as full as it had been earlier. The short deliberation period was the cause. I picked up a couple of glares from people who were with Hughes. It came with the territory. Didn't matter which side of the fence you were fighting on.

Mr. Hughes was sitting at his table, sandwiched between

his defense attorneys. His once confident demeanor had changed. He no longer had an unconcerned look. His face was now full of grave concern.

I sat in my chair and the court was called to order. The jury filed in. There was no attempt at eye contact between any of them and Mr. Hughes, or myself. I placed my hands on the table with my fingers interlocked, sat erect and looked straight ahead.

"Will the defendant please rise?" Judge Walters said. Hughes and his defense team complied. "Has the jury reached a decision?"

"We have, Your Honor," the foreman replied.

"How say you?"

"On the charge of possession with intent to manufacture and distribute, we find the defendant guilty. On the charge of embezzlement, we find the defendant guilty, and on the charge of transporting a contained substance across state lines, we find the defendant guilty."

Each succeeding guilty verdict sounded like a sweet melody to my ears. I gripped my hands tighter to repress my elation, not allowing my posture or expression to give my emotions away.

At the next table, there was no sweet song to sing. Each verdict fell like a bomb. In a matter of seconds, the empire that Hughes had built on ill-gotten gains had been reduced to rubble. He was stripped of everything right before our eyes. You could see the money, clothes, cars and women vanish in the blink of an eye. Paul Hughes was welcomed to the flip side of all that flash.

His Honor informed us that the sentencing hearing would be held tomorrow at 1:30 p.m. With that, court was adjourned for the day. Hughes slumped back in his chair amid tears and "Lord have mercies" from his supporters.

That tripped me out. A woman dressed in her hoochie best, sitting among three other women who were all dealing with the same thug, asked the Lord to have mercy. The Lord might forgive Hughes, but today's verdict was the legal consequence of his actions. He was getting his just due.

As Hughes was being led away, I glanced around as the courtroom began to empty. The judge's bench, the jury box, the prosecution and defense tables. The gallery behind me. The U.S. and North Carolina State flags that hung behind the judge's bench. I'd seen it all before, but today I wanted to take it all in, so that years later, I would still be able to savor every emotion of my first victory as lead prosecutor. I felt real good about myself and what I had done that day. Snatching up my briefcase with pride, I strode out of the courtroom.

"Mr. Pruitt, how do you feel?" asked a reporter.

"Were you surprised with the quick verdict?" shot another.

"Were you nervous prosecuting your first case?" This question and the familiar voice came to me clear as a bell. It was from Bob Campbell of WSTV-Channel 6.

I turned in the direction of the question. "I wasn't nervous; I was prepared." It was time for the dog-and-pony show to begin. "I don't think this case would have been given to me if I wasn't, but I had plenty of support from my colleagues."

"Sentencing is tomorrow. Any leniency," Bob said.

"No," I replied flatly. "The man broke the law and hurt a lot of people in the process. He didn't show any leniency to them. If he wanted leniency, he should have pled out before we presented final arguments to the jury. We are seeking the maximum sentence. Thank you, ladies and gentlemen." The elevator doors opened and I slipped into the car.

As I rode the elevator down, I thought, *Well, that was the end of my business day.* I was on my way to the South Park area to purchase an engagement ring for Denise. She co-anchored the news for WSTV, but was the sole anchor of my heart. I had made the decision to propose weeks ago. I just needed to get this trial behind me. The timing was perfect. We'd celebrate my first victory as a lead prosecutor on a major case, and I would ask her to be my wife. Yes, sir, things were definitely falling into place.

2

"Okay, man, stop playin'," Chuck said.

"Brother, I joke about a lot of things. This is not one of them." I was very matter-of-fact.

"Dog, it ain't too late. You haven't asked her yet."

"Right. We're here at Garibaldi's in South Park so you can talk me out of buying this ring."

"You know it wouldn't be me if I didn't take a shot at it. I hate to lose my boy."

Chuck and I had been friends since our first full contact practice at Eastern State University. I was the hot new freshman wide receiver from Asheville. Six-foot-one, one hundred and eighty pounds, clocked at four point three in the forty. Chuck was a six-foot, two hundred and twenty-one-pound junior free safety from Myrtle Beach, S.C. This guy was so cut, even his toes had muscles. He ran a four point five forty. The way I saw it, I didn't have anything to worry about. Oh, how wrong I was!

There was a crossing route that took me into the free safety's zone. The defense was in a cover two. I remember seeing the ball and thinking, *This is too easy.* I reached for the ball and heard a loud noise; then I saw that flash of white light. That was the last thing I saw before I lost touch with reality. Like a beaten boxer, I was out on my feet, but still managed to finish practice. Chuck later told me I caught the ball and had a great practice. To this day, I don't remember any of it. At that moment, we gained a ton of respect for each other. He started looking out for me like I was his little brother off the field. On the field though, he never let up.

Chuck played two years of pro ball with the Seahawks before a serious neck injury cut his career short. He'd only gained about fifteen pounds since he'd stopped playing ball, but the majority of it had settled around his waist. His hairline had begun to recede a bit, but not much else about him had changed, and the mustache and goatee that had become a fixture on his face still remained.

"Chuck, as long as you've been looking out for me, come on, man, I'm always going to be your boy."

"Just fuckin' with ya, dog. But you know Niecie ain't gonna let you hang at my clubs no more." Chuck owned two clubs—The Baha, one of the more popular clubs in Charlotte, and Big Ballers, without a doubt the hottest gentlemen's club in town.

"Chuck, you don't hang at your own clubs that much anymore."

"That's because I spend a lot of time working for you, and my clubs practically run themselves."

Chuck was a private investigator as well as an entre-preneur. He'd always been a hustler. In college he sold bootleg ESU tee shirts and sweatshirts after football games. We ate a lot of good pizza and drank plenty of brew off of that money.

"You're right about the clubs, but I don't catch all this grief about the work you do when those checks come."

"Good point," Chuck said.

The jewelry store clerk finished with another customer, and went into the storeroom.

"I'll be right with you Mr. Pruitt," Chuck mimicked. "Damn, dog, they know you like that up in here?"

"I was in here last week to pick out the diamond; they had to order it."

"Order it. What kind of ring did you get?"

"Not the ring, Chuck, the diamond. They had to order the diamond; but they set the diamond here."

"Why'd they order the diamond?"

"They don't carry the kind I wanted, in the store."

"You went all out, didn't you, player?"

I had definitely gone all out. The diamond was a flaw-less, half-carat solitaire. A one-carat, five-star solitaire usually cost four to five thousand dollars. A flawless, one-carat solitaire could cost twenty thousand. Needless to say, this half-carat number was going to have me on peanut butter and jelly sandwiches for the next year. Hey, a flaw-less woman deserved a flawless ring.

"You know Denise; she's worth going all out for," I said.

"Can't fault you for that," Chuck agreed.

"Here you are, Mr. Pruitt." The saleswoman returned with a ring box. She opened it and presented the ring to me with a jeweler's scope so I could inspect it.

"Damn, son!" Chuck always was good at expressing himself.

The diamond was set in a very nice, subtle band that didn't steal the focus away from the remarkable gem that was its centerpiece. I examined every facet of that rock with the scope and it was indeed flawless. I returned the ring to the saleswoman. She then gave me the documents that authenticated the diamond ring's value. Ten thousand, seven hundred and sixty-two dollars. I saw that price and I said, *Damn*. But I also knew I'd spend ten thousand more if that's what it took to have Denise with me for the rest of my life.

"Ten seven. Bruh, ten seven, she'd better say yes!"

"I hope so," I said.

"Is everything satisfactory?"

"Very much so." I wrote a check for seven hundred and sixty-two dollars. Then I pulled out my two-day-old Visa card with a ten thousand-dollar limit and promptly maxed it out in a matter of two minutes. I looked at Chuck and he just shook his head.

My cell phone rang as we were leaving Garibaldi's. I looked at my watch; it was 6:34 p.m. Just like clockwork, it was Denise. I had not spoken with her after the verdict was announced, and the six o'clock news had just ended.

"What's up, girl?"

"Congratulations, baby," Denise said.

That woman had a way of calling me baby that made my toes want to curl up.

"Thank you. You ready to leave?"

"No; looks like I'm going to be doing the eleven o'clock news tonight. Alicia's sick, so guess who owed her one? I wanted to celebrate with you."

"We can do that tomorrow night, babe. I wanted to do a little something special anyway."

"What up, Niecie?!" Chuck hollered in my phone.

"Tell Charles I said hello." Denise said this in an I-should-have-known-you'd-be-with-your-boy tone. "What are you two doing?"

"I was filling Chuck in on how brilliant I was with my closing."

"Well, I'll let you guys go so you can bond. Call me later. I want to hear about your great close, too."

"I will."

"I love you."

"Love you, too. Bye." Denise hung up after I said bye. She never said bye.

"Gotta go, right?" Chuck said. "It's already startin'."

"Actually, she thought we should hang out for a while."

"She's workin' late, huh?" Chuck smirked. "If she's workin' late, we could roll over to Ballers. I got this new girl in that…ah, hold up, man. I'll be right back."

Chuck was notorious for stopping conversations in

mid-sentence when it came to women. He was on his way to see three beautiful sisters who were leaving Montaldo's. It was an exclusive women's boutique. Chuck had a different walk for each category of woman he approached. Women coming out of a boutique, like these, got the smooth, suave Charles. He'd casually flash the Rolex while he tweaked his nose and introduced himself. "Hi, I'm Charles Mays. I played football with the Seahawks. Come check out my club, The Baha." No matter what they said, those would be the first three lines out of his mouth. The next move would be the club passes and some numbers exchanged. On the other hand, if he caught a woman a little more revealing in her dress coming out of a Victoria's Secret, she'd get *Chuck*. The head cocked to the side, leg-dragging player. The owner of Big Ballers. That was my man.

"Dog, did you see them women?" He loved meeting new women.

"Hell, yeah."

"Yo, the tall honey was checking you out."

"Really?" I tried to sound surprised. But a brother does love to hear that he's still got it.

"I got a number for you."

"Chuck, man, come on! I'm…"

"Just messing with you, Bruh." Chuck laughed. "You know I wouldn't do Niecie like that."

As much as Chuck ragged me about Denise, he did like the idea of us being together.

"Back in the day, you would have been all over that."

"Yeah, I would. I was a killer then. Thriller and killer."

"That was us. You ready to give all that up?"

"Yeah, I am. You reach a certain point, man. It's not about what you're giving up; it's about what you're getting to keep. I got the better deal in this one, Bruh."

"You did, ah, shheeo…don't tell Denise I said that."

"Don't worry; I got you covered." Denise knew Chuck was happy for me. I couldn't bring myself to break that to him; he was having too much fun thinking he had a secret.

"You hungry, Jimmy?"

"Starving"

"This one's on me," Chuck said as we headed to the food court. Chuck started to pat himself down looking for his wallet. "Hmph," he said.

"Ahh, damn!" My thoughts had already reached my mouth.

"What?"

"Man, I just spent almost eleven grand on an engagement ring; don't make *me* buy dinner."

"I think I left my…"

"Wallet in the car?" I couldn't count how many times I'd heard that one. That was my man.

Chuck and I ate dinner and had a couple of beers. We told a couple of lies and some jokes, but didn't hang long. I had some work to finish up and Chuck had his clubs to check on. We called it a night at 9:40 p.m.

At 9:45 p.m., I was driving home, recapping my day on the phone with Denise. I was tired and had some work to prepare for tomorrow, but in all honesty I wanted to keep the conversation short. If I talked to her for more than five minutes, I'd be telling her about the engagement ring and blowing the whole surprise. I told her my cell phone battery was low.

Denise promised to call after she got home. I usually stayed at her place or she at mine. The nights we didn't stay together, we would call each other to say good night. Seemed like my head wouldn't hit the pillow right if I didn't hear her voice.

3

I left my house a little later than usual on Friday morning. There was a lot of nervous energy within me. I'd almost backed into the garage door before I hit the button for the opener. I'd been living in this house six months and I was about two-and-a-half feet away from my first major domestic incident.

After I had hung up with Denise last night, I'd spent two hours rehearsing my proposal. Would I pull out the ring and get down on one knee, or get down on one knee and then pull out the ring? Should I ask before dinner? After dinner? During dinner? Maybe I should have it placed in the food? Hell nah, I wasn't putting that ring in any food. The only decision I'd made was where we would eat, Crawford's Urban Bistro. Crawford's specialized in soul food and live jazz. The jazz was great, but the food was even better. They made collard greens that tasted like my mom's. One time, I almost got up to check the kitchen to see if she was back there cooking away.

The garage door opened, and I backed out and closed it. I stopped halfway down the driveway so I could pick up my paper. Leaving late, I hadn't had the chance to scan it the way I'd become accustomed to. I grabbed it, tossed it on top of my briefcase without looking at it, and headed to the office.

It was shortly before 9:00 a.m. when I opened the door to my office.

"James," Michael Rucker called. He was the Federal Prosecutor for the Western District of North Carolina. My boss. He had Jason and several other prosecutors in tow. "Have you seen the paper today?" Michael was in his fifties. He was a stocky, gruff, bull of a man. Bushy eyebrows sat above eyes that were always intense, and could cut you with a glance.

"No, sir." I hesitated. For a moment I thought maybe I had dreamed yesterday. Maybe I had actually lost.

Michael opened the front page of the *Charlotte Observer*. The caption read, "Prosecutor Pruitt Prevails."

"Very nice; very well done." There was a trace of a smile on Rucker's face.

On the front page, in full color, was a picture of me besieged by reporters as I left the courtroom. I read the caption again. *Prosecutor Pruitt Prevails.*

"Thank you, sir." I took the paper and shook his hand.

"You're going to do very well, son." With that, he headed down the hall.

The handshakes and attaboys from my co-workers followed. Not all of the congratulations were genuine. Some of their comments were made for Mike Rucker's benefit, in an effort to seem like a part of the team.

Some of those rednecks hadn't said anything more than hello to me since the first day I'd met them. Big Ruck came around and tunes began to change. Once he was out of earshot, the crowd quickly thinned out. It was back to business as usual.

"Let me get that door for you. I know it'll be difficult to get that big head in there," Jason said.

"I'll go in sideways."

"How about that article?!"

"Front page, above the fold." I took a deep breath. "Business is going to pick up."

"So much for anonymity."

"It's the hot story of the day. It'll cool as soon as tomorrow's ink dries." One thing I had learned playing ball in college, you're only hot when you're performing. Tear your medial collateral ligament, meniscus and anterior cruciate ligament, and you're damaged goods. Even if the injuries happened after an All-American sophomore season.

"The ink won't be dry on this tomorrow. Hughes was a hell of a snag first time out. He beat two raps before you nailed him."

"He was ripe. I just got to pick him off." That was my attempt at being humble.

"Jimmy, quit the modesty bit. This is me and everyone else is gone. Talk to me, dude."

"Man, I knew it was heavy, but I'm tripping. Front page of the paper." We sat on opposite sides of my desk.

"And more to come. Local news ran some shorts yesterday."

"Denise told me. They'll be running more coverage after sentencing."

"Got the inside scoop, huh?"

"Relationships have their privileges. What'd you think about Rucker?"

"Very nice; very well done." Jason furled his eyebrows and spoke in a deep tone to imitate Big Ruck. "That's huge. It took three years before he knew my name, five until he complimented me."

As sharp as Jason was, I knew then that this was one heck of an achievement. The adulation was a reward for a job done well. It felt good, but it wasn't why I'd approached the law with passion. There's something to be said for giving your best effort every day. My pop always had said not to look for rewards, but to work hard and they would come.

"Big Ruck must be getting soft on us."

"You know better than that. It was damn good work." Jason shot that one to me straight.

"Thank you."

"So how'd you celebrate?"

"A little shopping. Chuck and I drank a couple of cold ones."

"And you didn't call me?"

"Like you could get out of the house."

"Did you go to Ballers?" Jason was leaning in and almost spoke in a whisper.

I had taken Jason to Ballers one time about six months ago. One time was all it took. I thought he was going to sign over his paycheck the way he was handing out money. He'd been begging me to take him back ever since.

"No, we didn't."

"If my best friend owned a spot like that, I'd be there like every day."

"Blah, blah, blah." We both knew this was just talk. Jason knew the way to the club, had an open invitation from Chuck. If he'd really wanted to go, it was there for him. Jason's biggest kick in going to Ballers wasn't the women, although that was a large part of it. He'd tip them and they'd back that thing up for him. It was more about hanging with the guys, suspending the reality of the day-to-day life and talking about what the women had done.

"Can't eat pizza every day. Sooner or later you'll pass up a slice."

"Good point. You and Denise celebrate?"

"Tonight."

"Anything special?"

"Oh, yeah." I let the response hang in the air. I could sense Jason waiting for more details, but that was all the goods he'd get for now.

"I'm getting back to work. Take a few minutes and read your article. You should be proud. I am." Jason stood up and extended his hand across the desk. I grabbed his hand and shook it as I stood.

Something as simple as a handshake could convey a

myriad of things. With that one, Jason, who was essentially my mentor and friend, who'd requested that I work for him and do his grunt work, who had helped shape my growth in the legal profession, conveyed to me that he respected me as a peer.

"Jason, thank you. Not just for the compliment, but for the influence that you've had on me."

After Jason left, I settled in to read the article. It encapsulated every step of the case. The tracking of evidence, Hughes's manufacturing and distribution operation. Manufacturing and distribution? Sounded like the CEO of a plastics company. There were a couple of quotes from me. Justice prevails, etc. To be honest, the article bored me. I knew the case; I knew the evidence inside and out. It was good pub though. Something to send home to Mom and Dad.

Two or three more cases like that and some more good press, and I'd get a bigger office. Not that I was complaining, but I'd often thought this one could have doubled as a broom closet. If my dad had heard me thinking like that, he'd have said, "A boy who puts on britches too big for him will fall down real quick." Of course that was when I was a kid. Not too much he could say now, with all the kids and rappers running around with their clothes hanging off of them. Whenever he saw that, he'd suck his teeth.

I continued reading the paper. As I was scanning the Carolinas section, an article caught my eye. *Stay of Execution*

Denied. It was another article about Warren Johnson. I recalled there being one about him yesterday that I never got to read. He was on death row for rape and murder. Now this was truly a high profile case that was pushed back to page six in the Carolinas section.

The phone rang as soon as I began to read the article. My first impulse was to let the voice mail pick it up, but with the article and the news coverage on me, it might be important. Looking up from the paper, I realized it was my direct line.

"Hello."

"Oh, Mr. High-and-Mighty can't call his own mom and dad!"

"Mom?… I was getting ready to call you."

"Boy, don't start that with me. I know you too well. I'd bet ten dollars to a dime you're working on your next case."

"Actually, I was reading the paper and relaxing a little bit."

"You'd better not tell your father that."

"Don't worry, I won't." My dad didn't believe in idle time when you were supposed to be at work. He rarely believed in idle time when you were asleep. A man with nothing to do would have nothing to do with him. Doing something, anything, let him know he was still kicking.

"You didn't have to tell us you won. No, we got people callin' us. Jimmy's in the paper; Jimmy's on the news; but Jimmy can't call Mama," she said, snickering.

Mom always had a smile and a joke. It was her way. She was my father's counter-punch. He was a hard working, hard driving, get the mission accomplished type. That's how he showed love. Mom was nurturing, compassionate, and when need be, the comedy relief. Two halves that made a great whole. Mamie and William Pruitt.

They had provided me with great direction. Dad may have been a little coarse around the edges, but that is what he understood about his manhood, and he had no qualms with it. At the core of everything he and Mom did for me was love. They had adopted me when I was less than a year old. If they hadn't told me, I would have never known.

"I was going to call later, talk to you and Dad at the same time." I found myself attempting to manage my father's time for him. He'd had a heart attack four years ago. The last year had been pretty rough on him. "He's awake. Let me get the phone to him."

"How is he?"

"He's...well, you know your daddy. He won't admit to anything bothering him."

Something wasn't quite right. Mom hesitated and her voice had become pensive. She handed the phone to my dad.

"Congratulations, son, how are you?" Dad asked.

In spite of his attempt to sound upbeat, I knew he wasn't feeling very well today.

"Doing good. What are you doing up so early?"

"Otis come callin' this morning. Talk about gettin' me up to go huntin'. I told 'em Bernice done put one knot on your head this week; mess with me and ya have two more."

Otis was Dad's closest friend. They'd been friends and neighbors for the last forty years. Dad was sixty-six and Mr. Otis was sixty-two, same age as my mom.

"Feeling good, huh, Dad?" I asked, but I could hear his breathing. It was slow and labored.

"Yes, sir; feel like I'm only fifty. Might go run a mile." He laughed and slowly started to cough. "I gots to take some medicine," he managed to say in between coughs. "Talk to your mama."

"Is he okay? Really, Mom, how is he?" I could tell by the receding of my father's voice that she was turning to leave the room.

"Not too well. He's trying to be strong, but he gets short of breath. His heartbeat is irregular and his arms and legs have numbness from time to time. He's just as stubborn as an old government mule. He's not used to listening to nobody."

"You all right?"

"Sometimes. Boy, don't you fret none over us. Your father and me 'bout to bust with joy; couldn't be any prouder. You know you are our gift."

"Thanks, Mom. But you know, without you two I wouldn't be here today. Love ya, Mom. Kiss Dad for me and tell him I love him.

"All right, baby; we love you, too."

"I'll call you later."

I enjoyed talking to my mom and dad, but for some reason, this conversation had felt awkward to me. My father always ended our talks with him giving me some tidbit to chew on. My building blocks of character, I called them. That had begun to change in the years since the heart attack. There were good days for him and some days like today. Tomorrow, hopefully, we'd be back to a good day, and he'd be handing me another block.

It was a special bond I had with my parents. I'd always fit with them. Most adoptees felt like they were missing something. They needed to put some pieces together. I didn't. Part of that might have been because I was an only child. But I had realized early in life how lucky I was to have parents like William and Mamie Pruitt. I had no idea who my biological parents were, didn't need to, but I could not have been raised better. The way I saw it, there must have been some reason why I needed to be adopted. For me, it wasn't necessary to know.

That type of thinking was due to Mom's influence. She could find something positive in any situation. When I blew my knee out, she said I could go to law school sooner if I didn't play ball. There was always an "up" side with her, even during the most trying times.

My best friend, Bruce Wells, had been killed at sixteen. He was a good kid, bright student, phenomenal athlete; showed more promise than me. His older brother, Keith, was always into one thing or another, and it was never good. He had a beef with this twenty-three-year-old guy named Demar Hooks over a girl. She was with Demar and seeing Keith on the side. Demar got wind of it and had it in for Keith.

Bruce drove Keith's car every now and then. On one

particular night, he borrowed Keith's car to go to the Circle K on Lynmore Drive and that's where Demar found him. Demar hadn't wasted any time checking to see who was in the car. He'd assumed it was Keith. It was a cold day in January, at 6:47 p.m., when that punk put three bullets in Bruce's chest.

Demar was arrested, convicted, and sent to prison, but it never had to happen. Two years prior to that incident, he had killed someone else and gotten off. That time, Demar had killed a small-time pimp. Same type of situation—over some girl. His story was he was trying to save her from prostitution. The claim was self-defense, but other people had said it was done in cold blood. The prosecution didn't care about the dead pimp. The way they saw it, two niggers got into a fight; one nigger's a pimp; pimp nigger's dead. Who cares? It wasn't *nothing* but some nigger mess.

If it hadn't been for that attitude, Bruce, my best friend, would still be alive today. I wanted to kill Demar myself. It made no difference to me what the consequences were. My dad asked me if I wanted to go to jail instead of Demar. My mother asked me if that would bring Bruce back. She said there was nothing I could do about what had happened to Bruce. That's when she had planted her seed. She asked me what I could do to prevent someone like Hooks from killing again. By the end of that day, my course in life had been charted. The decision to become a prosecutor had been made. That would prove to be my positive.

4

Sentencing for Paul Hughes was over by 2:30 p.m., and as far as I was concerned, that was the end of my day. It was Friday and I was ready to put this week away. It had been a good week, but I didn't mind ending it.

I got into my Pathfinder, opened the sunroof, threw in my old school CD, inhaled deeply, then pulled out of the parking deck onto College Street and headed straight to my house.

I still referred to my dwelling as a house instead of a home. It was missing something, but that was going to change soon. Six hours from now, Miss Denise Brown would be accepting my proposal. Leaving early would allow me to get everything in line before I popped the question.

By 3:50 p.m., I was shaved and my mustache was meticulously trimmed. I started to take a shower, but thought it might be cool to soak in the Roman tub for a while. I thought it might help me to relax and prepare myself for this next step.

I knew this decision was a major one in a man's life, as well as a woman's. For me, it was the next phase. A lot of my friends, partners back in college and, especially Chuck, avoided commitment as if it was the plague. I was sure part of this had to do with what they'd seen or hadn't seen in their own houses. I saw a black man and black woman who loved and respected each other. They'd had disagreements and argued like anybody else, but it hadn't prevented them from staying on the same page.

My mother had once told me to find a friend and fall in love. She had said that as long as you had a friend whom you were in love with, you could always talk. My father had a little different take on the matter. Oh, he'd agreed on the friendship stuff. He'd said I should experience some different women; according to him, that was only natural for a man. But when you found *The One*, playtime was over. He said that if you truly loved someone, you'd be willing to put their well-being first. You'd still both have your own goals and ideas, but you'd try to accomplish them as a team.

I finished my bath and got out of the tub. I put a towel around my waist and draped one over my shoulders, a habit I'd developed back in junior high. It was also a habit that irritated my mom to no end on laundry day. I brushed my teeth and hair, put on my deodorant and some Polo cologne, Denise's favorite. I stepped into my closet and picked out my beige linen slacks and the five-button, oversized linen shirt that matched. This was a different type of power suit. I matched this with a white ribbed t-shirt, a pair of light brown Cole Haan loafers, and a light brown belt. After I placed my ensemble on the left side of my bed, I lay down on the right side and turned on the television. The bath had really allowed me to unwind. I set my clock for 6:00 p.m. in case I dozed off. I remembered seeing 4:44 p.m. on the clock before I flipped thru a few channels and drifted off to sleep.

When the alarm clock went off, I shot straight up. Usually I'd lie in bed. Open one eye, then the other, yawn and stretch. Not this time. I was in the bathroom brushing my teeth again, and touching up my hair. I put lotion on, checked my deodorant, and hit myself with one more shot of Polo. Back in the room, I went to my dresser and put on a white pair of boxer briefs, then the ribbed t-shirt. The linen slacks and belt followed. My feet slid comfortably into the shoes, no socks. I picked up the shirt, keys and my wallet and proceeded to the garage. The shirt was laid carefully on the back seat. I started the Pathfinder and thought I was missing something. *I'll be damned—I forgot the ring.* I went back into the house and got the ring. I put it in my pocket, and was ready to go.

Denise had a condo in the heart of Charlotte. At 6:30 p.m., there was no traffic going into Charlotte, especially downtown. It was virtually a ghost town by 5:30 p.m. on Friday and wouldn't revive again until 7:00 a.m. Monday morning. There were a few restaurants and small clubs that drew heat on the weekends, but not the bustling you would expect from a burgeoning large city. For tonight, this would be the ideal setting.

I pulled into the parking deck for the Franklin Square

Con-dominiums, and parked next to Denise's black 535i BMW. Deep breath to savor the moment and relax. It was 6:53 p.m. Time to go see what my woman was wearing.

Exiting the elevator on the fourth floor, I checked myself one last time and patted the ring that resided in my left pants pocket. I turned the key to unit 4B and opened the door. The room was dimly lit and two aromatic candles were burning. Vanilla spice was the scent of the month.

"Denise, you ready, baby?" My nerves were in check.

"What do you think?" she asked seductively.

Then she came into the living room. She was wearing a black, sleeveless dress with spaghetti straps. It didn't cling to her, but it hit all the right curves and screeched to a stop at her knees. She wore black heels that caused her calf muscles to bulge ever so slightly. She walked slowly toward me and I could hear that slight friction as her pantyhose gently grazed the fabric of her dress. This woman knew how to reach me without putting a hand on me. She was smart, beautiful, and oh my God, was she sexy.

"You look all right," I said after I picked up my jaw and put my eyes back in their sockets.

"You're all right, too," she said, after she eyed me from head to toe. Then we both laughed.

We stepped to each other, kissed and hugged. Denise was five-foot-six and with three-inch heels, that made her five-nine. Her head fell to my collarbone and she arched her head slightly so her soft, gentle lips were brushing my neck. I pulled her tighter to me and tilted my head toward her as she gripped my waist more firmly and slid her hands upward to my shoulder blades. I wanted to hold her, protected in my arms forever.

"How are you?" she whispered in my ear.

"Very good, now. You hungry?" I asked, but didn't let her go.

"Starving. It's your night; where do you want to go?"

"Crawford's. A little dinner, some jazz. We can walk down there."

"Walk?"

"It's been a long time since we walked on a date, maybe college?"

"Did you make reservations?"

"Seven-thirty; we'd better get moving. The longer we stand here like this, the less likely we'll make it to dinner." We finally broke our embrace, but it was difficult.

"We'll make dinner. Make sure you get enough to eat; you're going to need the energy when we get back." Denise smiled.

On that note, we left for Crawford's. Riding the elevator down, I was anticipating our return. We would be newly engaged and there was no doubt that both of us would require plenty of energy. Emerging onto the street, the air was still and the temperature felt as if it was still in the 70's. It was a perfect evening for a stroll to and from the restaurant.

"I remember we used to do this all the time when we were in school," Denise said.

"I thought it might bring back some memories."

"Why'd we stop walking on dates?"

"We got cars. Besides, those weren't dates when we walked everywhere. We were just friends hanging out then."

"They were buddy dates."

"The operative word there is buddy."

Denise had hit campus as a bright-eyed freshman as I entered my sophomore year. She immediately caught my attention. The sister was holding, but I never stepped to her then because I actually liked her. Something in the back of my mind said, *Don't mess over this one.*

Being a rising star on the football team, I had girls coming at me left and right. Didn't have to work for it. Denise was far more interested in my mind and we could talk about anything. Our conversations stimulated and challenged me intellectually and, on occasion, emotionally. We'd hang out at her dorm, the student union, whatever; we were just friends. The guy she was dating at the time didn't believe it, even though it was the truth.

Our relationship changed during my junior year when I tore up my knee. It was the fifth game of the season. Almost immediately, the girls quit coming around and calling. Some of the fellas would hang with me, every now and then. Chuck would call two or three times a week while he was trying to make his way in Seattle. But

Denise was a constant presence. She was the first face I remembered seeing after the surgery. She was there with my mom and dad.

That was early October; by the following March, we were a couple. She was with me during rehab, pushing me when I couldn't or wouldn't push myself. She didn't do it because she was looking for a gold mine. Denise did it because she'd come to know me and realized I had something to prove. She observed how other people reacted and treated me after I was put on the shelf, like I was damaged goods. But Denise was my friend in the truest sense of the word.

"When we started calling ourselves a couple, I was driving that Cutlass."

"That raggedy silver Cutlass," Denise added.

"Funny, I don't remember it being classified as raggedy when we were rolling and everybody else was walking." Denise and I laughed.

"Then, it didn't seem raggedy, but looking back, you know it was. Admit it. Baby, it had rust spots and the springs in the seat would jab you in the butt. It's okay, baby; everybody's had a hoopty. Admit it; you'll feel better. Baby, you had the rearview mirror duct-taped in place," Denise teased.

"I don't care what you say; I'm not selling out on the Cut."

We laughed and joked and arrived at Crawford's in no time. As we entered, "Happy Blues" by Chicago greeted our ears. The lights in the restaurant had been dimmed for the evening dinner crowd. It would prove to be the perfect setting.

"Good evening," the hostess said. "Your name, please."

"James Pruitt. Reservation for seven-thirty."

She scanned the reservation book. "Yes, Mr. Pruitt, right this way."

The petite hostess ushered us to our table. I pulled out Denise's chair, waited for her to sit before I took my place across from her. The tables were covered with burgundy tablecloths. They matched the burgundy walls in the stairwell that led to the jazz club upstairs.

"So how do you feel now that it's over?" Denise inquired as she opened her menu.

"I feel really good."

"You were pretty stressed out for a while."

"Stressed? No, baby, I was focused on a mission." I looked at Denise. She wasn't sold on what I was saying. "Maybe a little stressed, but now I get to enjoy my personal life."

"Gives me more of a chance to enjoy your personal life, too."

I smiled and stared into her beautiful, deep brown eyes. This woman had totally captured me. The same way I had been since the first time I laid eyes on her, although I would not admit it then.

"What are you thinking?" Denise shook me out of her spell.

"I'm glad I'm here with you in my life." The time was getting near.

"Do you know what you'd like to order?" Tiny asked, cheerfully. Tiny was our favorite waiter. How he became known as Tiny at three hundred and fifty pounds, I would never know.

Denise ordered jerk chicken with collard greens, squash and onions. Collard greens were a specialty dish at Crawford's. The restaurant hung a poster that traced the history of the arrival of greens to Jamestown, Virginia, in the 1600s. I ordered the blackened catfish with macaroni and cheese and green beans. The food here was perfectly seasoned, but some Texas Pete hot sauce was still needed to make the meal complete.

"What do you think about the Johnson execution?" Denise asked.

"Not much. I haven't been able to keep up with it. Channel Six is all over it though."

"Tell me about it. I'm not too happy with it."

"Why? The man was found guilty of the crime; it's time to pay up. Doesn't seem to be bothering your co-workers," I added.

"I'm sure they don't mind. But you should know being found guilty of a crime and committing the crime are two different things."

"What are you saying?"

"That brother is going to be executed for rape and murder, and I simply haven't been convinced of his guilt."

"Baby, they found that brother's seminal fluid. Not around her, not by her, but *in* her."

"You don't think there was a rush to judgment?"

"Maybe. But look at the situation. A young white woman is brutally beaten, raped and killed. Not just any woman—Sheila Thurgood. Congressman Louis Thurgood's daughter. The suspect is a black man, a known drug dealer who..."

"Thought you didn't know the case?" She looked at me.

"I caught some bits and pieces," I said.

"I see. But you know being a convicted drug dealer doesn't make him a rapist or a murderer, and circumstantial evidence shouldn't get him the death penalty." Denise went into a Southern drawl. "This is good ol' North Caroliny, where justice can be determined by color."

"That's not just North Carolina; that could be anywhere. And this isn't about color. It's simple guilt or innocence. Based on evidence presented to the jury, Johnson was found guilty."

"Here's something for you." Tiny gave us a bottle of Merlot. "Compliments of Mr. Crawford. People have been in here all day talking about you." Tiny turned his attention to Denise. "And I talk about you all day, every day." Tiny smiled and politely moved on to his next table.

Thank God for Tiny. Denise and I needed to stop this debate. I had no vested interest in the Johnson case, and I certainly didn't want to spend this evening with Denise weighing the pros and cons of his situation. But I loved her fight. We might not have agreed, but I did respect her position.

Mr. Crawford came to our table to greet us. I shook his hand, and then he slowly cupped Denise's hand and kissed it. Mr. Crawford was a refined, slim, older gentle-man with a dark chocolate complexion and wavy gray hair; the kind of waves that came from a can of Murray's and a stocking cap. Looking at him, it was immediately apparent that he was the kind of man that women of all ages couldn't help but be attracted to.

We talked with Mr. Crawford until our food arrived. Needless to say, there wasn't an opportunity to pop the question. As had become our ritual, Denise placed her hands in mine, and we closed our eyes and said our grace before digging into the best soul food in Charlotte that wasn't cooked in someone's mama's kitchen.

After dinner, Denise and I were relaxing, listening to "When You Think Of Me," the old Eric Benet cut play-ing in the background. The cover band was beginning to set up upstairs, and my window of opportunity was presenting itself.

"Tell me how you see yourself in the next five years," I said.

"Career-wise or personally?"

"Either." I would ease my way into this.

"Professionally, I'd like to move into producing. I don't picture myself on the box forever. As far as the personal, I'm sure you play a part in that. Why do you ask?"

"This case had me doing some personal and professional inventory. Seeing where I want to go and how I want to get there. Sometimes you have the plan all figured out, then three, maybe five years on the road, you take some time to re-evaluate. That's all."

"Re-evaluate? How do I fit into all this?" Denise was smiling.

"Perfectly, if you want to." The moment had arrived. I started to reach for the engagement ring in my pocket when my cell phone rang. *Damn, I had meant to turn the thing off before I got to this.*

"Sorry, baby," I said to Denise. "Hello."

My father's best friend, Otis, was on the other end. My mom wanted him to call me. He was quick and to the point. I needed to come home as quickly as possible. My father had been rushed to the hospital and he wasn't doing well. I blurted out that I was on my way and hung up the phone before he could start his next sentence.

"I gotta go home." I was shocked. My mood had taken a complete one hundred and eighty degree turn in a matter of seconds. I was about to propose one minute and the next minute I was rocked to my very core. "My dad." It was all I could manage.

"When, now?"

I nodded my head. There were no words able to pass the knot that had lodged itself in my throat

"Want me to go with you?" she asked.

God, I wished she would. I wanted to tell her that I needed her. But I shook my head instead. *I can handle it,*

I told myself. If I kept telling myself that, maybe I would believe it.

"Are you okay?"

I looked at her, tears welling up in my eyes, shrugged my shoulders and very weakly said, "Yeah." I think I put the money on the table for the bill, but I'm not sure.

5

Denise hugged me at the door and told me to call her when I knew what was going on. I nodded my head and mumbled an okay to her. I made my living arguing cases before judges, communicating with fellow prosecutors for hours at time. I cross examined defendants without missing a beat, but since I had received the call from Otis, I hadn't been able to put more than three words together.

I left the parking garage and was home in a record fourteen minutes. I left the Pathfinder running in the driveway and went in through the front door. I kept my luggage upstairs in my spare bedroom. I bounded up the stairs two and three at a time. A hanging bag and a small luggage bag were all I needed. I snatched them up quickly and turned to my room. I put a pair of slacks, two pairs of jeans, a suit, a shirt and tie and some dress shoes in the hanging bag. Underwear, socks, along with my sweatsuit and sneakers went in the other bag. I grabbed my shaving kit out of the bathroom, gathered the other two bags and I was back out the door in less than ten minutes. I tossed my gear in the back seat and left for Asheville.

Interstate 77 North leads to Interstate 40. East heads to Winston-Salem and west goes to Asheville, and west was where I was headed. This was a trip that should take two hours and forty minutes; normally I could make it in two-twenty. Tonight, it would take me just over two hours to get there.

My cell phone rang at 10:49 p.m. It was Otis again. He told me which hospital room my father was in, and then he asked how long it would be before I got there. By my estimation, it would be another twenty to thirty minutes. He said he'd see me when I got there and was off the phone before I could ask him anything.

This didn't sit well with me, not the fact that Otis had called, but that my mother hadn't. I'd driven this highway so many times before, and only one time under conditions similar to these. When my father had had his heart attack, my mother called me after my father was in recovery from emergency triple bypass surgery. She told me he was doing fine and that he was going to be okay. But this time, I hadn't even spoken to her. That wasn't like her. My father was in trouble; that was something that no one had to say to me.

It was 11:16 p.m. when I arrived at Nations Memorial Hospital. I parked at the emergency entrance and hurried inside. I made my way to the elevator and rode it up to the fifth floor. The closer I got to my father, the longer it seemed to be taking for me to get there. I heard the bell ding as I passed each floor. When the door finally opened, I thought I had stepped off of what had to be the slowest elevator this hospital could have.

The waiting room was straight ahead. I looked through the Plexiglas window and spotted Otis. Once he noticed me, he began walking toward the door. Mr. Otis made his living as a mechanic, but he was now semi-retired. If it hadn't been for the size of his arms, one would never have guessed what he did for a living. Mr. Otis couldn't stand to be dirty away from his job.

My dad would tease him about the size of his arms. Said he'd been down at the shop bench-pressing transmission cases and engine blocks. My father had me call him Mr. Popeye. He weighed a hundred and sixty pounds, and forty of those were probably in his arms.

"How yah doin', Jimmy?"

"Okay. And you?"

"Fine. Let me take you to your mama." It was then that I noticed his eyes. They were slightly bloodshot. "She's been with him since they got here. It's not good."

Otis led me to the room. I looked at Otis, but I didn't know what I was looking for. Maybe I wanted him to tell me that my father was going to be okay. I opened the door to the room and sitting beside my father, holding his hand, was my mom. She was holding on for dear life. I don't think she heard me come in. At that moment, it seemed as if all her energy and focus were directed toward him. I walked into the room. There was a nurse and Dr. Gaines at the far right corner of the room.

Looking at my father in the condition he was in was the hardest thing I'd ever had to do. He was hooked up to different monitors with one tube running into his mouth and another into his nose. This was the man who had taught me about life, who still did, and he was barely clinging to his.

I went beside my mom and kissed her on the cheek. Barely able to maintain my composure, I said, "Hey, Mom." It broke the hold my father had on her.

"Hey, baby," she said. The look in her eyes told me every word I would need to know. She never let go of his hand.

I pulled a chair to my father's right side and sat down. I wiped at the tears that had begun to flow and tried to prevent any others from falling.

"William, William, James is here," Mama said, leaning in. "You were asking for him."

My dad opened his eyes and strained to see me. His breathing was slow and lumbering. I clutched his open hand and he smiled at me.

"Love…you…Love you," he said.

"I love you, too, Dad."

"Have…brother." His breathing was even more of an effort now. "Help him."

The words were muddled and barely audible. I couldn't understand what he was saying. They were also the last words he would speak to me in this life. His breathing became slower and deeper. There was a short breath and a wince. The EKG began to flat-line, and then a calming peace came over his face and I felt him slipping away. I looked at my mom and she already knew. She was gently letting his hand go; she couldn't hold him here anymore. It seemed to me as if she was able to hold him here long enough for him to say he loved me and give me the chance to say it back to him. And now, her job done, she was letting him go.

Dr. Gaines had been my father's primary physician since his heart attack. He was preparing to take my father's pulse when it dawned on me that nothing was being done to revive him.

"What are you doing?!" I yelled.

"I have to report the time of death," Dr. Gaines replied calmly.

"You're just gonna let him die? Get the crash cart. Do the thing with the paddles!"

"James, I can't," he said.

"What!!? What in the hell are you talking about?" I let go of my father and sprang from my chair. I snatched Dr. Gaines up by his collar.

"Jimmy!" my mother snapped. "Let him go," she said in an almost pleading tone.

"Mama, they're not doing anything." There were tears in my eyes. I was angry. "Why won't they help him?"

My mother walked around the bed to me. She put her hands on my right arm. Looking into my eyes she said, "Please, let him go."

Respecting my mother's wishes, I let go and sat back down in the chair.

My mother put her arms around me and pulled my head to her abdomen. I rested my head as she held me like I was still nine years old.

"Your father didn't want to be revived," Mama said, pointing to the D.N.R. notice on my father's chart.

"Time of death, eleven-thirty-seven p.m.," Dr. Gaines said before he and the nurse left us.

I looked at my father and clung to my mother even tighter and I began to cry like a nine-year-old child. This didn't make sense to me. Why would my father give up his fight so easily? I had just seen him during Christmas. He wasn't his old self, but he was okay.

"Why would he do that?"

"Shh, baby. It's okay," she said.

We sat in our chairs for another forty-five minutes. I didn't want to leave and couldn't bear to stay. Over and over again, I kept saying to myself that it was okay to go; I urged myself to just get up and walk out of the room. But my feet wouldn't move. I couldn't leave him there. If I didn't get up and leave this room, then this wouldn't be true. The reality of my father's death was on the other side of the door. There would be no more time to talk, or laugh, or sit beside each other and watch a football game. Once I was on the other side of that door, all I'd have of my father would be the memories. One day, I'd be happy when I remembered them, but it sure wouldn't be anytime soon. I was not ready for that.

I looked at my mother, who seemed to be accepting my father's death a lot better than me. Her strength amazed me. She rubbed the face of the man she had loved for more than forty-seven years with such care. As much as that moment hurt, I was being extremely selfish. Until now, my only concern had been what I was feeling. The woman who provided balance to my father and me was left without the biggest part of hers. She needed to be able to lean on me as much as I needed to lean on her.

Standing up, I leaned over my father and kissed him on his forehead. It already felt cool as my lips touched him.

"Thank you for all that you've done for me. I love you," I said softly, and then I walked around the bed to my mother. I stroked her beautiful gray hair and kissed her cheek.

"Mom, I'll be right outside."

"Okay," she responded quietly.

"Whenever you're ready, I'll be right out there." I was trying to maintain my composure, for her sake. She looked at me and nodded.

There was so much more that I wanted to say; to tell her that it would be okay. We'd get through this, and he wouldn't suffer anymore. This was how it was supposed to be, but I couldn't bring myself to tell her something I didn't believe. Instead, I went to the door and looked back at my dad with my mom beside him. Mom needed time to say goodbye to Dad alone. I turned and walked out the door.

"How ya doin', Jimmy?" Otis asked.

I nodded my head, then clenched my teeth and shook my head, not able to utter a word.

"I'll take ya'll home." Otis put his arm around my shoulder.

"It's okay; we'll be fine."

"Looka here, boy, me an ya daddy was like kin and I know how I'm feelin'. You's his only boy, an in there's the onlyest person he could love more'n you. You been through a lot tonight. I'm a see to it ya get home safe."

"Yes, sir." What I wanted was for my dad to be the one to drive us home.

6

Otis drove us home. What little conversation we had was stiff and awkward. Otis pulled into the driveway of my parents' home. My mother was in the front seat and became very rigid as Otis stopped in front of the garage. Then I turned and said, "Yes, sir, I like it."

"Ya get good mileage?"

"Whew, Mr. Otis, I don't want to talk about gas. The mileage is good, but the price of gas is what kills me."

"What you need is a little car that gets good gas mileage. That way, when you take long drives, you can save some money."

"I might have to do that." We were attempting to make small talk. What we were really doing was allowing my mother time to go inside, when she was ready.

This would be the first time she'd enter the house without my father. The first time she would cook in there, clean, sleep in her bed alone, and eat. All of these things would be tremendous undertakings. So we sat there and waited.

"We'd better go inside," Mama said after a few minutes.

"You sure you're ready, Mamie?" Otis wanted to make sure.

"As ready as I'll ever be." Mama took a deep breath.

"Let me get that for you, Mama." Getting out of the back seat, I opened the door for her.

Otis also got out. "Do you want me to go in with you?"

"No, Otis, I'll be fine. Jimmy's with me."

"Now it ain't no trouble at all."

"We'll be fine." Mama was already heading for the door.

"I'll get Bernice to take me back down to the hospital tomorrow and pick your car up."

"That'll be fine, Otis."

"Thanks for all your help, Mr. Otis." I tried to smile.

"If ya'll need anything, anytime, call. We right down the road."

"Yes, sir."

Otis looked over my shoulder. "Take care of your mama. You ain't got to say much; just sit with her. She'll tell ya all ya need to know when she ready." He watched Mama as she opened the door and went into the house.

"I'll take care of her."

"I know you will. You're ya daddy's boy. Let me get on to the house; you know how Bernice is. She was upset when I told her."

We shook hands; he pulled me to him and hugged me much like a father would hug his son and patted me on the back. Then Otis made a beeline down the street to his house. He and Bernice lived just two doors away.

I grabbed my bags out of the back seat, shut the door and made my way up the walkway to the front door. Twenty yards to the door now felt more like two hundred. The shrubbery was trimmed and the azaleas were blooming. The grass was neatly cut in front of my parents' ranch-style brick home. Everything was the same as I had always remembered my parents' home to be; yet none of it would ever be the same again. I walked into the house.

"Do you want something to eat?" Mom was already going to work in the kitchen.

"No, ma'am, I'll just put these bags in my room." Funny how easily you could fall back into old habits. "Let me put this up and I'll fix you something to eat."

"I'm not hungry," she replied.

Not knowing what else to say, I moved on to my room. Everything in my old room was in the same place, exactly the way I had left it when I left for school. Trophies on the dresser, plaques on the wall next to the Michael Jordan poster I'd refused to take down as a kid. I put my luggage in the closet. I'd unpack tomorrow; it was almost 1:30 a.m. I wanted to call Denise, but I could wait until morning. I heard a noise. It couldn't be what I thought it was. Mom was in the dining room vacuuming a clean rug.

I hurried downstairs. "What are you doing, Ma?" Not hearing me, she kept vacuuming. "Ma!" She looked up. "What are you doing?"

"Cleaning up," she said as she turned off the vacuum.

"There's gonna be a lot of folk comin' by. I don't want them comin' to no junky house."

The house was spotless, as usual. Growing up, whenever Mom had something on her mind, she cleaned. You could tell what she was thinking about by what she cleaned. If it was money, she'd start in the kitchen. Family sick, bathrooms. But whenever it was Dad, she'd start vacuuming the living room. There wasn't any stopping her once she got started.

"Mind if I help?"

"Not at all, baby. You can start dusting."

Mom started the vacuum again, and I got a rag and the polish. Mom was wasting no time; she was halfway across the floor when I came back in to start dusting.

"Jimmy, move that couch over and get the coffee table out of the way." Mamie was on the move, and cleaned behind them. "Put those back and slide the love seat out."

She was barking out orders like a drill sergeant. What had I gotten myself into? She finished behind the love seat and I put that back before she could get the words out. Mom started working up a sweat, and I had one going, too.

"Give me a minute to sit down," Mom said as we sat on the couch.

"Mom, you don't need to push yourself so hard."

"I need to get this house ready for company."

"I'm not saying don't do it; just take it a little easier."

"Okay. I'm surprised the phone's not ringing off the

hook. You know Otis called Bernice from the hospital. I'm sure half the town knows by now."

"If not now, they will by tomorrow. Mrs. Bernice sure can get the word out."

"Yes, she can." We sat there in silence for a few minutes. Mom started looking around. "Your father proposed to me in Big Momma's living room. Did you know that?"

"No, I didn't."

"He asked me in front of everybody, Big Momma, Paw Paw, everybody. Ever since then, it's been my favorite room in the house."

"Did he get down on his knee in front of everybody, too?"

"He sure did." Mama smiled. Paw Paw was her father. "Your father came over to our house that evening and he was so nervous, the poor thing. He was wiping his sweaty forehead and clearing his throat every twenty seconds. He had a suit and tie on, and sat straight up in the chair beside me. Finally, he asked Paw Paw and Big Momma if he could talk to them in the kitchen. A few minutes later, they came back into the room. Big Momma was smiling, but Paw Paw was all business. He pointed to a spot on the floor and that's where your daddy went. Then Paw Paw called all six of the other kids in. When everybody was in there, he said, 'Go on, boy.' Your father had been standing there waiting so long I thought his knees were going to knock. He bent down to one knee and asked me to marry him." Mama paused.

"So what did you say, Mom?"

"I told him yes soon as he got it out his mouth. Big Momma hugged me and Paw Paw grinned, stuck out his hand and welcomed him to the family. Willie smiled and shook Paw Paw's hand so hard I thought he'd pull his arm off. He kept saying thank you, Mr. Garret, thank you."

"I'll bet that was something to see." I'd never known my dad to be nervous about anything. The silence returned and we sat there for a few more minutes, neither one of us ready to move to the next topic.

"Have you thought about any of the arrangements?" I hated to ask that question.

"We…your father and I…let's start on the next room."

It was something we needed to discuss, but I had no qualms about cleaning more before we got to that. I would try to be patient and take the advice that Mr. Otis gave me. The routine changed in the den, me with the vacuum, while Mom started polishing and dusting. I took my time with the vacuum. Mom would cut her eyes every so often to make sure I was getting every spot. Nobody could clean her house the way she could, she'd always say. When I finished with the vacuum, I grabbed another rag to help her dust.

"You did real good on the floor," she said, inspecting.

"I'd better; you'd be right behind me if I didn't."

"Hmph. Make sure you get behind that TV."

"Yes, ma'am." I did the best I could to try to clean what

was already spotless. If that's what it took to keep my mother company tonight, that's what I would do.

We worked our way from the den to the kitchen. Mom swept the floor and I got the mop and bucket ready. When she had finished sweeping, I took the mop to the vinyl floor. Mom sat down for a quick break.

"You don't have to worry about the arrangements."

I stopped mopping. "I'll take care of it, Mama. I don't want you…"

"It's all taken care of," she said, cutting me off.

"Ma'am?"

"Your father and I have taken care of it. Otis will call Barkley's Funeral Home first thing in the morning to let them know it's time."

I stood there dumbfounded. Again, the words failed to find a way to my mouth. My mother looked at me for a second, allowing the comment to settle before she spoke.

"The funeral will be on Monday at 2:00 p.m. All the details have been handled." She paused and took a deep breath. "We did that about a month ago."

"A month ago?" I sat down at the kitchen table.

"Your father wasn't doing well for a while. Ever since he had that heart attack four years ago, he's had trouble. The last few months he was getting worse, and he didn't want to leave me, you, or anybody with the burden of tending to his affairs. We talked about it and decided to get everything set before this happened."

Sitting there listening to my mother tell me they'd

decided to get his affairs in order made me angry. I'd been cheated. I was angry at him; I was angry at her... and I was angry with myself for being angry.

"Why didn't anybody tell me what was going on? I should've known!"

"Your father didn't want you to worry about him. He asked me not to tell you. As much as I wanted to tell you, I did what your father asked me to do." Mom maintained a calm, rational tone.

"Why didn't he want me to know?"

"What would you have done?"

"I would have dropped everything. I would have been here with him."

"That's what your father knew, and he didn't want that to happen. He knew you were in the middle of that case with that Hughes fella. He didn't want your thinkin' about him to mess up your first big case. Your father was so proud of you, he didn't want anything to stand in your way."

"I could have been here."

"You were here. You got to say goodbye to your father and tell him you loved him and so did I." Her eyes began to water. "Being here any sooner or longer wouldn't stop what happened, but he left knowing how much he was loved."

I sat there, quiet. Not knowing what to say and still feeling like I'd been cheated. As what she had said began to sink in, I was sinking deeper into my anger. I had been dropped in a forest of conflicting emotions and struggling to find my way out of the darkness.

"I know you're upset about how we handled this, and I'm sorry. Your father and I had come to grips with what was going to happen to him. It was four years and he was tired; he was ready to rest. You can be upset, but it won't bring your father back."

There it was. A way to climb out of this dark place I was heading into. My anger wasn't with him or my mom or the way this issue was handled. I was angry because my father was gone. Mom had just knocked down the first tree. She had started to clear the path, but it would be up to me to work through the rest of the forest.

"I had no idea that he was…"

"He wouldn't have it any other way." She shook her head and had a slight smile on her face.

"I never heard him complain about being sick or hurting, even when I was young."

"That was your father's way, always worried about someone else, but didn't want anybody taking their time for him."

My mother explained to me that the bypass surgery my father had had after his heart attack solved only part of his problem. Eventually, he would have needed to have transplant surgery. The diet and exercise program he was on was a struggle that had gotten progressively harder to follow and the last year it was virtually non-existent. He also knew the chances of a sixty-five-year-old man receiving a heart transplant weren't going to be very good. He told her that he wouldn't quit fighting, but he also said he wouldn't fight in vain either. He understood what was ahead of him, and he was okay with it. What would have bothered him more than anything was being kept around as a guinea pig. They'd talked about that too many times to count. As much as she couldn't bear to be without him, it would be worse for her to watch him live a life he didn't want to hold on to. Finally, she understood what he wanted and reluctantly agreed.

I understood it, too, but right now, I couldn't accept that. It was too hard. This was the first time I'd heard it. There were so many more trees I would need to clear.

I finished mopping the kitchen while Mom kept busy cleaning counters. We talked more, mostly about Dad. We laughed some and cried a little more. The conversation stretched to Denise, my case and then we just kept each other company. She needed me and I sure needed her.

By the time we had finished talking, the sun was just beginning to come up. The bathroom, the dining room, living room, den, and the guest room were spotless. My mom said she would sleep in the guest room this morning. It was too soon for her to sleep in their room. We put everything away and called it a night, or in this case, a day.

7

At 6:18 a.m. I was lying on my old bed, looking at my old digital clock, waiting to fall asleep. Rest wouldn't come easy, but it was much needed for the hectic day that lay ahead. My mind danced with all the things that my mom and I had talked about. Trying to understand what my father wanted, and why he wanted it. My mom was trying to do the best she could by him; I got that. But understanding it and accepting it were two different things. This was bullshit. If I'd had the chance to sit with him, talk with him, if I knew what had been going on, maybe I could have changed his mind. We could have done something different.

Tossing and turning, trying to put these thoughts out of my mind so I could go to sleep wasn't working. The more I tried to force sleep, the more my mother's words bounced around the inside of my head. I stared at one spot to fall asleep, but I saw my father. When my eyes were closed, I saw myself walking into the hospital room. There he was, lying in bed with tubes running into his nose and mouth. The sound of his breathing penetrated my ears; it was slower and heavier, uttering words that couldn't be understood.

If I could get outside of my own head, lay this hurt down for a little while, I'd be better for it. Yesterday seemed like a week ago. I had been on top of the world, feeling as good as I'd ever felt. Now, less than twenty-four hours later, life had turned so fast. The life I knew had collapsed around me.

This was supposed to be the day we announced to my mom and dad that Denise and I were getting married. It was slated to be another good day in my life. It definitely hadn't turned out that way.

Giving up on the futile attempt at sleep, I decided to busy myself by hanging up my clothes and putting my socks and underwear in the old dresser that was hand made by my father; his hands were everywhere around me. I picked up my slacks and turned them upside down to put them on a hanger. The box containing Denise's ring slipped out of the pocket. It was on me the whole time I was cleaning and talking with my mother. I put the ring in the side pocket of the luggage bag and stored it away in my closet. Then I hung the jacket and slacks in the closet.

It was time to call Denise. We hadn't spoken since I had left her place last night. The charge on my cell phone wouldn't hold up much longer, so I'd use the cordless phone in the den to call; my parents had never put an extension or a TV in my room. It was my designated homework area and there was no room for distractions. The cordless phone hadn't made its appearance in the Pruitt home until after my first year of college. When I went looking for it, I decided that since I was up anyway, I might as well catch some ESPN.

The den had been my father's favorite room; he had built it as well. I had helped him, as much as a fourteen-year-old with raging hormones and a short attention span could. I was the fetcher. Dad would say 'fetch me that hammer, fetch me some nails, fetch me some water'. My father had been a mechanic by trade, had owned his own shop until the heart attack. But looking at the skill and craftsmanship of this room, he could have been a carpenter. If you hadn't seen this house before, you would never have known this was an add-on.

I sat down in my father's favorite chair, a well worn leather recliner, and used the remote to turn on the TV. Growing up, I was the remote. I would sit next to my dad and a tap on the side of my head signaled the time to turn the channel.

The phone was on the end table next to me. I stared at it, trying to figure out what to say. Denise needed to know what had happened, but I didn't want to lose it while talking to her, so I waited.

At 7:00 a.m., *SportsCenter* was coming on again, and I realized there was no need to keep delaying the call. So, I picked up the phone to call Denise.

"Hello." She was groggy, and her voice was raspy.

"Hey, baby."

"Jimmy! Are you okay?" Denise was suddenly wide awake.

"Yeah." I was very hesitant.

"I woke up at three-something and called you on your

phone and didn't get an answer. I didn't know if something had happened to you, but I didn't want to call your parents' house that late," she rambled on in concern.

"I'm okay."

"You sure?"

There was a brief pause. "Yeah, babe."

Denise knew something was wrong. "How's your father?"

"He ahh…ahh…he didn't…make it."

"Jesus, baby. I'm sorry."

"Thanks, me too." *Come on; come on; hold it together*, I told myself.

"How's your mother?" She hated to ask that.

"I don't…they knew it was coming." There was too much to explain and I couldn't explain something that didn't make sense to me.

"What do you mean?"

"His heart was in bad shape. He needed a transplant. They never told me about it."

"Why?"

Because my father thought he was protecting me. He didn't want to stop me from doing my job, or be a burden on my life. Because William Pruitt was too stubborn to let me help him. That was what I wanted to say, but instead I said, "I don't know."

Denise knew me. I didn't want to talk, not about this, not right now.

"Does your mom have any idea about the funeral or the arrangements?" she asked gently.

"It's already been taken care of."

"Taken care of?" Denise was caught off guard by that.

"They made all the arrangements. Mr. Otis is going to call Barkley's Funeral Home this morning. The funeral's going to be Monday at two p.m." My voice cracked. She was the first person I had given the information to and my emotions were about to get the better of me. How do you speak about your father, in these terms? Never in my life had the thought of losing him crossed my mind; I couldn't imagine it. Not even when he'd had the heart attack.

"Jimmy. Jimmy!" Denise could hear me in my silence; she could feel me slipping. "Baby, talk to me."

She offered me balance. I needed it, but I was a man and I would get control of it. As much as I wanted to let her help me, I had to get to my own place of understanding before giving in to her.

"I'm okay, just not used to hearing myself say that." It was coming back together for me.

"Jimmy, let me get a couple of things together and I'll be there in a few hours."

"Denise, you don't have to—"

Denise cut me off. "I want to be there for you."

I wanted to tell her how badly I hurt, how I was sitting in my father's chair in a room that we built together, how bad I already missed the rudder that guided my ship. None of these things came out.

"Thank you." That was all that came out.

"Have you had any rest?"

"I haven't been able to sleep."

"Try to get some rest. I'll be there before you wake up," she said.

Denise knew as well as I did, there wouldn't be much sleep coming my way.

"I will."

"I love you."

"I love you, too. Bye, babe."

"See you in a little bit. Do you need me to get you anything?"

"No. I brought some stuff with me. I'm good."

"I can stop by your house if you want me to."

Now she was just stalling to keep me on the phone.

"Baby, I'm straight; you can hang up and I'll see you in a little while, okay?"

"All right." Then she hung up.

Denise's father had died when she was four years old. She never had the opportunity to know her father the way I knew mine, but she knew the emptiness she felt when he was gone. We had stayed up many nights talking about it. It made me realize how fortunate I was as a black male to have a father, a male role model in my home. And based on those conversations and knowing how I had felt about my Dad, she knew I was hurting.

The refrigerator was full as usual. Some scrambled eggs would hold me over. I grabbed two eggs from the fridge, and the Lawry's that was always in the cabinet to the left of the stove. Mom didn't burn without the Lawry's nearby. I pulled her favorite cast iron skillet from the drawer below the stove. My mother had had the skillet since the day she got married. It was well-oiled and blackened from the many years of good use. I thought all skillets were made like that until I bought one for my house. Mom had told me it would take at least three years of cooking in it and oiling it up before it would begin to turn black.

I finished my eggs, washed the dishes, and cleaned up my mess. After all the time my Mom and I had spent cleaning up, I didn't want to leave anything out of place. Not that Mom would complain, but I was just trying to keep myself busy. I needed to check on her, but I also wanted to let her have some time to herself. We had covered a lot of ground last night; a little time wouldn't hurt me either.

SportsCenter was still on, so I sat back in my father's recliner to watch it. Ten minutes of trying to watch was all I could stand. I started dialing numbers on the phone.

"Hello," a voice answered warily.

"What's up, Chuck?"

"Jimmy. 'Sup, man? Hold on a second." Chuck grunted and there was a slight squeak. I could tell he was sliding out of bed and changing rooms.

"You alone?" I sat back in the recliner.

"Nah, bruh. You remember the women I talked to at the mall Thursday night.

"Yeah?"

"The tall one, Shelly. We kicked it last night. Bruh, she's off the hook."

"Yeah?"

"Don't get me wrong, dog, I didn't hit it. We went to the Baha, grabbed something to eat, and came back here and just rapped. She's good people. Hold up, dog. Congrats, right. I need to get my tux, don't I?"

"No, not yet."

"Wait a minute." Chuck's tone changed to serious. "You flashed that big-ass ring and she ain't down with you?"

"I didn't get a chance to ask her."

"Why not? Ya'll fall out?"

"Something came up."

"You at the crib? I'll be over in a little bit."

"I'm not at home, Chuck."

"Where you at, man? You straight?" Now Chuck was getting concerned.

"I'm in Asheville."

"Asheville?" Chuck had been to my parents' house a couple of times. He had even flown out to visit when my father had his heart attack. Chuck took to my parents. "How your peeps?"

"My father passed last night." It still wasn't coming out any easier.

"Shit, I'm sorry, man. I'll be down there this afternoon. You talked to Denise, right? She coming?"

"Yeah, she's coming."

"Good. How's your moms?"

"I don't know. We talked a lot this morning. She knew it was coming, but I know it hasn't hit her yet."

"Be ready when it does, dog. When it hits, it comes

hard. Look, I can't bullshit you. I got no words for you on this. Your pops was good people. You were lucky you had him."

Chuck never really knew his father. He had met him and seen him a couple of times when his old man was between jail stints, but he didn't know him. He didn't have the luxury of a father playing catch with him, taking him fishing, or teaching him to drive. When I was younger, I took those things for granted. They would have been luxuries for Chuck. His grandmother raised him; his mother was sixteen when she had him. She was more like his older sister than his mom.

"Yeah, I was lucky that I had him."

"What happened?"

"He needed a heart transplant, and his heart gave out on him." That wasn't the complete story, but I didn't have the energy to rehash the details for Chuck. Chuck was my man; he didn't need them, anyway. "The funeral is Monday at two."

"Monday?" Chuck said, shocked. "Damn, that's as fast as white folks."

"How'd I know you would say something like that?" I smiled.

"Because you know me. Look, man, I'm gonna get some breakfast with Shelly, and I gotta straighten some things out down at Ballers, and then I'll be headed that way fo' sho'. Give your mom my condolences."

"Alright, man."

"Keep your head up; your moms is gonna need you."

"I will."

"I'll holler." Chuck hung up.

Nobody I rolled with said good-bye. I put the phone on the end table and sat up in the recliner. It was time to check on my mom, but before I could get up, the phone rang. I had been telling my parents for years that they needed call waiting.

"Hello."

"Jimmy, how ya doin', baby?" Mrs. Bernice said in her fast-paced, Southern drawl. Her family was originally from Charleston, S.C., which accounted for that hint of a Gullah accent she had.

"I'm okay. How you doing, Mrs. Bernice?"

"Oh, chile, we fine. Worrin' 'bout ya'll. Look, na, Otis gonna call the funeral home directly. We gonna take care of ya."

"Yes, ma'am. My mom told me. Thank you."

"Glad to help, chile. Where your mamma at?"

"She's sleeping in the guest room."

"Guest room, good. She don't need to sleep in her room yet."

"I'm sorry?"

"My mamma told me dat. When you lose your husband, you don't sleep in the room you had wit him until after he's buried. Give the spirit time to move out, or dey can drag you to the grave wit 'em."

"I've never heard that before." That was the best response

I could come up with. Every now and then, Mrs. Bernice would come up with one of her sayings that would stop me in my tracks. This was one of those times. "Did you want to talk to her?" I stood up from the recliner.

"Only if she's awake. I'm going to bring you two some food after while. If you need anythin' else, you let me know."

"Yes, ma'am, I will." I was already at the door of the guest room.

"Hold on, Mrs. Bernice." I put the phone to my side and lightly knocked on the door. I didn't want to wake her if she was sleeping.

"Come in, Jimmy."

"Mrs. Bernice is on the phone; you feel like talking?" I said as I entered the room. Mama was sitting on the bed reading her Bible.

"That's fine; let me have the phone." She placed her bookmark in the Bible and set it beside her as I handed her the phone. I kissed her on the cheek, turned and left the room.

I went back into the den and turned off the television. It was almost 8:00 a.m. and my mom was on the phone. When she and Mrs. Bernice got going, it could keep her busy for a few hours. Mom would be fine with Ms. Bernice on the phone, so I went back to my room to relax for a little while.

8

"What the hell?" In the midst of my sleep there was pressure on my right shoulder and chest and I could barely breathe. I tried to sit up, but could not. Someone was leaning on me. Then the scent of fresh green apples hit my nostrils.

"Hey, girl, what are you doing?" My eyes were still closed, but there was a grin on my face.

"What do you want me to do?" Denise kissed me on the temple and stroked my hair.

"I know what I want you to do; we just can't do it here."

"If you're scared, say you're scared."

"Yeah, right. As soon as I'd say come on, you'd be backing off." I reached up, hugged her close to me and took a deep whiff of that apple-scented shower gel that she used. "I'm glad you're here."

"Me, too. I've been here almost an hour."

"What time is it?" I glanced at the clock; it was almost 1:00 p.m. "Man, I've been asleep that long?"

"You needed to get some rest." Denise lay down beside me.

There were other voices in the house. I picked up Mrs. Bernice's voice immediately, and there was no mistaking the unique sound of my Aunt Sarah, my mother's sister who lived in Morganton, N.C. There was a third person whose voice I didn't recognize.

"Who's in there with my mom?"

"Your Aunt Sarah, Mrs. Bernice, and some woman named Martha who came in about ten minutes ago."

"Martha? Light-skinned, heavyset woman with a gap in her teeth?"

"Yep, who's she?"

"My dad's nosy sister. I haven't seen her in fifteen years."

"Fifteen years?"

"She and my dad fell out about something and he told her not to come back around here no more. She didn't."

"What did they get into it about?"

"Tell you the truth, I don't know. I was a kid then. They told me plain and simple, it was grown folks' business. That's all they had to tell me."

"Listening to her talk in there, it doesn't take long to realize she can work a nerve. She was nosing around in there like she was the cleaning inspector."

Denise picked up on her quick.

"Yeah, that's Martha. Did my mom say much to her?"

"They talked. Well, your Aunt Martha talked about her big house in Knoxville."

"She should have a big house. She's buried three husbands and from what I understand, number four is a banana peel away from the grave."

"What?"

"She didn't mention that, did she?" I watched as Denise shook her head no. "Did you bring your bags in?"

"Already stuck them in the closet."

Oh no, I thought. The engagement ring was inside the pocket of my bag lying on the closet floor. Denise had never been one to look through my things because she trusted me and I gave her the same respect; but with the ring in there, I was a little paranoid. I hoped she hadn't picked now to start taking an occasional look. "What are you doing putting stuff in my closet?"

"You mean my closet," Denise said with a smirk. "Your mom gave me your room while I'm here."

"Every time we come here, she does that to me. It's usually the guest room for me, but this time it's going to be the pull-out couch."

Denise and my mom had shared an instant bond the first time they met. That was when we called ourselves just friends. My mom met some of the other girls I had dated, but she always said she could see those heifers coming a mile away. But Denise was like the daughter she never had and I had been the odd man out with my mom whenever Denise came around.

"You'd better get in there and speak to everybody."

"Kicking me out of my own bed," I said, getting up.

I picked up my shaving kit and went to the bathroom to brush my teeth. If I remembered Aunt Martha correctly, she'd be talking about my stink breath all over the state of Tennessee.

When Denise and I walked into the living room, the ladies, with the exception of one, greeted us warmly. Aunt Martha was a little reluctant to say anything and I noticed her cutting her eyes at Denise and me. That is when the unmistakable sound of her sucking her teeth made its way to my ears. I had never spent much time with her; didn't take long to remember why. She always had this aura about her when I was young. Seeing her now, I realized it was negative energy.

"How are you, Jimmy?" Aunt Sarah said, hugging me.

"I'm fine, and you?" I'd answer this question a lot over the next few days.

"Doin' good. Your Uncle Johnnie here, but he went with Otis to the funeral home."

Aunt Martha snorted as she listened to Aunt Sarah. Everyone heard her, but no one acknowledged it.

"We appreciate all of you being here."

"We been talkin' with your friend girl," Bernice said in that Gullah accent. It seemed to lighten the mood.

"Mrs. Bernice, don't start," I said. Mrs. Bernice had a way of twisting words that reached back to her Gullah roots.

"Please, don't," Denise said.

Every time Denise came home with me, Mrs. Bernice would always start in on us. How cute we looked together. *That boy ain't causin' you no worries, is he? That girl ain't causin' you no worries, is she? I wonder what ya'll's kids would look like.*

"Don't worry, chile, I wouldn't think of it today. We didn't wake you, did we, Jimmy? Carryin' on an' such."

"No, ma'am; Denise did." The women, including my mom, chuckled. Everyone except Martha.

"Mmm, I bet she did," Martha mumbled; then, when she realized she'd spoken those words out loud, she tried to play it off by chuckling, too.

"Do you remember your father's sister, Martha?" Mom said.

"Who?" I knew good and well who she was, but she was already working my nerves and I didn't want to fool with her.

"Your Aunt Martha. You haven't seen her in sixteen years," Mom added.

"Oh, yeah, how are you?" I feigned enthusiasm and gave her a halfhearted hug; couldn't wait for another sixteen to pass.

"Oh, darling, I'm just so torn up." Here was her moment to be in the spotlight and she took full advantage of it. "Oh, Lord Jesus, my brother's gone." She hugged me tighter. I looked over my shoulder at Denise, my mom, and everyone. They all had the same expressions on their faces—one that said, *Would you look at this bitch?* I guided Martha toward the chair behind her, and helped her sit down. If I could have pushed her over it, I would have.

"My brother's gone; what am I going to do?" And she sat there with crocodile tears in her eyes.

I looked at her putting on her big show and thought about what she said. *What are you going to do? The same damn thing you've been doing for the last sixteen years. Going about your business.*

This woman who had had a decade-and-a-half-long beef with my father succeeded in pissing me off. She hadn't been around here when my father was alive and now here she was after he was gone, acting like she didn't know what to do without him.

"I need something to drink. Can somebody get me something to drink?" Martha asked.

Nobody budged. Everyone just stood there looking at Martha, waiting for her to move for herself.

"I'll get you something," Aunt Sarah said and went into the kitchen. She quickly came back with a glass of water.

In that short span of time Martha had gotten herself back together. She took the glass of water Aunt Sarah gave to her and carefully inspected it.

"They don't have no soda in there?"

Aunt Sarah looked at her as if to say, *You don't drink that water, your husky ass will be wearing it.*

"Thank you," Martha barely mumbled.

"How's J.J. doing, Aunt Sarah?" I asked, to change the subject. Aunt Sarah was one of the sweetest women I knew, but she couldn't stand Martha. In that regard she wasn't different from anyone else in the room. I remember when I was about nine-years-old, Martha made a pass at Uncle Johnnie. What did she do that for? Aunt Sarah gave her a beating right in the front yard of our house. Judging by the looks on their faces, Aunt Sarah remembered and Martha damn sure remembered it, too.

"He's fine." She was still looking at Martha. Then she finally eased up and looked at me. "He's down in Atlanta at school and done fell all in love with a girl. He don't hardly come home no more."

"Not J.J. He told me he wouldn't get caught out there like that." J.J. was John Jr. By his definition, he was a sworn player committed to the game, not committed to a woman.

"She's a sweet girl, but got his nose wide open."

"I got to call little cuz and talk to him about that thing."

"What you gonna tell him?" Mama said.

"You know—how to keep his game tight."

"What game?" Denise chimed in.

"Your nose is open so wide we can all see what you're thinking," Mom said and all the women laughed. It was good to see Mom laughing, even if it was brief.

"Dat boy is sho nuf sprung," Mrs. Bernice added, and the women roared with laughter.

The house almost seemed normal for a minute. Then there was Martha trying to fake a laugh, but also keeping an eye on everyone. She just didn't fit in.

"Sprung nothing. I got this." This was comeback number seventeen in the players' handbook. I looked at Denise and then at my mom. Oops, note to self, don't use that line in the presence of your woman, your mom, and a gathering of three or more women. This set off a chorus of *oohs* and *aahs*.

Mom looked Denise square in the eyes and said, "Get 'im, girl."

"Who are you talking about?" Denise said. Then she smiled as the other women came with their *that's right* and *amens*.

I glanced at the faces of these women who were waiting for the other shoe to drop, and then there was Denise anticipating another verbal blunder. My next move was to keep my mouth shut. I wouldn't be able to get a full sentence in with these women ready to strike. I walked slowly to Denise, stopping just inches from her, leaned in and kissed her.

"You got this, too," I said. Then I winked at my mom.

"Dat's right; you better fix dat up," Mrs. Bernice said.

"Oh, Bernice, you leave those two alone. They just happy. Now J.J., he need to find him somebody who gonna look at him, like she do you. That girl he's with is gonna tear him up," Aunt Sarah said.

"Sarah, you know it's gonna take some tearing up in order for him to find the right one to fix it," Mom said.

"I know, but that's my baby."

"Well, look at my baby over there; he did very well."

"Where you from?" Martha asked Denise.

"Virginia Beach, but I live in Charlotte now."

Everyone sat back to see where this conversation was going. Martha had the floor for the moment.

"Oh…you and Jimmy live together?"

"No, I live downtown and Jimmy lives on the north side."

"And who do you work for?"

"WSTV News Channel Six." Denise was being polite, but quickly becoming irritated with Martha's fifth degree.

"A secretary or something?" Now Martha had successfully alienated everyone in the house.

"No. I co-anchor the five-thirty and six p.m. evening news, and I have two secretaries. You should call one of them sometime when you're in Charlotte and we'll try to schedule you in for a lunch."

Don't insult my baby; she don't play.

"You're a news anchor? Well, isn't that wonderful?! A celebrity!" Martha said.

In the span of fifteen seconds, Denise went from a golddigging hoochie, who was shacked up with me, to a wonderful celebrity. No wonder they couldn't stand that old bag.

"How long have you worked for that station?" Martha was now just as sweet as she could be to her new buddy.

"Excuse me; I need to get something to drink." Denise went into the kitchen.

"Baby, let me get that for you." I followed her into the kitchen. "You and Martha seem to be getting along well."

"What is wrong with that woman?"

"I don't know a thing about her."

"Every time I make a move, she's staring at me. She

sucks her teeth when somebody says anything. I tell her I work for a TV station; instead of asking me what I do, she makes an assumption about me. When she finds out I'm a news anchor, she's all over me like lint on a cheap suit. And I was hoping your Aunt Sarah would knock her ass into next week when she started bitching about that water."

"All it would have taken was one more word and she would have."

"How is she gonna ask for something to drink, someone is nice enough to bring it to her, and then she complains about it? If that's not some low-budget bullsh…"

"Babe, so I guess you didn't like her."

"That woman has issues."

The sound of the garage door opening interrupted our conversation. Uncle Johnny and Mr. Otis were back from the funeral home. We entered the living room as Uncle Johnny was coming into the house. Martha was skinning and grinning as her eyes met Uncle Johnny's. He almost backpedaled when he saw her. Denise elbowed me to make sure I didn't miss a thing, I was already checking out Aunt Sarah. So was Mom.

"Hello, Johnny," Martha said, still grinning and flashing the wide gap in her front teeth.

"Martha? How are you?" Johnny was surprised both by her presence and the fact that she had the audacity to speak to him.

Uncle Johnny was not very tall and a little overweight.

He was always the life of the party. Back in his younger days, a party didn't start until Uncle Johnny had a drink in one hand and Aunt Sarah in the other.

"I'm fine." Martha snickered. "You're still looking good."

That was the kind of stuff that had gotten her ass whipped by Aunt Sarah years ago. Judging by the look on Aunt Sarah's face, if it hadn't been for the reason we were there, Martha would have found her butt in some shrubs again.

"How you doing, Unc?"

"Hey, boy, who you got there wit ya? Shoot, that there's Denise. How you, girl? He takin' care of you? Better be." Uncle Johnny would answer his own questions before you could.

He shook my hand and hugged Denise. Johnny was an old-school Southern brother. He didn't believe in hugging grown men. It didn't mean he didn't love them; it was just his way.

"Where's Otis?" Bernice asked.

"He took the truck back to the house. He said he'll be up here in a little bit."

What Uncle Johnny was saying in a nice way was that Otis needed a little time to get himself together after going to the funeral home. Johnny was family, but Otis had been my dad's best friend. With Otis and my dad, their friendship meant a lot more than the relationships they had with some family members. They hunted to-gether, worked on cars together, fished together and watched each other's lives grow and change. There were things Otis knew about my father that I would never know, and probably some things my mom wouldn't know, either. It was quite understandable that he would need some time to himself before he came back to the house.

At some point, I'm sure we would all need some time to ourselves.

9

"Ain't no way in hell you bowled a two-seventeen, Johnny," Otis barked.

"Did too. What I got to lie to you for? I ain't tryin' to impress you. You ain't no woman."

"Two-seventeen? How would you know? Hell, you can barely count past a hundred."

It was almost 7:00 p.m. The sun was setting and I was sitting on the porch and listening to those two go at it tickled me to death. Dad had been the mediator for them. Now here we were sitting on the porch and I was playing fill-in as the middleman. Neither one of them meant any harm. They just liked to see who could get the best of the other.

"Jimmy. I know you ain't laughin'. You know I keeps a pocket knife on me. I'll cut ya both. I'll cut ya quick," Uncle Johnny said.

"Uncle Johnny, if you can bust the rust off of that old knife, then you do what you gotta do."

"You think 'cause you family, I won't cut ya. C'mon, I ain't never cut me no lawyer before."

"Shoot, you ain't never cut nobody before, least not

on purpose," Otis said, laughing. Johnny looked at him and began to smile.

"Don't forget nothin', do you?"

"What are you talking about?" I asked.

"Your uncle damn near cut his fingers off one time when we went fishin'. Must'a been thirty years ago. We was drinking the night before and leaving to fish 'fore sunrise. Hell, somebody never stopped drinkin'. We get to the fishin' hole and somebody's alcohol started talking for him. Oh, I caught this, oh, I caught that. Fool went to cut his line and cut three fingers instead. Alcohol makes ya blood thin. Blood was runnin' out of him like he was a faucet. Fishin' trip was canceled; women flew hot at us 'cause we ain't take care of him right. And me and ya daddy was hot at him for a month 'cause we got no fish and no lovin' comin' to us."

"They wouldn't let me fish with 'em again for almost a year. That's about how long it took for my damn fingers to heal."

"Look at what just turned down here," Otis said.

"What ya see? Oh, that there is sharp," Johnny said.

"Yes, sir, she is a tight one all right. I could handle her."

To listen to those two men talk, you'd have thought the finest woman on earth had graced us with her presence. What they were talking about was a silver Lexus GS. That was my boy Chuck; sure knew how to make an entrance.

"It's pullin' up here," Johnny said.

"Don't look; act like you don't see it," Otis said.

Now those two have showed out. They were falling all over themselves for a car.

Chuck got out of the car and walked up the driveway toward the house.

"That's your buddy, Chuck Mays, ain't it? Yeah, that's him. Didn't he play with the Seahawks? Uh-huh, that's right, the Seahawks. They always been my favorite team."

"Calm down, Johnny. Favorite team, you can't even spell Seahawks. What happened to the Falcons?"

"Hell, they's all birds."

"Act like you been somewhere before," Otis chastised.

I walked to the edge of the porch and stuck out my hand. Chuck shook it and put his other hand on my shoulder.

"How you doin'?"

"I'm straight. Thanks for coming, bruh."

"You got that. I know you'd do it for me."

"How you doing, Mr. Otis?"

"Okay. I see you doin' good, Chuck."

"Trying to."

"Chuck, you remember my Uncle Johnny, don't you?"

"Oh yeah, he's the Cardinals' fan. Or was it the Eagles?"

"That's a mighty fine ride out there, boy. Won't you take me and Otis for a ride? I know I'll look good ridin' in her."

Otis looked at Johnny and just shook his head.

"I'll do you one better." He tossed his keys to Johnny. "Why don't you and Mr. Otis take it for a spin?"

Johnny was already in the driveway.

"That what you call being calm!" Otis shouted at Johnny. Otis looked at us. "You believe him." Then he hopped off the porch and quickly followed Johnny to the car.

"They'll argue for the next five minutes over who's going to drive. Hope you have some gas."

"Let 'em have some fun."

Johnny got into the driver's seat and leaned it back further than Chuck had it. Otis slid into the passenger side. They were leaning so hard you couldn't see either one of them. Within seconds, the car was back on the street, music pumping.

"This is how you do it, young bloods!" Johnny shouted.

He hit the gas and spun the wheels. He couldn't have gone more than twenty feet before he hit the brakes and stopped. Johnny and Otis bolted straight up in their seats at the same time. Four eyeballs as big as fifty-cent pieces stared straight ahead. Otis put on his seatbelt and Johnny adjusted his hands to the ten and two driving position. The music was turned down.

"Got some kick to it, huh, Unc?!" I yelled to them.

"Uh-huh." Johnny never took his eyes off the road as he mumbled his reply toward us.

"Dog, you might want to go check their shorts."

"I'm not checking no grown man's shorts."

Johnny must have gotten some of his nerve back. He headed to the corner doing about ten miles per hour. He looked both ways twice before making his move. He eased around the corner and was gone.

"How you doin'?" Chuck asked again once we were alone.

"I'm fine. You want something to drink?"

"Not right now." Chuck paused. "How you really doin'?"

I smiled and shrugged my shoulders. "I'm fine." I looked at Chuck.

He stared me straight in the eyes. "How are you doing?" he asked again slowly.

I shook my head. I didn't have any words.

"I feel ya, dog."

We sat down on the porch, realizing what Chuck had done. He never let anybody drive that car, and he knew there was a house full of people. It might be the only chance that we'd get to kick it for a minute.

"I was trying to figure out what I was going to say to you all the way up here. I didn't come up with much. You know, my pops wasn't shit. I don't even know him and don't want to. My pops never taught me nothing. Not one thing! Wait, I take that back. Watching him go in and out of jail showed me what I didn't want to be. I didn't want to be a loser in life, football, or whatever business I was handling. Your pops gave you a blueprint to manhood. Showed you how to carry yourself by how he carried himself, how to treat a woman by how he treated your mom. Any fool can see that by how you treat Denise. Him being driven showed you how to motivate yourself. I never heard you say a bad thing about your pop. That's a blessin'. I wish we could all be led into manhood by our fathers, but that shit's hard to do when seventy percent of our fathers are actin' like kids themselves. But you got that in you, dog, from him. You'll carry it with you and pass it on to your seeds, and they'll grow and pass it on to theirs. Tough as this is, you can hold on to that."

"I will."

The cool, spring, mountain air filled my lungs and Chuck's words filled my thoughts. I sat there in silence and let both of them sink in.

"How's your mom?"

"She's strong. People have been coming and going all day. She faces every one of them and holds up better than they do."

"Some women have amazing strength, but like I told you, dog, she's gonna break down," Chuck offered.

"Sooner or later everybody does."

"Not everybody. Not everybody's got a reason to."

I looked at Chuck and I knew this wasn't just about my dad. Death, the finality of it, made every person it touched retreat into themselves. The where am I, who am I, and where do I go from here thoughts.

"What do you mean?"

"Like if my old man kicked it, I wouldn't give a shit."

I stared at Chuck.

"I wouldn't. That nigga…"

I glared at Chuck.

"Bruh, there ain't no better word for him. That nigga's part of the seventy percent I was talkin' about. He didn't care nothin' about my mama. Knocked her up when she was sixteen and trickin' for him when she was nineteen. He damn sure didn't care nothin' about me. Nigger saw me on the street one time and walked away, like he didn't know me. After I got drafted, he started trying to call; wanted to come around. It was too late by then. I was grown. That dude could go missing tomorrow and it wouldn't faze me."

"As much as you want to believe that, Chuck, it would. You wouldn't want it to, but it would."

"Man, you trippin'."

Every child craved love and attention from his mom and dad. Chuck's grandmother raised him and he got the best he could get from her. He knew he missed out with his mom and dad, but it was their fault, not his.

Chuck might not have liked his father; he might have even hated him, but he'd talked to him before, touched him, and smelled him. Chuck might have thought he wasn't worth shit, but that was his father. His blood ran through Chuck, and if only for that reason, Chuck would feel something.

"Me and my pops ain't nothin' like you and yours. I know who he is and I know his name. But we don't share anything. I can't feel nothin' for him." Chuck sat there for a few seconds thinking about what he had just said, or maybe about what he was preparing to ask.

"Have you been to the funeral home?"

Chuck was looking out over the neighborhood when

he asked that question. So was I. There was no eye contact.

"No, I haven't. Mr. Otis and Uncle Johnny took some clothes over there earlier, but they won't have my dad ready until...until...my mom and Aunt Sarah are going over there before the wake tomorrow."

"I'll take you over there before the wake if you want."

The one thing Chuck kept stressing to me was to be there for my mom. He also knew I needed somebody to be there for me. Obviously, Denise would be, and I would confide in her. Chuck also knew that I kept things to myself to process them in my head before releasing them onto other people. He provided me an out in case I needed it.

"Denise and I are going when they go. You can go with us."

"That's more like a family thing." Chuck didn't want to intrude.

"You are family," I said. Chuck looked at me and nodded his acceptance of the comment. "You've been family since the first day I stepped on that practice field. As many times as you slept in this house, ate my mom's food, fished with my dad and me, rode..."

"All right, nigger, you made your point. Don't get corny. Too much more of that and some slow music will start playin' in the background."

"That's more like a family thing," I said, mocking him. "Man, get in there and get you some food."

"You straight?"

"Yeah, man." The two of us got up to go into the house. I put my hand on the storm door and looked back at Chuck.

"Wait until you meet my Aunt Martha. You're just going to love her." I smiled at Chuck.

"You got a young aunt in there?"

"No. Trust me; it won't take you long to want to get away from her. Denise met her this morning and in less than an hour she was done with her."

Denise and I had bet an over-and-under on how long it would take Chuck to ditch Martha. Denise said it would be over ten minutes. I said it would be less. The wager was my bed versus the pull-out in the den. We both knew that was a useless bet with Chuck here. We'd be in the den and Denise would get the room.

"Hold up a second," Chuck said as he stepped back. "You didn't ask Denise, did you?" We backed further from the door.

"Nah, this isn't the right time."

"Just wanted to make sure, dog. You know me. I'll go in there and say the wrong thing in a second."

Chuck had been known to put his foot in his mouth, and then there were days like today. Chuck paid attention, he saw very clearly, he heard what had been said. Chuck knew I was struggling emotionally, even though I wouldn't admit it. So he threw me a couple of ropes to cling onto. I knew they wouldn't immediately pull me out of the jungle of my feelings but they would give me something to hold onto until I did.

10

Saturday afternoon rolled into the early evening hours and the visitors rolled in with the cover of night. The walls closed in on me as the number of people grew. This was the place that I needed to be, to show support and strength for my mom, allow Denise and my family to see the man that my father had raised. But the house had become a pressure cooker and I wanted out.

Relief came in the form of some of the guys from high school. They dropped by to offer their condolences. Two of the guys were basketball teammates of mine in high school—Wayne Watkins and David Meeks.

I introduced Wayne and David to Chuck. I hadn't seen either one of them since the day I had graduated from high school. The athletic talent pool in Asheville ran deep. Wayne had been a talented athlete in football and basketball who could have gone to nearly any college if he'd had the grades. He was one of Asheville's local legends who never made it out of the city. David had been one of those guys who was on the team, but never played much. Heart of gold and hands down the smartest kid I ever knew growing up. Unfortunately, he hadn't taken a dip in the same pool that we did. David kept Wayne academically eligible, barely, when we were in school. David now lived in Texas and earned his living as a mechanical engineer. I had always hoped that some of David's smarts would rub off on Wayne and some of Wayne's athletic prowess would rub off on David.

Keith Wells, Bruce's older brother, came over to see us as well. He had two well-behaved children with him. He looked good; his life appeared to have taken a turn for the better. We sat around and ran the gift of gab about the old days until Wayne suggested we go over to Reedy Park and shoot some balls. He wanted to do it like we used to. Headlights on the court at night with the car radios playing, we killed more of our parents' car batteries than we could count.

Denise declined the invitation to join us; she wanted to stay with my mother and help out at the house. She'd also just met Kim King, one of my ex-girlfriends from high school who came by to pay her respects to the family. Personally, I think Denise wanted to pick her brain about me. That would surely make for an interesting evening when I got back.

At the court, Wayne wasted no time trying to show us that he was still the best player among us. He exploded to the basket and laid down a vicious dunk that shook the rim and left the chain-link net jingling. Wayne used these rim-rattling dunks back in high school to intimidate the competition.

We played a couple of games of Twenty-one. It didn't take long to discover that Wayne wasn't the same athlete he used to be. He still had some of the same moves, but he lacked the endurance he once had. David was dropping shots on him left and right. He had developed some skills, and didn't hesitate to let Wayne know it.

Listening to David talk trash pissed Wayne off. The harder Wayne went at it, the worse he ended up playing. This was no longer high school and Wayne didn't run the show anymore. It was hard to tell what pissed him off more, the fact that things had passed him by or David's incessant trash talk.

In those few short minutes of playing basketball, we were able to catch a glimpse of how our lives had changed. David was a mechanical engineer. He wasn't the high school smart kid who kept the bench warm; he was more confident having grown into his own skin. I'd been through law school, won my first major case and my career was on the rise. Wayne, though, had become stagnant; he hadn't changed or grown. He was living at home in his old room, and selling bootleg tapes out of the trunk of his mom's old Buick. Every story he told or comment he made related to high school. For all intents and purposes, his life had peaked then and he had yet to find a direction in which to go.

Keith picked up a case of beer while the rest of us played our last game of Twenty-one. That is where things began to get blurry for me. I shot-gunned three beers in less than two minutes. Fifteen minutes later, there were five empty beer cans in my column. I don't remember how much I consumed after that, but it wasn't a stopping point. Drinking on an empty stomach compounded the issue. I was physically there, but mentally shot.

Keith and David had called it a night after we finished balling and drinking. Chuck and I hung with Wayne at a liquor house where Wayne convinced me to try some clear, home-brewed corn liquor. White folks called it white lightning; we called it Buck. If this concoction sat too long in a Styrofoam cup, it would melt the bottom off of it. And people still drank it!

Needless to say, the corn-brewed whiskey didn't blend well with the beer. Chuck couldn't get me out of that juke joint fast enough. The queasiness in my stomach had risen to my throat by the time we hit the door. What little food I'd had and the majority of the alcohol I'd consumed was left in the doorway of the liquor house.

I passed out on the way home and I don't remember what time it was when Chuck was able to get me back home. He was careful not to let my mom see me in that condition, but he made sure Denise had a front row seat to how the night had gone. She was the person he had help him with the door.

Denise woke me at 12:15 p.m. I was sleeping in my old bed. Apparently, getting drunk won me the privilege of sleeping there. Still hung over, I couldn't see straight or think clearly. Judging by the sound of the rattling pans in the distance, my mom was cooking. The smell of bacon, eggs and grits confirmed it. Normally this would have stoked my appetite; today it made my insides churn.

As time moved in fast forward, breakfast was over and I was at the funeral home, looking at my father, and not quite sure if this moment was real or not. I cried some, but I was detached from the moment, and that allowed me to hold up pretty well.

For the first time, though, my mom began to let her emotions go. I could not begin to fathom how my mom must have felt looking down into a casket at the man she had loved since she was sixteen. The good and bad times they had shared, all of life's storms that they'd weathered together, had come to an end forever. The enormity of the moment had finally hit her.

I held her as she cried. Everybody left us alone. We sat there, and as I listened to her cry, I felt ashamed of myself. I was embarrassed by the way I had behaved last night, ashamed that I wasn't totally connected to this moment. I used getting drunk as an excuse to assuage the emotions I had toward my father's death.

We stayed in there for the better part of a half hour. I don't remember much of what was said or who decided we should leave. My head was still foggy and the best I could do was just be there while Mom worked this out for herself and was ready. My mother's family had a long-standing tradition of holding the wake the day prior to the funeral, I was beginning to understand why.

When we arrived back home, Mom was much more composed. I didn't see her cry anymore. She warmly greeted people, and accepted their condolences without giving in to her own feelings.

I was surprised by her strength as she carried on. The comfort she gave to others as they attempted to comfort her. Part of me wanted to be able to do the same thing, but I couldn't. I was still a step behind everyone else. I couldn't catch up and it was quite possible that I didn't want to. Hangovers never lasted this long for me, not even in college. The other part of me wondered how Mom could be so calm and seemingly at peace right now. Maybe she didn't want to show her vulnerability to these people. Maybe what we had shared earlier was just between us. The more I tried to make sense of this, to understand how Mom could cope with this so well, the more the throbbing pain would return to my head. And in moments when the pain would subside, I kept hearing my father's low voice, struggling to say something. I heard him all the way back to my parents' house as his voice and the pain alternated.

"How you doin'?" Chuck's voice snapped me back to reality. He was standing beside me. "You were pretty caught up in those thoughts."

"Yeah. Not too many people left, huh?" Chuck, Denise, and I were the only ones left in the den.

"Everybody's in the living room. People couldn't decide on how to get you to talk, so they left us in here," Denise said.

"I'm gonna get something to eat." Chuck promptly excused himself.

Denise and I looked at each other for a minute. There was an awkward silence between us.

"What?" I asked.

"I don't know what to do for you."

"What are you talking about? You're doing it."

"What am I doing? Please tell me what I'm doing."

"You're here."

"Then talk to me, baby; that's why I'm here."

I thought she was upset with me, but that wasn't it at all. She wanted me to open up to her.

"I will. I need some time. I'm not trying to shut you out; I'm just at a loss right now and I don't know how to handle it."

"Nobody does." Denise got up and walked towards me. "It takes time." She eased down into the recliner and onto my lap. "But you need to talk about it to help that time pass." She kissed me on the cheek. "Okay?"

I nodded and wrapped my arms around her. I leaned my head against her breast and listened for the sound of her heartbeat. If I could focus on that, hear each thump, find its rhythm, then I would know my mind was clearing. There it was. A little faint at first. I closed my eyes and pressed a little harder to her. The beat became louder, and stronger. Even though I was perfectly still, I could feel myself slipping back into gear, catching up to her rhythm.

"Sheeiit, should'a known I couldn't leave you two alone for one minute," Chuck said.

Denise looked up at Chuck. "Should'a known you'd only be gone for one minute." She was mocking him.

"Hell, you're in my bedroom."

"Like you're going to bed anytime soon."

"I would if I ran up on the right one in here. Yo, J, your old girl who was in here last night; she coming back?"

"Please," Denise said. "I tell you what; I have Kim's number in my cell phone if you want to call her."

"You think I won't?"

Denise had thrown down the gauntlet and Chuck didn't hesitate to pick it up.

"I talked to that sister last night for over an hour. I'm telling you now, ya gets no play." Now she was challenging his manhood.

"You talked to her for an hour?" I wanted to make sure I'd heard her right.

"Oh, yeah." Denise looked at me and smiled. "She's very intelligent."

I looked at Denise, then Chuck, then back to Denise. I wasn't taking that bait.

"Intelligent, I'll show you intelligent. Go get me that number." Chuck wasn't going to back off.

"I'll be right back." Denise smiled at me and got up slowly. I smiled back. I had just dodged a bullet. I watched Denise as she left the room.

"Damn, cuz, she hollered at your old girl for an hour. You know that was a fact-finding mission."

"I thought they might talk when we left, but damn.

It's no big deal, though. There wasn't much she could tell."

"Sheeiit, she could make up some stuff. How's your head?"

"It's getting there. I've been in a fog all day."

"See, messin' with that Buck will tear you up every time. That stuff is high-grade battery acid."

"Now you tell me."

"Shit, dude, you from here. You know about that stuff; that was your call. If that's what you needed to do, so be it. I just had your back in case you got into trouble."

"I was in trouble when I started drinking that stuff."

"What you want to do tonight? We can get in touch with Wayne if you want."

"You're not going out again, are you?" Denise came back into the room and handed Chuck a piece of paper.

"I'm going to look out for him."

"Well, why not, look how well things went last night."

"C'mon, Niecie, J needed to let off some steam."

"I did that. It didn't change anything." I eyed Chuck for a second and then looked at Denise. "I'm not going out drinking or anything else."

"Good, because you…"

"Let me finish." My voice was low, but firm. I was in full command of my faculties now. "Last night and most of today was a waste. Drinking and hanging out didn't help me worth a damn. I just went through the motions today. I was lost, couldn't tell you what people said to me or what I said to them. Chuck, you told me to be ready when my mom broke down. Well it happened, and I wasn't worth two cents to her. I won't let that happen again. It can't. I won't embarrass myself or anybody else like that again."

"It's cool. I feel you." Chuck got the message.

"I'm not going to have another day like today. I will be clearheaded and ready to help my mom get through tomorrow, and I'm sure that she'll be ready to help me as well." I would lean on my mom, as well as Denise and Chuck. I felt much better knowing they were here for me, regardless of which way my moods swung. "I'm going to sit with my mom."

"Want me to come with you?" Denise offered.

"I'd like that very much."

"I might be in there in a little bit and I might not." Chuck looked down at the piece of paper Denise had given him. "I'm gonna holler at ol' girl for a minute; see what's up."

Denise cut her eyes back to Chuck. "See you in a few minutes."

"You can doubt my skills if you want to." Chuck tried for a comeback, but it was time for him to show and prove.

Denise and I went into the living room and sat down with my mom and the other folks who were still there. A few minutes later, Chuck joined us. He wouldn't look at Denise or me, but without saying a word, we knew this was his destination for the rest of the evening.

11

Mt. Olive Baptist Church was established in 1868, not long after the end of the Civil War. My parents had been members of the church long before I came along. We arrived for the funeral at 1:45 p.m. The parking lot was already full. Folks around Asheville were well aware that Barkley's Funeral home didn't play. If the service was called for 2:00 p.m., the service started promptly at 2 p.m. The two limousines provided by Barkley's pulled up to the front of the church. Our driver hopped out of the car and hustled back to our door.

The mountain air was cooler today than it normally was in April, and there was a light drizzle. It met us as soon as the limo doors were opened. We lined up two-by-two and proceeded to the church door. I escorted my mom, Chuck was paired with Denise, and Johnny with Sarah. In the other limo, Otis and Bernice had the pleasure of riding with Martha. My cousin J.J. had the unenviable task of escorting her in.

When we entered the church, the only thing visible to me was my father lying in that open casket, and I felt my mom weaken and begin to shake as she held onto my arm. I put her arm around my waist and put my arm around her shoulder to steady her, and we moved forward.

If only somebody had been there to steady me, and in that moment, when I felt I couldn't go any further, I heard my father's voice telling me to come on. He once told me that a short walk can carry you a long way. I didn't understood what that meant back then, but on this day, it all made perfect sense.

I took a deep breath, and let the tears fall from my eyes. I looked at my mother, who also had tears streaming down her face.

"I'm here with you. It's okay," I whispered to her.

There was nothing for her to say. She simply nodded her head, and we continued on. We made the short walk to my father. I watched my mother as she stood there and gazed at him. She seemed to be replaying a lifetime of memories while she stood there. Finally, she put her hands on his cheeks, leaned toward his face and kissed his lips for the last time, and then she lost it. She cried uncontrollably, and I tried to console her and maintain my composure. An usher and Chuck walked her over to her seat while I stayed with my father to say goodbye.

I managed to smile at him through the hurt and pain. There were still many questions in my mind about why we had come to this, but looking at him, I knew he'd given me all of himself that he could. Wiping my eyes, I leaned down and kissed him on his forehead, thanked him for being my father and told him I loved him. I took my place to the left of my mother.

The rest of the family and friends filed in and viewed my father's body on the way to their seats. We shook hands with them as they walked past us. Again, there were so many faces that I recognized, but their names escaped me. Former co-workers, employees, hunting and fishing buddies, people Dad had bowled with. So many of my mom's friends were there as well. I was surprised to see Jason and several of my co-workers. As Jason made his way by, he told me that Chuck had called him on Saturday, let him know what had happened, and given him the address to the church. I looked at Chuck and nodded my head to acknowledge my thanks.

Once the congregation was again seated, the funeral director began to prepare everything for Reverend Wilson's home-going service. I watched as they placed the white silk fabric inside the silver coffin, and eased the lid down. Then I heard the metallic ping, as the lid locked into place. That sound shot through me and I fought to hold my composure, but I was losing it. Mom was trying to regain hers, but hearing that lid lock didn't help her either.

I held my mom and tried to find comfort in the eulogy that Reverend Wilson gave for my father. We listened to the choir sing "His Eye is on the Sparrow." It was my father's favorite song. He loved to hear it any time, anywhere. Every member of his home church knew it and they honored him by singing along with the choir.

The limousines were waiting to carry us to the burial site after the service was complete. Barkley's was a stickler for the starting time, but the end of the service was left to the families of the departed. They patiently waited to take us the three miles to Grace Cemetery off of I-40.

The ceremony at the gravesite was brief and much smaller due to the rain that had picked up. That was fitting for my father; he'd always said he didn't like being at funerals for a long time.

"Chuck, get my mom and Denise back into the car," I whispered to him when the service concluded.

"You straight?"

"I'm good."

He led them back to the limo. I stayed and watched as they lowered my father into his final resting place, inside the concrete walls. Then they placed the concrete lid on top of it. I listened to the sound of that heavy concrete slab being maneuvered into place, and watched the first shovel of dirt go in. I'd seen enough, but I could not move. I closed my eyes and heard those shovels dig into the dirt and dump load after load onto my father's coffin. I could feel myself becoming unbalanced.

"J, you ready to go?" Chuck had gotten my mom and Denise into the limo and come back for me.

"In a minute," I said. I wanted to be anywhere but here. I just couldn't make myself move.

"It's hard to leave, I know, but there's nothing you can do. Your mom needs you." Chuck waited for a few seconds before continuing. "C'mon, let's get out of the rain."

There's no telling how long I would have stood there

if it hadn't been for Chuck. I backed away from the gravesite, looked for a few more seconds as more dirt continued to be thrown in, then turned and walked toward the limo.

"You know, all these folks waitin' on you so they can go back to the church and eat, don't ya?" Chuck smiled.

He was trying to pick me up, but I didn't have a smile to give right then.

"My bad, I just wanted to…"

"It's cool."

There was no need for apologies. He knew I was having a hard time, and he was just trying to help. "Thanks for pulling me away from there."

"No problem, dog."

Life is full of obstacles. Some you can clear by yourself and other times you need some help. My dad had taught me that a man can handle his own business, but sometimes it takes a bigger man to ask for help when he can't find his way through a situation alone. He told me that if I was willing to give a shoulder to somebody, at some point, I'd have to be man enough to accept someone else's shoulder when it was offered to me.

12

"I tell ya, that boy was crazy." Otis was holding court with Johnny, Bob T. Mason, and me. "We was out huntin' deer in February. It was 1972."

"Now that's where you went wrong," Bob T. cut in.

Bob T. was another one of my father's good friends. He stood six-foot-five, a strapping man, and he always maintained a stoic demeanor with people he didn't know. To look at him, the size of his hands and arms, you'd immediately have thought he could snap your neck as easily as he could snap a number two pencil. He was a gentle giant, though. Truth be told, he was scared of his own shadow.

One Fourth of July, when I was thirteen years old, we were having what had become known as the "Pruitt Fourth of July Annual Cook Out" and Bob T. fell asleep in the rocker that was sitting on the front porch. Dad and Otis told me to sneak up on him and yell in his ear. I eased up behind him and when I yelled, he shrieked in a high-pitched voice, jumped out of the rocker and ran top speed on his tiptoes all the way to Otis's house. Dad and Otis laughed so hard they broke into a sweat.

"What ya mean?" Otis said.

"What business three black men got in the woods in February with guns, huntin' deer?" That tickled the hell out of Bob T.

"So now that's funny, huh? You still mad as fire 'cause your wife wouldn't let you go out in the cold with us." Now everybody was laughing. "Anyways, we in Tennessee on the side of the mountain near Knoxville, when Willie spots this ten-point, three hundred fifty-pound buck. The boy got so excited, he lost his footin', the buck got spooked and started to take off. Now as he's fallin', he pulls the trigger, hits the buck and slides half a mile down one side of the mountain. The buck fell the other way."

"Sho did; I was right there. Tell 'em what come next. Tell 'em," Johnny said.

"We settled in and waited for Willie to come back up. He done circled around the mountain to where the buck went down. 'Bout half hour later, here he come grinnin', and draggin' that damn buck with'em." Otis was seeing it all over again.

"That's right; that's as true as I'm sittin' here right now." Johnny was playing testifier today. "That was your daddy. He sho nuff was a determined man."

"That was Pop for sure. If there was something he needed to get done, he wasn't stopping until he was finished," I said.

"Hey, dude." There was no mistaking Jason's voice as he came out of the house.

Nobody on the porch had missed hearing him, either. As soon as "hey, dude" came out of his mouth, all eyes locked on him. It was not the ordinary setting for those words. Otis and the guys weren't in the habit of seeing white men from Southern California up around here. I jumped in to save him by introducing him to everybody.

"Sit down with us for a while," I said.

"Love to, but I've got to get back to Charlotte. Chuck's gonna show me out. He was saying goodbye to your mother."

"That could be all night."

"He said he'd be right behind me."

"You don't know his mama," Johnny said.

I looked over my shoulder at the storm door and saw Chuck in the living room. I nudged Jason and directed his attention there. Chuck's bags were on the floor; he'd pulled a chair up next to my mom, and he was starting to go to work on some of Aunt Sarah's sweet potato pie. Bob T. pulled out a chair for Jason.

"It could be a while," Bob T. mumbled.

"So you work with Jimmy down there in Charlotte?" Johnny asked.

"Yeah, but at the rate he's going, I might be working for him pretty soon," Jason teased.

"How's that?" Otis asked.

"Jimmy's banging out a hell of a name for himself in Charlotte. The city's really buzzing about the case he won last Thursday."

Last Thursday seemed like last year. Paul Hughes was a distant memory. I hadn't thought about that case, the law, or how my career might have changed since my father had died.

"That boy might turn out to be something," Otis joked. "If you'd seen what I done seen of him growin' up, you'd know what I mean."

"Details. Please?" Jason was begging for the goods.

"He was just strange. Run around here dressed like that MC Mallet fella." Otis butchered the name.

"Hammer, what they call him," Johnny said.

"That's what I said. Haircut slanted to one side, and he'd run wind sprints up and down this street all summer long. Hottest part of the day, too. Looked like Gumby flyin' through here. Guess you was just tryin to catch somthin'." He looked at me with genuine sincerity. "Sounds like you're gettin close to it."

"He got fight just like his daddy." Johnny nodded his approval.

That was high praise from some of the people closest to my father. I hoped I'd be able to live up to it.

"Rest assured, you can be very proud of what this young man is doing in Charlotte," Jason said.

"Let's roll, Baines!" Chuck yelled as he came stumbling out of the door with bags in his hand and crumbs from Sarah's sweet potato pie around his mouth.

"Dude, slow down, there some good scoop happening."

"Cuz, if you rollin' with me, you'd better be ready to make a move. Didn't you want to stop by Ballers?"

With that, Jason was on his feet and couldn't get out of there fast enough. Otis and Johnny didn't miss a beat. As soon as they heard Ballers, they looked at each other and winked.

"Well, gotta go. I enjoyed meeting you gentlemen."

"Let me walk you guys out," I said.

I grabbed one of Chuck's bags, and he and Jason shook hands with everybody. I excused myself and escorted them to their cars.

"Wait until I tell Beverly you were hanging out at Ballers."

"James, come on, dude."

"Don't let him bust your balls, Jason. He ain't gonna say nothin'." Chuck put him at ease.

"You know I wouldn't do that to you."

"I know…so, ah, when are you coming back?"

"To work? I don't know. Probably next week. I haven't really thought about it."

"If you need me to cover anything for you, let me know."

"I will. Thanks for coming, Jason."

"Glad to do it." Jason got into his car.

"Yo, J., if you need me to hang a litt—"

"Don't worry about it, bruh. I'm good."

It was time for Chuck to go. He couldn't sit in one place for too long. It was all over his face. Work was calling him; his clubs were calling him; his women were calling him—and not necessarily in that order. We loaded his bags into the trunk.

"Last chance," Chuck offered.

I just looked at him. I appreciated everything he had done for me, but I needed him to go just as badly as he wanted to go. It was time for me to start working through this with my mom and Denise. As long as Chuck was here, there would be an excuse for me to avoid my issues.

"I'm good. Don't keep Jason out too late. Beverly will kill him."

"Jason's got some work he needs me to do. I figured since he's always askin' about Ballers, I'd take him over there so he can have some fun while he fills me in," Chuck assured.

"Yeah, okay. If Big Lex is still in there doing that trick with the beer bottle, he's not going to get any work done." I said this loud enough for Jason to hear me. He winked at me. "You two aren't going to get anything done. I'll give you a call when I get home."

Chuck got into his car and pulled out into the street. Jason followed him. Chuck stopped his car and looked toward the porch.

"Mr. Otis!" he yelled. Then he hit the gas, spun the wheels, and smoked the street.

Otis, Johnny, and Bob T. stood up from their chairs to get a better view of Chuck's show. They howled and cheered as he pulled away. I went back to the porch to join them.

"Those some good friends you got there," Otis said. "That Chuck coming down here, stayin' the last couple of days. Can't ever replace good friends." Otis was talking as much to himself, as he was to me.

I sat on the porch with my dad's friends and listened as they continued their stories. Every time one of them told a story, the next one had a better one to tell. The stories continued until they couldn't remember any more, or make any more up. As I pondered their memories of my dad, a smile came to my face. I was gaining new insight into him. I hadn't known him the same way that they had. My father had had a profound effect on a number of lives. Learning more about him through their experiences made me feel closer to him.

After the house had emptied and all the tales had been told, I sat on the porch by myself, replayed them in my head, and reflected on those last moments that I was able to spend with my dad. If only I could have understood what it was he was trying to say to me in that hospital room, maybe it would help give me some closure. It seemed like he was hanging on for something.

"Why are you sitting out here by yourself?" Denise came out of the house to join me.

"My dad's friends were out here telling stories about him. Just thinking, seeing him the way they saw him."

"There were a lot of people here today," Denise said.

"Dad couldn't go anywhere without making a friend. Mr. Otis said he could make a friend at a Klan rally if he had two minutes alone with one of them."

"Mr. Otis is a trip." Denise checked over her shoulder

to see if anyone was there. "That Martha's the real trip, though."

"Who you telling? She and my dad were like night and day. What'd she do?"

"Before she left, she was in there trying to get your uncle's attention, and Aunt Sarah kept looking at her like it could be on at any time. She was lucky she got out of here when she did."

"Aunt Sarah got a new hip last year, but I'm willing to bet she wouldn't have minded wearing it out on Martha's tail."

"Martha and your dad certainly weren't two of a kind."

"Funny how two people can grow up in the same house and be that different from one another. It's like they didn't take the same thing away from there."

"It happens more than you think."

Denise and I sat there in silence for a few minutes. She was waiting for me to move the conversation in any direction, and she would follow.

"He looked good, didn't he?"

"Yes, he did," Denise said, stroking my hair. She kissed my forehead as I leaned my head against her shoulder. "I know you'll miss him."

"More than I can put into words. He gave me everything he had. Most of the guys I know, barely knew their fathers. I was lucky to have him. You've heard people who are adopted say that they feel like there's a void in their life."

"Uh-huh."

"I never felt like that. I've always been at home here. I never felt out of place."

"That is a blessing. Most adoptees want to find their biological parents. Something to close a circle for them, you know, find out why they were left out."

"That's true. I just never had a need for it." I lifted my head and looked towards the house. "I don't need to find my birth parents. Dad's gone...but that's my mom in there...I wouldn't drag her through anything like that."

"Do you think it would bother her if you wanted to find them?"

"Don't know; we never talked about it. But I'm sure she would support me if I did."

"If that was what you needed to do for yourself, there's no doubt that she'd support you."

Denise pulled my head back to her and placed it in her lap. She took one hand and stroked my hair and placed the other one on my chest. This woman had a way of knowing what it took to make me feel at ease even before I did.

"The first time I came to your parents' house, I felt love. Pure love. The way your parents were toward each other, toward you and me. They had a way of reaching people, pulling them in, and accepting them for who they were. Well, probably not your Aunt Martha. But I've always had a sense of that. Even now, with your father gone, it's still here. It's a little harder to find right now, but eventually things will settle back down and that love will ring through just as clear as it always has."

I closed my eyes as I listened to Denise tell me in her way that everything was going to be okay. She was right, but it would be a struggle to get to okay.

13

I woke up early Tuesday morning. Denise and I had fallen asleep on the couch in the den. Mom was sleeping in the recliner. After Aunt Sarah and Uncle Johnny had left, we sat in the den and talked, played Gin Rummy, and Mom pulled out my old Monopoly game. She waxed Denise and me the same way she used to wax Dad and me. She was ruthless when it came to the game; oftentimes she would keep her opponents alive but strip them of all their property. If that wasn't bad enough, she was talking smack to us. But we didn't mind; it allowed her to focus her mind on something else, at least for a little while.

I eased away from Denise and the blanket that was covering us. Mom must have covered us up sometime during the night. I washed my hands, brushed my teeth and went straight to the kitchen to start preparing what my mom called the Jimmy P. World Famous Omelet.

The refrigerator at my parents' house was always fully stocked, whether it was food from Food Lion, deer meat from one of Dad's hunting excursions, or that half a cow in the deep freezer that Dad and Otis had split after they had slaughtered it themselves. Mom and Dad made sure you could always get a full belly at their house.

It only took a few seconds to find the ingredients I needed. Tomatoes, onions, green bell pepper, sliced ham, and some shredded cheddar cheese. I went about the task of carefully dicing my ingredients and placing them in a bowl. I selected eight eggs that would hold the masterpiece I was about to create.

"Boy, what are you doing?" Mom said, with a knowing smile.

"I was trying to surprise you two." Mom and Denise loved my omelets, and I wanted Denise to have one of my treats before she left. "Now you relax and let me finish, okay?"

"You're gonna need this." Mom reached under the stove and pulled out her well-used, blackened iron skillet. "You know you can't make an omelet in here without that pan."

I nodded my head and smiled. She was right; that pan sure had a way of frying an omelet. I'd almost swear that if you turned your back on the pan, it would cook the omelet by itself.

"Thank you, Mother. I'll take it from here." I knew she wouldn't sit down or relax. She would let me cook, but she would not give up her domain. My mom had to know what was going on in her kitchen at all times. She used to tell my father it was unnatural for another woman to cook in her kitchen, and I don't recall anybody else cooking in there except me, Aunt Sarah, and

Mrs. Bernice. If I hadn't been her son, I'm sure I wouldn't have been cooking in there.

"Is that what I think it is?" Denise came into the kitchen rubbing here eyes when the aroma of the first omelet caught her attention.

"My boy is in here burnin' up something," Mom teased.

"You know how I do."

"Yes, I do," Denise said with a hint of a sexual overtone.

"Well, let me go freshen up." Mom never missed a thing. She went to the bathroom.

"What's up with you?" I asked.

"Nothing; what's up with you?" Denise smiled.

"Just trying to get my grill on." I leaned over and kissed Denise. "Damn, baby, you might want to freshen up, too," I joked.

"Oh, now see, you don't try to play me like that when we're at home." She grabbed me and started kissing my whole face.

"All right now; I'll really burn this food."

"Okay. Do you need me to do anything?"

"No, just relax and enjoy breakfast."

Mom and Denise set the table while I finished cooking. I placed each omelet on a plate and garnished it with some salsa. I was a little light on Mom's; she didn't go for a lot of spices anymore. I took Mom and Denise their plates and went back for mine. I sat down at the table and noticed Mom was already looking at the dishes.

"I'll take care of the dishes after we finish eating," I said.

That put Mom at ease. I looked at Denise and thought I'd better get to blessing the food real fast. I recognized that look in her eyes; her mouth was watering for that food. After the blessing was finished, there was no more conversation for at least three bites.

"Mmm, mmm," Mom uttered with her eyes closed and inhaling through her nose, savoring the flavor.

"Uh-huh, uh-huh," Denise mumbled in total agreement.

I couldn't cook a lot of things, but I could cook the hell out of an omelet, that was for sure. It made me feel good to see them enjoying their meal. Sometimes doing things for other people brought more joy than one ever thought possible.

When I was in college and came home during Christmas break, I'd make omelets and creamed beef for breakfast on Christmas morning. It had gotten to be a tradition. Wherever we spent Christmas, I'd be making omelets and creamed beef. I wondered if that would change without Dad around.

"You know you put the whup on this," Denise said.

"I try."

"Oh, stop being humble," Mom said.

"Well, you know I hooked it up."

We laughed, and talked while we enjoyed the rest of our meal. When we had finished, Mom immediately tried to clear the table.

"I'll get that," Denise said, as she collected our plates and glasses, and took them to the sink.

"So how long will it take you to get back to Charlotte?" Mama asked.

"A little more than two-and-a-half hours."

"Two-and-a-half. It only takes Boogie two hours."

Boogie was the nickname that I'd always had growing up. As far as Mama was concerned, I wouldn't ever grow out of it. But she limited when she used it now.

"Mama P., have you taken a ride with Boogie lately?"

I knew that she'd be calling me Boogie for the next week now. Happened every time she'd been around my mother.

"No, and I know better. That boy drives faster as he gets older."

"Okay, okay, break it up. I knew it wouldn't be long before you two started teaming up on me." Playfully, I tried to divert Denise's attention back to the sink and the dishes that needed to be cleaned.

I heard Mama scoot her chair back, so I knew she was standing up and then I heard her clear her throat. I turned and looked at her. She slowly moved her gaze from me to the bottom drawer near the refrigerator, and flashed a devilish grin. I straightened up with a quickness. That move was lost on Denise.

"I don't get it." Denise was confused.

"You going to tell her?"

"Come on, Ma." *Please, not now*, I thought.

"What is it?" Denise was dying to know what had stopped me in my tracks. "It's got to be something in that drawer."

That bottom drawer contained a belt that at times I had gotten a little more familiar with than I would have liked to remember. It was a well-worn, brown leather belt. The leather was so old it was cracking in places, but it still held strong. That drawer was where I marched every time I was in serious trouble. I'd retrieve the belt, take it to my parents, receive the spanking and then I'd have to take it back. That was some lazy discipline if you asked me. Some people had to pick their own switch; me, I had to get my own belt.

"That's the drawer where my parents kept the straightening belt."

"Straightening belt?"

"The belt I got spankings with. Whenever I got out of line, they used it to straighten me back up." I looked at my mom. "You know you could go to jail for that stuff now. They've got DSS for people like you."

"Well, I hope you got the number. The way you're talking, you're gonna need them."

"Ohhh, get the belt, Mama P." Denise was instigating.

"All right, I'm going to leave you two right where you're at." It was time to remove myself from the situation.

"He remembers that belt, doesn't he, Mama P.?"

"Sure he does. Look at him over there trembling. I got him in check." Mama and Denise cracked up.

I laughed, too, but it would have been a lot funnier if I hadn't been the one on the receiving end of those whippings.

We all pitched in and had the kitchen cleaned in no time. I packed Denise's clothes while she took her shower. She had to leave soon; she was doing the 5:30 and 6 o'clock news today. She was leaving early enough so she could get back up to speed before the broadcasts.

I put Denise's suitcase into the trunk of her car, picked up the newspaper and went back inside. I sat down in my father's recliner in the den and opened up the paper.

The sports section was usually the first thing I read. It was a ritual I could trace back to high school. Saturday morning, after a football game, I'd scan the sports section to see if I had gotten my name in the paper. The local section drew my attention today though.

An article about Warren Johnson caught my eye. It was a small article, but it was on the front and continued on an inside page. It covered the same information I had read in the Charlotte paper last Friday. The news had now traveled to Asheville. I kept reading until Mom interrupted.

"Is that the local section?"

"Yes, ma'am," I said, handing it over to her. Dad had always taken the front page, while Mama took the Local and I took Sports.

"You finished reading? I can read it later."

"I was skimming some things I've already read."

She didn't give me another chance to reconsider; the words were barely out of my mouth when she swiped the section from me. She was already turning pages by the time she sat down.

When Denise had finished getting dressed, I was through with the Sports section and working on the national news. Denise had another carry bag in the room that needed to go into the car. The cute grin and the batting eyes were the signals for me to go get it. "It's about that time," Denise said to us.

"You sure you have everything?" Mama asked.

"I think so, but if I forgot anything, Boogie will get it for me."

"I heard that!" I yelled over my shoulder.

I grabbed Denise's carry bag and turned around to go out of the room when I noticed my closet door was open. My bag was hanging partially out. I hoped she hadn't been in there. After a real quick check, I found the ring box was still in the side pocket and the ring was still there, but had she seen it? I put the ring back up. It was better not to say anything about it unless I had to.

I took the bag outside to where Mom and Denise were hugging by the car. I walked past them, trying to pick up any indication that my surprise had been blown, but could not. I popped the trunk, placed the bag in, and listened.

"You call us when you get home."

"Yes, ma'am, I will."

"And don't you be driving like Boo…" Mom looked at me as I shut the trunk. "Like Jimmy."

"Don't worry. I won't drive like *that*." Denise was laying it on thick.

"You drive worse than I do."

"Now don't you start nothin' with her. Come on around here and tell her goodbye." Mom walked over to the porch and piddled around.

"So what were you two talking about?" I asked.

"Just making sure she was all right. What about you? You okay?"

"Yeah. Hey, thanks for everything." I put my arms around Denise and pulled her to me. I was still searching, but I was pretty sure she didn't know about the ring. "I love you."

"I love you, too."

"Be safe, okay?" I started to kiss her, but I noticed Mom staring at us. I hesitated; couldn't kiss her with Mom looking. Moms put her hands on her hips, looked at me, looked at Denise, and then back at me.

"She's waiting. Go on and kiss her."

So I did. Denise got in the car, started it and backed out.

"See you tomorrow," I said.

Mom stood beside me and we waved at Denise as she pulled off.

"That's a winner there, Boogie."

"She sure is."

"She should be my daughter." Mom smiled.

I smiled back. I waited to see if there were any questions to follow. There weren't. Maybe this was just a coincidence and neither one of them had a clue about my intentions to propose. Only time would tell.

14

T he door to my parents' bedroom had been closed since I had arrived here early Saturday morning, a barrier I hadn't crossed. My mother had gone in there as little as possible over the last four days. Maybe to get a change of clothes or some odds and ends, but she would not spend a lot of time in there. For all the cleaning we did to the house, this was the one room that had not been touched.

Mom told me it was time, the hospital bed was being returned today. That came as a shock to me. Hospital bed? I had no idea that there was a hospital bed in there for my father. Things here at home had gotten far worse for him than they had ever let on.

I stood at the door for five minutes trying to go in there. It seemed like hours. This lack of mobility, the trepidation of moving forward was becoming all too familiar to me and getting old. When I finally opened the door, my eyes locked on that hospital bed. It was next to my parents' bed. Adjustments were made to the nightstand and dresser so the hospital bed could be next to their bed. As far back as I could remember, when my parents slept under the same roof, they slept in the same bed. Apparently, not even a hospital bed could keep them from being beside each other.

Thankfully, there wasn't a substantial amount of hospital equipment in there. Seeing the bed was enough to make my stomach drop. The room was stagnant, lifeless. It reminded me of death. I opened the window to let some fresh air flow through.

"Take the sheets off the bed. I'll wash them." Mama entered the room.

"Yes, ma'am." I looked at the hospital bed and then to her. "I didn't know it was in here."

"They put it in here in early February. It was getting hard for your father to get in and out of our bed, so we got this for him."

"He must've hated it."

"He didn't mind the bed; it was easier on him. He didn't like not being in our bed. They'll be here to pick it up any time now."

No sooner had she uttered the words than there was the sound of the doorbell ringing.

"That's probably them now." Mom went to get the door.

Mom wanted to start boxing up the clothes and other items that only Dad would use, and take them to the Salvation Army. I looked around the room, trying to decide where to start first when I recalled Mom's instructions. I pulled the sheets off the bed, folded them and put them to the side; I'd take care of it later. Friday's paper was sitting there near the bed. It was the last one my dad would ever have had a chance to read. I should have found something else to do while the bed was being taken out, but as with a car accident on the highway, I watched them anyway.

These guys knew what they were doing. They operated with precision and had the bed broken down in less than fifteen minutes. It was out of the house and they were gone in under a half-hour. The room was now back in the same order it had always been in.

"I think I'm going to change this room around," Mom said.

She tried to be upbeat for my sake, and probably hers, too. But underneath that, she knew that even though the room looked the same, none of it would ever be back in the same order.

"You want me to throw this paper out?" I handed Friday's paper to her. *That's odd*, I thought to myself, there was an article that was cut out of the paper. Mama looked at the paper and also noticed the missing article.

"Go on and throw it out."

I cleaned out the items my father had in the bathroom. Shaving kit, razors, combs, even an old can of Murray's that had been in there since I was eight years old. I cleaned out Dad's dresser and boxed up all the clothes that were in there. All of his T-shirts were in one drawer, folded the same way. Socks and underwear in another drawer, folded the same way. Sweatshirts, same thing. He believed there was a place for everything and everything was in its place.

I set the boxes outside the bedroom door so Mom could mark them. I'd start on the closet. Everything was uniformly hung. Suits, slacks, long-sleeved shirts, short-sleeved shirts, work clothes. Those had to be folded and boxed, too. The last things to be boxed up would be the shoes.

While gathering up the shoes, I came across a few shoeboxes and a large boot box. One had some items in it that Mom should probably have taken a look at. Match books from weddings, a pressed flower. Sentimental things she might want to hold onto. One box was empty; but the boot box had a bunch of newspaper clippings in it. The article on the top was from Friday's paper; it was an article about Warren Johnson.

There were many other articles underneath this one. They were about Warren Johnson as well. His trial, conviction and sentencing, even articles about his appeals. There were articles from the Asheville, Charlotte and Raleigh papers, and it was all in chronological order. Underneath the articles were some pictures of a young African American male at different ages, but it was the same person. These matched the person whose picture was in the paper: Warren Johnson.

I studied the pictures and articles. Why would this stuff be in here? Why was it placed under shoes in a boot box in the back corner of the closet? Then it hit me. Could it be? No, not my father. He wouldn't have done anything like that; he couldn't have done anything like that. But there was no other explanation. My father must've had another son.

"Are you finished in the closet?" Mom asked, standing behind me.

I was so engrossed in the articles and the thoughts that were racing through my mind I never even heard her come back into the room. I tried to cover the box up and put it back down. If this was what I suspected it was, I didn't want Mom to see it.

"What's in that box?" She was shifting her weight on her feet trying to look over my shoulder. "What is that, newspaper?"

"It's nothing, just some stuff that needs to be thrown out."

"Thrown out? I haven't looked at it yet."

"I went through it; it's nothing." I knew this wouldn't work, but I had to try something to keep her from looking at the box.

"Jimmy, give me the box."

There was no way for me to avoid this. I stood up, with the box in hand, and turned around to face her. Reluctantly, I stuck the box out to meet her outstretched hands.

She took the box, sat down on the bed, and opened it up. Mom probed the first article for a few seconds. Then she started leafing though the rest of the articles until she got to the pictures. She took a deep breath and looked at me. She had a curious look on her face, but I couldn't read it, had no idea what she might be thinking. She turned her attention back to the box, closed it, and walked out of the room, taking the box with her.

I watched her leave and didn't know if I should follow her or let her be by herself. If my father had another son, she would be devastated, and she would need me. I left everything where it was and went to sit with her in the living room.

We sat there for a half-hour and I listened to Mom flip through the articles one at a time. There was so much to say, but neither one of us seemed to be able to get the ball rolling. So I waited some more.

"Are you okay?" I asked when I couldn't bear to listen to the deafening silence any more.

"Yeah… How about you?"

"Fine." I waited for her to continue. She didn't. If this conversation was going to move forward, I would have to be the one to move it. "Ma, do you think Dad had another son?"

"What? Is that what you think?"

"I don't know. The box was hidden in the closet, so I don't know what to think."

"It wasn't his son."

"Well, can you tell me what that stuff is about?"

"Yes, but I want you to keep an open mind," she said.

This wasn't a good sign to me. Usually, whenever somebody said keep an open mind, it was always before they got ready to lay something heavy on me.

"I always thought you should've been told about this, but your father thought it would be best to let things be. We've never talked about your biological parents. Have you ever thought about them?"

"No, well, I mean, yeah, but what does that have to do with Johnson?"

"He's related to you."

"Related to me?"

"He's your half-brother, by your biological mother."

"What? You know who my birth mother is?"

"Yes, both of your parents actually."

"You know who they are?" I watched as Mom nodded. I stood up, not able to sit down on this. "Who are they? What are their names?"

"Let me tell it, okay?" Mom calmed me with her voice and I sat down again. "Your father and mother were murdered when they were twenty-two...by Warren's father. Silk was what they called him."

"Why?"

"He never wanted to let your mother go. He was a no-account, involved in dealing drugs, and your mother and father was on 'em pretty bad. Heroin and marijuana. It was just a bad situation all the way around."

"What happened to Silk?"

"They say Warren killed him."

"How? When?"

"The same night Silk killed your mother and father."

"Same night? How old was he?" My head was spinning again.

"Six or seven."

"How did he manage that?" I couldn't comprehend a six or seven-year-old boy killing a grown man.

"They say he had a butcher knife. When the police arrived, he was sitting on his father's stomach in the middle of the floor, stabbing him in the chest."

I heard what she was saying, but I still couldn't figure out how he had pulled it off.

"How old was I when all this happened?"

"You were only one. You were barely walking. The police found you in your bedroom asleep. Your mother and father were shot by Silk. I don't know if you slept through it or not, but that's how they found you."

One year old. I tried to picture this, dredge up some type of memory of it. It was a traumatic event; surely there was something I would remember, but I was drawing a blank.

"We adopted you after we found out about all this. I wanted to adopt Warren as well, but your father didn't want to."

"If a kid could kill his own father, I could understand why Dad didn't want to adopt him. There's no telling what kind of danger anybody could have been in." I couldn't believe the words I spouted, but it was an honest reaction.

"That wasn't his only reason."

"What else is there?"

"It had more to do with your father and Warren's father." Mom paused for a few seconds. Something heavy was coming. "Your father was our son."

There it was, a bombshell. My biological father was their son. My mind started to race through what this meant. My parents, William and Mamie Pruitt, were actually my grandparents.

"I wanted to tell you, but your father always said it would be best if we let it be."

"Why?" None of this was making sense.

"We lost Billy. That was what we called your father. We lost him long before he died. He was wild and high-strung. Your father and I couldn't do anything with him. William and Billy fought all the time. Words mostly, but the older Billy got, the more physical he became with your father and me. He was arguing with your father one time and hauled off and hit him in the face. William hit him back so hard I thought he'd killed him. I ran between 'em and covered Billy to keep your father from him. Billy threw me to the floor and cussed me. Said he hated me, and didn't need my help. Then he threatened to kill both of us. He left not long after that."

"How old was he?"

"Fifteen. He left with our car and almost seven thousand dollars your father had buried in the back yard. We never saw him alive again."

"Never talked to him?"

"I wanted to, but Billy and your father were just alike, both stubborn as hell. Your father hated Billy for leaving; he hated him more for not coming back. After a year or two, William started erasing Billy from our lives. I heard about him from time to time, especially when he got hooked on drugs. Your father didn't want to hear anything about him; when he was 'bout to change his mind on it, that was when Billy turned up dead." Mom let this settle for a few minutes before she pressed on. "Now your birth mother, I don't know too much about her. Her name was Evelyn Johnson. That's all we ever found out. We didn't even know you existed until Billy died. We'd lost all contact with him by then. Your father thought it would be best if we raised you as our son and let the past be the past. It became a Pruitt family secret. Us Pruitts have taken too many secrets to the grave."

My head was swirling with all this information my mom was telling me. It wasn't done swimming in the other pool of mess and it just got deeper. Biological parent, half-brother, all of this on top of my father's death.

I looked at the box my mother held in her hands. There was no need to back up now. Whatever came to mind, it was time to ask.

"Why did he keep up with Warren's life these last eight or nine years?"

"He began to feel guilty about not adopting him, too, especially when he saw he was in trouble behind that white gal. Before that, he never talked about Warren.

Deep down, your father still loved Billy. When this first happened, he felt like he couldn't bring the son of his son's murderer into this house. Over time, his feelings changed, but by then, he was with Evelyn's family. That was that."

"And now Warren's on death row."

"Your father thought that he could have made a difference in his life. Friday was the day he read that Warren was going to be executed in two and a half weeks. He wished you knew each other, even hoped you could help him."

My father passed shortly after I had arrived at the hospital. I had been trying to figure out what it was he was trying to communicate to me, but couldn't make sense of it then. Now it was crystal clear.

"The last thing he said to me, it was—*have brother, help him*, wasn't it? He was talking about Warren."

Mom nodded to me. This was my father's dying wish for me. To help the type of person that I was usually trying to put away. There were a whole lot of things coming at me right then. I was trying to make sense of it. This was something I didn't know if I could do, and I certainly wasn't about to make that decision then.

We talked and cleaned a lot more. We made the decision that I would go back home that day. Mom knew my plate was full and decided not to add to it with any additional portions. She would let me digest what I'd already been given.

Bob T. stopped in to check on us. He and Otis had gone fishing early that morning. He volunteered to take my dad's belongings to the Salvation Army. We took the boxes outside and loaded them into the back of his pickup. There was little conversation between us as was typical of our relationship. It was the kind of interaction I was accustomed to having with Bob T. Last night with him, Otis, and Johnny, that was a circle I'd never been in-vited into before.

"Me and Otis was s'posed ta do this for ya'll. Otis wasn't ready to pick through this stuff of Willie's yet."

"I understand."

Bob T. studied me. My voice told him something other than what I said.

"When ya goin' back?" he asked.

"About an hour." It would actually be as long as it took to get my Jeep packed. Bob T. stared at me, a piercing stare.

"Your mama told ya, didn't she?" He turned his attention back to the bed of the truck.

"Told me what?" I acted like I didn't know what he was talking about. Bob T looked back at me and just stared. "Yeah, she did."

"Your father was human. He ran off of emotions. Emotions can make you do some wrongs. The wrongs he made were because he thought it was the best for you and his family. He never had a chance to fix what happened wit' Billy. That's why he worked so hard wit' you. He was a boy hisself when Billy come; he was a grown man when you hit. He taught you a lot. Showed you a lot and told you a lot of things. He just couldn't tell you about Billy."

In a roundabout way, Bob T. was telling me not to hold this against my father. It was the most he'd ever spoken to me in my life. I wondered how many people knew about this. Everybody who knew my parents for a long time had to know about Billy.

"We gonna see to your mother now. Don't worry 'bout her. She'll probably stay down to Otis and Bernice's for a couple of days." Bob T shut the tailgate and walked to the front of the truck. "You want to go wit' me?"

"No, sir. I'll be leaving before long."

"Be careful." Bob T. got in the truck and left.

An hour later, I was packed and ready to go. Mrs. Bernice stopped by to sit with Mom. I knew she was in good hands. I gave Mrs. Bernice a hug and then hugged my mother as tight as I could.

"I'll call you when I get home," I said when I let go.

"You okay?"

"I will be." I hoped that was true.

"I know you will. You'd better not be speedin' up and down that road."

"I won't."

"Don't waste your breath and tell that lie," Bernice said. "Before you get gone, stop down there and holla at Otis now."

"I will." I'd blow the horn and speak, but I didn't plan to stop.

I got into the Pathfinder. The time had come for me to head home and try to make sense of everything that had happened, and everything I'd learned.

15

"That's some heavy shit, dog," Chuck said.

Chuck was getting the rundown on my family history and the new addition to it. This was more weight than I wanted to carry alone. I called Denise during my drive back, but it was 4:20 in the afternoon and she was preparing for the newscast. I was able to give her some of the highlights, but none of the specifics. She was coming by my house after work and we would talk about it at length then. It was almost 7:00 p.m.; she would be here soon but this albatross that hung around my neck wouldn't hold until then. So for now, Chuck was the lucky candidate who got to hear me out.

"And that was the last thing he said to you? 'Have brother, help him.' Wow. You gonna see him?"

"Don't know." That was the million-dollar question for the day. I had gone back and forth with that decision while driving home. Focusing on it didn't allow me to think about my father. "There's no reason for me to get involved with this guy."

There was a look on Chuck's face; he wanted me to justify that statement. He knew what was coming, but I had to be the one to say it.

"This guy's on death row. A convicted rapist, murderer and a known drug dealer. You've read the papers, seen the news; you know what's up. I'm a prosecutor. That's where I send people and yes, I like where he is. It's where he should be."

"Uh-huh, so you straight with that? Skip the law thing; you gonna just let that go?"

"Yeah, I can let it go, and I can't skip the law thing. It's who I am. It's what I do!"

"Bruh, take it easy. Just wanted to know where you were coming from, dog."

How could he know where I was coming from when I didn't? Things were coming at me so fast; it was getting hard to hold on, much less keep up.

"It's not something I can do right now."

"I feel you. But don't let your gig make the decision for you. That's blood." Then he smiled at me. "Plus, if you gonna do something, do it soon. Dude's on the short list."

Dude? Chuck had spent too much time with Jason yesterday.

"How long did Jason hang with you?"

"I got him home before his curfew. Yo, that food is smelling right; hook a brother up." Chuck was staring at the Chinese food in a wok.

"There's not enough for you."

"That's cold. I'm supposed to…" Chuck stopped in mid-sentence when he heard the garage door opening.

"Oh, hell no! Tell me she don't have a garage door opener to your crib."

"Yeah, and...?"

"She wearin' the ring yet?"

"Keep it down. I haven't had a chance to ask her; time hasn't been right.

"She got keys, a garage door opener, probably got clothes in your closet, and no damn ring on her finger?"

"It's coming; trust me. Soon as everything settles down."

"You'll be waiting forever. It never settles down; you just hold on."

Chuck wasn't just talking; he had the gift of gab and could say a lot and not say a thing, but he was saying something today, and I heard him. All I was doing right now was holding on.

The garage door was closing. Denise wouldn't be far behind that sound. The door to the garage was off to the left of the kitchen. Chuck and I were talking near the island that stands in the middle of the floor. As soon as that door started to open, Chuck was hung out to dry. I made a beeline to meet her.

"Damn, cuz, you need to get you some speed bumps in here." I knocked Chuck off balance as I went by.

When Denise had the door open, my open arms greeted her. I hugged her tightly, her breasts pressed against my ribs and I kissed her softly. She slid her hands to my waist as I slid my right hand down to the small of her back and pulled her hips toward mine.

"Hey, baby." She leaned her head back to look at me.

"Hey, yourself." Mom wasn't here to inhibit me. There was no doubt about my arousal, and I definitely wasn't trying to hide it until...

"Ahh, shit. Look at these two here. Like ya'll didn't see each other yesterday."

"Hello, Charles, damn," Denise said.

This was a new record for Chuck. It took him only fifteen seconds to bust up our groove.

"Hey, bruh, thanks for coming by. I'll holler," I said.

"Dog, you gonna play me like that?"

I looked at Chuck, and then I looked at the beautiful woman in my arms.

"Hell yeah, cuz, you got to go," I said.

Chuck looked at me, then slowly turned his head toward the wok where the stir-fry was going.

"I ain't budging 'til I get some of that."

"Well, look here, my brother, if it will help you get out of here, then by all means," Denise said, as we broke our embrace.

"That's what I'm talkin' 'bout, sister; unity."

"Man, get your food and get out of here."

Chuck and I had taken so much food out of each other's houses, we knew exactly where to go. He pulled a Chinet out of the cabinet. In no time, he had his plate loaded up, reached into the drawer of the island for the tin foil, slapped it across the top and he was ready to go.

"Look at the time. You two haven't seen each other for a minute, know what I mean. I need to raise up."

"Good lookin' out, dog. Thanks for comin' by," Denise said, mocking Chuck.

"Always. I'll let myself out."

We shook hands and he hugged Denise. Once he hit the door, Denise and I turned our attention back to each other.

"So, tell me about this half-brother."

"I will, after we eat. Hungry?" I wanted to start the story of Warren Johnson, tell her about Evelyn Johnson and Billy Pruitt. So far, I'd only told her that I had a half-brother; no names had been mentioned. After explaining all of this to Chuck, I was mentally exhausted and needed to recharge my batteries. Nourishment would come first and spending time with Denise was a top priority. Putting these issues to the side was necessary at the moment.

Denise didn't hesitate. "I'll fix the plates." She pulled two plates down from the cabinet and placed a bed of rice on each. She followed that with an ample amount of the stir-fried chicken and broccoli.

She was graceful as I watched her move around my kitchen like she was at home. Eventually she would be. That was the first thing I'd take care of once I straightened out all this other chaos that had become my life.

I lit a candle that was part of the centerpiece on the dining room table. When Mom bought me it as a housewarming gift, I thought it was corny. Had to remember to thank her for it again. I turned the lights down, put on some music and poured two glasses of wine. Denise joined me and placed the food before us. We sat across from each other and began to eat.

Denise teased and tempted me by eating her food slowly and sensuously. I definitely enjoyed watching her, but acted as if I wasn't moved. Other parts of my anatomy would tell a different story. I kept imagining it was me she was placing her lips on, but didn't let her know how turned on I was.

"So, what's for dessert?" Denise asked when she had finished eating.

"I didn't make any dessert."

Without changing the blank stare I gave Denise, I started unbuttoning my shirt very slowly, pulling my arms out of the sleeves and letting the shirt fall where it was. I stood up, unbuttoned my jeans and pulled the zipper down. Far enough to expose my manhood. The look on Denise's face was priceless. I stepped out of the jeans so Denise could enjoy the full view of my attire. I leaned across the table until mere inches separated me from her, still staring blankly. I kissed the side of her neck just below her ear.

"I'll be upstairs," I whispered in her ear. I kissed her lips softly, placing her bottom lip between my lips and gently sucking on it. Before getting too carried away, I backed off and started for the stairs. "You coming?" I smiled.

"Uh-huh," she struggled to utter.

I took her hand and led her from the dining room,

through the foyer, to the stairs and up to my room. The smell of the Egyptian Musk-scented candle filled my room, and Luther Vandross' "A House Is Not A Home" floated to our ears. The candle lent a soft glow to the room, which allowed me to take pleasure in watching Denise as she slowly undressed. She removed her blouse to expose a burgundy lace bra that complemented her beautiful brown skin. She unzipped her slacks and slipped them down to reveal the matching panties.

The glow of the candle bounced off the contours of her body. The conservative news journalist had transformed herself into a sexy, sultry temptress in a matter of seconds. As the music played, I began to kiss Denise on the side of her neck and held her as we began to sway with the music. Holding her, I skillfully unhooked her bra, slipped it off. I gently began to remove her panties and bent to my knees. I wrapped my arms around her waist and pressed the side of my head against her lower abdomen. Denise touched my cheek and ran her fingers over my hair. I kissed her navel and kissed up her body as I stood. Then I felt her hands around my waist and she started to slide them down, taking hold of my excitement. Denise guided me to the bed where I began to caress her, and passionately kiss her breasts, moving up to her neck. I felt her soft, tender lips near my ear and heard her moan. I placed my lips on hers and looked into her eyes. She moaned with pleasure as we found our rhythm.

Everything I'd experienced over the last six days—joy, pain, grief and anxiety—I gave to her and she willingly accepted. Without a word, she communicated that to me. I didn't just connect with her physically. I was connecting with her soul as she was connecting with mine. That, to me, was pure love.

"Unbelievable. Your mom told you all this?"

Denise was sitting in a bubble bath with me sitting beside her on the edge of the tub. She now had the whole story of Billy Pruitt, Evelyn Johnson, and my half-brother, Warren Johnson.

"Mom always wanted me to know."

"Warren Johnson is your brother." Without any reservation came her next statement. "When are you going to see him?"

"The appropriate question is *will* I see him?"

"Aren't you curious? I know you have questions. I would."

"No. This is insane. I can't catch my balance. Every time I think I'm going to, something else throws me back off."

"It just takes time; you'll get it back." Denise sat up in the tub as something dawned on her. "No wonder you never felt a void."

"What?" The statement lost me, got me off kilter again.

"Yesterday, you said you never felt a void like most

adoptees. It makes perfect sense." She paused, waiting for me to grasp the obvious. "You were always where you were supposed to be."

I hadn't looked at it that way. I was caught up in thinking my mom and dad were actually my grandparents, my biologicals were junkies who had been murdered by my half-brother's father. My half-brother was on death row and I had just buried my dad. My mind was racing a thousand miles a minute, but it did make sense. Denise was right; I was where I was always supposed to be.

"Come here, baby." She extended her arms to me. I took off the towel that was around my waist, and climbed into the tub with Denise. Sitting between her legs with my back to her, she wrapped her arms around me. "It gets better; trust me."

"I don't know what to do about Warren."

"Yes, you do, and you know what your father wanted. Regardless of how or when or where you found out, or even what he did, Warren Johnson is your brother. The only one you have. If you don't go see him, one day you'll find yourself wondering why you didn't."

It may not have been something I wanted to do, but it was something my father needed me to do. She had a point.

16

"Thought you weren't coming back to work until Friday," Jason said as he entered my office. He put his briefcase down and shook my hand.

The door to my office was open. I had stopped in to see what had piled up on my desk over the last couple of days. It was also a good time to review some of the precedents set in death penalty cases involving rape and murder.

"I'm not here now."

"Suit and tie says different. Files and journals all over your desk. What's going on?"

"I'm going to visit my brother in Raleigh."

"I didn't know you had a brother. Was he at the funeral?"

"Ah…No. I didn't know I had a brother, either."

"Really." Jason wanted to know more. There was an inquisitive look about him, but he realized this could be a long story. He looked at his watch before picking up his briefcase. "You have got to tell me about it when I have more time."

"I'll tell you all about Warren Johnson." Just like fishing. Bait the hook.

"Yeah, well... Warren Johnson... In Raleigh...Central Prison." I nodded at him. He put down his briefcase. "I got some time." Hook, line and sinker.

Jason got the quick version of the Warren Johnson connection. No need to tie him up too long. He had work to do and I wanted to get out of there before too many people showed up. It was almost 8:00 a.m. and Charlotte traffic was already backed up. If I left soon, I could be at the Central Prison in Raleigh by 11:00 a.m. Jason had a few contacts at Central Prison. He was going to make a couple of calls to make sure I didn't have any problems getting in to see Warren.

At 8:05 a.m., I was out of the office and headed north on I-85. The traffic on 85 had been reduced to a crawl because of an accident near the university area. So much for being in Raleigh by 11:00 a.m.; at least I wasn't on a time schedule. The traffic slowdown cost me an additional fifteen minutes. The traffic picked up beyond the university exit. I followed 85 to Greensboro where it merged with I-40. It was on to Burlington and Durham until I reached Raleigh. The GPS led me on to Central Prison.

It was exactly 11:27 a.m. when I arrived at the prison, a little later than I'd aimed for, but not too bad. I'd been to Central Prison before when I was in law school. It was a tour with some other first year students. I didn't pay much attention to the surroundings then because my nerves were getting the better of me. We barely looked up the entire tour. I never met one convict's eye. I never had a reason to come back until now. Now it was different. I paid attention to everything. The prison grounds looked clean and fresh. The grass was rich, deep green and neatly mowed. Flowers were in bloom, and as I pulled up toward the main entrance, the facility looked more like a large high school or a small college than a prison.

I paid more attention this time to the twenty-foot-high gate with spiraling barbed wire on top that seemed to run for miles in both directions. Central was a maximum-security facility. As nice as it appeared on the outside, I knew there was some real tough education happening on the other side of those walls. *What was I getting myself into?*

I rolled my window down to speak to the guard at the gate.

"Your name, sir?!" he barked while looking at his clipboard.

"James Pruitt."

"Pruitt?" He began to scan his list.

"I'm with the District Attorney's Office in Charlotte."

"Warren Johnson, right?" He waited for me to acknowledge him. "You're here to see Warren Johnson?"

I nodded. He provided instructions on where to park and informed me that a guide would take me to the row. So I parked and waited. The longer I waited, the mental debate of whether I'd made the right decision in coming waged on. There was nothing between me and the guy who was inside those walls. It was 12:28 p.m. I waited over forty minutes for the guide to take me to death row and he still hadn't shown up yet. It was a wasted trip. It wasn't the place for me to be. I started my car and was prepared to back out when I spotted a corrections officer in the rearview mirror standing directly in my path. I turned off the engine.

"You the one here to see Johnson?" he said in a deep, Southern drawl as he approached my door.

That tone was one I was all too familiar with. There was no mistaking what element I was dealing with. "Yes, I am."

"Come on hea, den," he said.

Sure enough, I had me a bona-fide deep woods redneck. I got out of my vehicle to get a better look at this good ol' boy. He was no taller than five-foot-seven and if he weighed a hundred and fifty-five pounds, he'd need to be fully clothed and soaking wet. As I watched him move, it was evident he had the agility of a cat. He had red hair, graying at his brush-cut temples, a weathered face with steely blue eyes. I could just imagine what kind of things he would do for fun. I got a look at his nametag before he turned around.

"T. Carter, James Pruitt." I almost extended my hand, but I doubted he would take it.

"Uh-huh. Prosecutor with the District Attorney's Office in Charlotte," Carter shot back at me.

Good news traveled fast around these parts.

Carter got me signed into the prison. I had to allow

myself to be searched by one CO while another one searched my briefcase. After being satisfied that there were no concealed weapons or contraband, they turned me back over to T. Carter so he could escort me to the visiting area for death row.

As we walked the corridors, the cleanliness of the facility continued to surprise me. It wasn't a full representation of the prison, at least not from what I'd been told. To capture the full prison experience, you would have to pull some 24/7s, spend some time in solitary confinement as well as among the general population; then you would know.

When we arrived at the visiting area, Carter ushered me to a seat that faced a thick, bulletproof glass where Warren would be sitting on the other side.

"It'll be a few more minutes before the boy arrives."

"What boy, T. Carter?" I may not have known Johnson, but I wasn't going to let this redneck ridicule him.

"Johnson." He glared at me. "He's in lockdown twenty-three hours a day; gets one hour out of his cell. He works out during his time out, from eleven to twelve. He needed to clean hisself up for he got hea."

"Thanks for letting me know, T. Carter."

"It's just Carter."

"Thank you, T. Carter." I looked at him and let my eyes lead him to the door. "I'll let you know if I need you." Carter was incensed. I could only imagine the degree of his displeasure after being dismissed by me.

The seats in front of the glass were partitioned off. I

couldn't see anyone coming or going until they crossed the section directly in front of me. There was a massive figure that stopped in front of the partition.

This man looked to be six-foot-two. He had a bald head and there was a slight glisten to it. It was likely damp from his workout or shower. His orange prison jumpsuit barely contained his massive chest. The sleeves were cut out and revealed his hugely defined arms. Veins so thick you could almost see the blood pumping through them. This was Warren Johnson.

He seemed stunned to see a well-groomed African American in a suit on the other side of his partition. He studied me as if he were stalking prey, trying to recognize me. He motioned for me to pick up the phone to my right. I picked it up slowly and put it to my ear. Neither of us took our eyes off each other. Johnson, still sizing me up, sat down, snatched the phone to his ear, waited. So did I. "You ain't my lawyer. Who the fuck are you?" He wasn't loud, but he definitely was attempting to be intimidating. Although I wasn't about to let him know it, he was succeeding.

"James Pruitt," I responded calmly.

"What do you want?"

"To meet you."

"Meet me? What you looking for, a date, bitch?"

As much as I wanted to, I didn't flinch. I wasn't going to let myself be intimidated by him. Especially not with the glass between us. So I just stared at him and waited for him to make the next move.

"Who are you?"

"James Pruitt." I held up a business card to the glass. "I'm a prosecutor with the District Attorney's office in Charlotte.

He leaned in to look at the card. "I can read. You muhfuckers are somethin'. What you want to charge me with? Some unsolved cases you got since you know I'm scheduled to die?"

"No. I just wanted to meet you."

"Don't give me no bullshit. I got lawyers callin' me every day tryin' to pin shit on me; tryin' to defend me; and you don't want a piece of that? Come on, Bougie, you don't want to make a name for yourself, nigger?"

"I owed somebody something." I wrote my cell phone number on the back of my business card and put in the corner of the glass.

"James Pruitt, Pruitt..." his voice trailed off and he got lost in his thoughts.

I stared at him until it looked like he had snapped back into reality.

"You all right?"

"Pruitt...the name just made me think of someone I knew."

"I've done what I came to do, so I'll..."

"Hold up, son." He looked at the clock on the wall. "I got some time. I don't think you came all the way from Charlotte just to see me live. Where you grow up?"

"Asheville." It would be interesting to see where this went.

"I had a little brother, lived in Asheville...don't know what happened to him." Warren squinted his eyes and looked into mine. He was looking for his answer. There was none from me.

"M-I-C," Warren said slowly.

"See you real soon." It was out of my mouth before I could stop myself. In that split second, I had a vision of the old Mouseketeers show.

"K-E-Y."

I nodded. I couldn't explain it, but we had just made a connection. We used to watch that show together.

"Jimmy." He smiled for the first time and his eyes took in as much of me as he could. He held his head down for a few seconds and then slowly raised it. By the time our eyes met again, his expression had changed. "Get The Fuck Out! Now!"

Two COs rushed to restrain him when they heard that loud outburst. He was pounding on the glass when they grabbed him. Damn if it didn't shake under his blows.

"Punk ass nigger is a fuckin' lawyer. Now you show up. Where you been, bitch? I got nothin for you, nigger!"

The COs got control of him, but not before he spit on the glass in my direction. I watched as his saliva slid down the reinforced pane. They took him out of the visiting area. Now I was stunned. What had just happened? I came here to meet him, to fulfill a dying man's request, and that bastard cussed me out. He figured out who I was and got mad at me. What the hell was his problem? That pissed me off.

"I can show ya out if ya done hea," T. Carter said.

"Yeah, I'm done." I clutched my briefcase and stood up to go. I saw T. Carter pick up my business card, but I was too frustrated to worry about what he was going to do with it. Screw Warren Johnson, I had done what I had to do to assuage my conscience. It was time to go home.

17

"Looks like we'll have some great weather the next couple of days," Mike Nettles said. Mike was Denise's co-anchor at WSTV. He was fifty-eight years old and had a richly baritone, veteran news anchor voice.

"Sure does. For the Channel Twelve news team, I'm Denise Brown. Thanks for making us the choice for your news."

It was 6:27 p.m. and the evening news was over. I had crept into the studio during the last commercial break and watched the end of the telecast. I was lurking in the shadows behind one of the cameras to surprise Denise. After my experience with Johnson, I hoped to bring a smile to somebody's face. Denise unhooked her microphone, cleared the set and then I stepped out of the shadows toward her.

"Guess who's back?"

"Hey, you!" Denise's face lit up when she heard my voice and then spotted me. "When did you get here?" We met in the middle of the studio floor and kissed.

"James Pruitt." Mike interrupted our kiss. "Sorry, Denise, I'm real anxious to speak with your boyfriend."

My first inclination was that he must have gotten some information on my connection to Johnson. I looked at Denise. Had she told? With a look, she conveyed to me she had no idea where he was coming from.

"First of all, I am sorry to hear about your father," Mike said.

"Thank you." I'd only known Mike since Denise had started working with him, but every time I'd encountered him, he'd always been genuine.

"I also wanted to congratulate you on your victory in the Hughes case. I speak on behalf of WSTV when I say we're all very proud of you." He extended his hand.

"I appreciate that, Mike," I replied as I shook his hand.

Mike continued to hold my grip. "Can we get a better sound bite next time?" He gave me a wink and a smile. That had been his trademark for the last twenty years. It was his sign-off.

"I'll try." He released his grip and left the newsroom.

"So, did you see him?" Denise asked, scanning the room to see if anybody was in earshot.

"Yeah, I saw him. How long until you get out of here?" A newsroom was not the place to openly discuss Warren Johnson.

"About ten minutes."

"I'll meet you outside."

We drove to the NoDa area. North Davidson was five minutes from downtown Charlotte. It used to be an industrial area with thriving mills, warehouses, and manufacturing plants. But as Charlotte really began to grow in the late '60s, and four- and five-story buildings gave way to high-rises and skyscrapers, the industrial areas moved further and further from downtown. By the time banking was king of downtown in the mid-70s to early '80s, the old buildings and warehouses were pretty much abandoned. It started springing back to life in the early '90s with restaurants, clubs, and a very strong artistic community. North Davidson became known as NoDa. It was Charlotte's answer to Manhattan's SoHo. We parked at the Sanctuary Bar on Thirty-sixth Street and before we went in to have some drinks, I poured out my Johnson experience.

"The thing that surprised me about him was that his movements and his thought process seemed calculated. Before we ever spoke, he was already trying to figure me out."

"Did you talk long?"

"No. Didn't have a chance to. Once he started thinking about my last name, he blanked on me for a couple of seconds, and then he knew I was his brother. He asked one or two questions and he was sure of it."

"What did he say?"

"He started singing the Mickey Mouse Club theme song."

"The M-I-C thing?" Denise was puzzled

"Yeah. I fell right in on it. Strange thing was it carried me back to something I couldn't totally piece together.

But for a split second, we connected." I wanted to end the conversation at that, although I knew it wouldn't be over that easily.

"Is that how you left it?"

"Not hardly. He smiled at me and called me Jimmy; then he went on a profanity-laced tirade and told me to get out."

"What?"

"He kicked me out, and I left."

"So what now?"

I looked at the woman who meant so much to me as if I didn't know her. *What now?* Where did that question come from?

"Nothing. I did what my father wanted me to do. I went to see him, exchanged words with him, and he cussed me out. Done deal. He wants as much to do with me, as I want to do with him." Denise looked at me and before she could speak, I blurted out, "He's a criminal, Denise, and he is short on time. I can't do anything for him."

Denise conceded the point, for now. She realized that there was no convincing me to see this situation differently.

"Have you talked to your mom?" It was her last shot.

"Not yet. I'll call her later on."

"And tell her about this."

"I'll tell her that I met him, that we talked, but that's as far as it'll go. It's too late to fix the last twenty-seven years. Two days ago, I didn't know anything about him.

Today, I still don't. He was a name in the paper. I went there for my dad, not for me. He's on death row for rape and murder, and if I was the prosecutor on his case, I'd be glad to put him in that same hot seat. I don't have the time or the energy to be concerned about him. I've got too many other things going on right now."

There were two things that were for certain. One: those would be the last words Denise and I would speak on the subject of my half-brother for the present. And two: I wasn't finished dealing with Warren Johnson.

18

The sound of my ringing cell phone woke me. I glanced at the alarm clock. It was already 9:41 a.m. and Denise was gone. Thursday morning was when she got her hair done. I fumbled with the cell phone. "Hello." I tried to sound coherent.

"What up, dog?" Chuck said. "I would ask you where you're at, but I know you all hemmed up under that woman."

That woke me up.

"Hemmed up? Come on, man, this is me. No woman gonna hem me up unless I say so. I run this, hear me?!"

"Uh-huh." Chuck paused for a second and I heard him suck his teeth. "Let me holler at Denise."

"Ahh, beg your pardon?"

"You just played yourself, homes. She ain't there, is she?"

"No. She went to get her hair fixed. What's going on?"

"Chillin', man, thinkin' about ballin' over at the Y on Morehead around lunchtime. You down?

"Yeah, I have some gear over here." There was silence.

"You ask her yet?"

My mind was so caught up with my father and Johnson that I hadn't even thought about proposing to Denise.

"Not yet; been a little preoccupied."

I told Chuck about my road trip yesterday and how it had ended. Brief and bitter and I was done with it. To my surprise, Chuck let it go. There was no, "When you going back?" or anything. He told me if I was cool with it, then it was cool, and to meet him at the Y at 11:30 a.m.

It was almost 10:00 a.m. and I was just getting out of bed. Ordinarily it felt good to sleep in. Not this morning. I had slept late because there was little sleep to be had the night before. It wasn't a simple matter of not sleeping in my own bed; Denise's bed was like my own.

At 3:18 a.m., I'd been wide-awake. I'm not sure if it was my father or Johnson that woke me. Dad was on my mind, but I focused my energy on Warren because it allowed me to be angry. Anger was easier for me to handle than the pain I would encounter trying to sort through my emotions about my father. There was love, hurt, anger and guilt for feeling angry. I wasn't ready to continue that, so the anger toward Warren was much easier to stay on.

I went back to bed around 6:00 a.m., after I had cleaned, polished and dusted throughout Denise's condo to rid myself of the excess energy. As I focused on Johnson, I got angrier. I should have cussed Johnson out. The fact that I didn't only served to make me angrier, and the angrier I got, the more I cleaned. I was turning into my mom.

Balling with Chuck and some guys would be a good distraction for me. I could run, hang with some people and sweat. I wouldn't have to think about anything but putting the ball in the hoop.

I sent Denise a text to let her know what my plans were before I took a shower. I'd leave for the Y at 11:30 a.m. Chuck would show up late, swearing that it was traffic that had held him up.

"You okay, man?" I asked Chuck. We were playing four-on-four full court and Chuck was wearing down. This was our fifth game, and we'd split two games with the other team.

"Yeah, I'm good."

"Point game, Chuck, suck it up. We ain't gonna lose to these scrubs. They over there talking shit about you. What you gonna do?" That was the incentive that Chuck needed to fire him up and get him over the hump.

"They talking shit?" Chuck was burning. "All right, give me the rock. I'm taking it to the rack and hangin' my nuts on somebody."

One thing about competition and sports, the guys on your side are always the good guys. The people across from you, they're the bad guys. Didn't matter if it were your best friend or family. In competition, the only goal was winning. If you were not there to win, then you had no business being there.

The ball was inbounded at half-court. I got the ball

on the left side of the high post and drew a double team. Chuck found an open spot on the other side of the floor. I passed to him. He pump- faked the defender who flew at him. One dribble and he exploded to the basket. Chuck laid down a thunderous tomahawk dunk.

"Ball game, suckers," Chuck said, as he slumped to the floor, exhausted. He was shot.

"You out there dunking like you're still in college," I said, leaning over Chuck.

"One difference: back then I could stand up after a game. Help me up so I can take a shower."

"Let's see if some of these guys want to get some wings or something," I said as I helped pull Chuck to his feet.

This was part of our male bonding tradition. After we broke a sweat together, we'd break bread together.

We gathered at the Chophouse on Morehead. They promoted themselves as having the best wings this side of Buffalo. If you liked hot hot wings, this was your spot. They had a sauce so hot it was called *suicide*. The first time I asked for it, they brought me some in a plastic container with a lid on it. I popped the top, took a whiff, and thought I had singed my nose hair. That stuff was strong.

Two pitchers of beer and an order of wings had already cleared the table and more were coming while we rehashed the game. Two of the guys from the other team joined us. Cotton and Big E. I'd played ball with or against those guys for the last two years and still didn't know what their real names were.

"Bet you guys didn't think I had hops like that no more," Chuck said.

"Shit, nobody doubted your hops. Nobody thought you'd be able to finish the game," Cotton said. He was a fairly short guy with a handle for days, but his jumper was suspect.

"What you talkin' about, Cotton?" Chuck asked.

"C'mon, man," Big E said. "Your eyes were as big as fifty-cent pieces. Hard as you were breathing, I thought them joints was going to pop right out."

I laughed. Hell I had thought the same thing when I was looking at Chuck.

"Hell, yeah," Cotton added. "Sweatin' like a ho in the first row in church." Everybody laughed except Chuck.

"What the hell you laughing at?" Chuck was looking squarely at me, trying to contain his laughter.

I couldn't think of anything to say. Fortunately for me, my cell phone rang. I dug through my bag to avoid Chuck and keep laughing. I fumbled around in the bag and found the phone before it stopped ringing.

"Hello… Hello?" I waited for a few seconds to hear if anyone was on the other end. I started to hang up when I heard someone on the other end. "Hello." That was the last try. Normally I would have hung up by now, but I hung on and I didn't know why.

"Hello, James Pruitt?" the voice said on the other end.

"Yes?" I didn't recognize the voice.

"It's Warren."

I was frozen. Was this guy calling me after the way he

had acted when I was at the prison? I turned away from the laughter at the table to hear the phone more clearly. I didn't say a word.

"Hello?"

"I'm here." My voice was ice cold.

"I got... I can't ask f... I ain't no good at this. I don't have much time. If you in this piece, I'll speak."

From the sound of his voice, there was a change in attitude; it was decidedly different from what I had encountered yesterday. This sounded like a man who had tried the best way he could to open himself up to me. Maybe there was something genuine underneath his massive, brooding exterior. I didn't know and I sure as hell didn't want to know.

"We got nothing to talk about." I hung up the phone. I had done what was asked of me. This was as far as my bus went. I turned my attention back to the guys.

Chuck was looking at me. He was laughing and sizing me up, trying to figure out what was going on with me.

"What's up, J?"

"Nothing." I shook my head as I spoke. "You guys keep talking about that dunk and none of you are giving me mine for that assist I gave Chuck."

"That's because you suck," Cotton said.

The jokes kept coming, so did the beer and wings. I kept my head in the conversation as much as I could, but the brief conversation with Warren kept replaying in my mind. When lunch was over and the party was breaking up, Chuck and I shook hands with Cotton and Big E. They said they'd be ready for us the next time we showed up. We promised them we'd be ready as well.

"You all right?" Chuck asked me after they were gone.

"Yeah, why?"

"You've been a little preoccupied since you got that call."

"It was Johnson. You believe that? My big brother."

"Really. What's up?"

"He wants to talk. No, I'm not," I said before Chuck could get the question out.

"You sure about that?"

I looked at him, but didn't respond to his question. My mind was on lock when it came to my big brother, Johnson. How had he gotten my number? I had left a business card by the phone where we spoke. But I remembered T. Carter picking it up and throwing it out. At least I thought he did. You can get anything you want in prison just as fast as you can get it on the street. Sex, dope, a hit on somebody or even information. Good to see the wheels of justice were still turning at Central Prison.

19

"Are you going to Raleigh?" Denise asked.

The call I'd received from Warren had had an unsettling effect on the rest of my day. Nothing I did could shake the guy from my mind. Maybe I didn't want to. I wish my dad had been here. He was someone I could talk to. He'd help me figure out what to do. That was no longer an option available to me and the void was deep and wide.

"James!" Denise pulled my attention back to her. "Are you going back to Raleigh?"

"No."

"But he said he would talk, right?"

"So?"

"So see what he has to say."

"I've heard what he has to say. I'm done with it. There isn't any scoop here, baby."

"That was a cheap shot."

"I just… I'm sorry. I'm just on edge."

"What I'm talking to you about right now has nothing to with what I do for a living. I can separate the two. This is a private, personal thing that we're talking about.

I would not use it for my own gain without letting you know first." She smiled, trying to loosen me up. "I want to help you work through a problem, any way I can, not be your adversary. So let's try this again."

I nodded and waited for her to continue.

"So, do you think he'll kick you out again?'

"I'd have to be there for him to have the opportunity to do that. You're operating under the assumption that I'm going to Raleigh."

"Why not go? You don't have anything to lose. There's information that he can give you about your parents that nobody else can provide. This isn't about bonding; it's just information. I know you're curious. Hear him out."

Her arguments were very strong and to anybody else they might have made perfect sense. It just wasn't clicking for me. There was too much happening. My mind was overloaded and I couldn't figure out my next step.

One week ago, I'd been on top of the world. I had successfully prosecuted the biggest case of my young career, and was ready to move to the next phase of my life. But before I could ask Denise to marry me, I had lost one of the most consistent influences of my life. With that loss came the knowledge of Johnson and my dead biological parents. Since then, it seemed as if I had lost control of my own life. That was something I wasn't used to. I had to find a way to get it back.

"We'll see." It was the best I could offer her. "I'm caught up in this and don't know what to do. My father wanted me to help him, but there isn't anything I can do."

"Hold it right there. You've always tried to do what your father wanted, right?"

"Yeah, but this isn't the same thing."

"What do you think your father meant by help him?"

"Get him off death row, I guess, but there isn't enough time for that."

"You're probably right, there isn't enough time to save his life. That's also not the only way you can help him."

Denise paused to give me the opportunity to see where she was going. She must have realized from the lost look on my face that I didn't have a clue.

"You were worried about me not being able to separate myself from my profession, and actually it's you that can't. Helping him doesn't necessarily mean legally. Whatever it is that's on his mind, whatever made him call, there is something he wants to say to you. Listen to him. That's how you can help him. That's how you can do what your father wanted you to do."

Denise was done. She'd laid it out and left the rest up to me. She would not say another word on the topic unless I did. Needless to say, that was the end of the subject for the night.

We played dominoes, ate pizza and capped off our evening by watching *Grey's Anatomy*. As much as I wanted to put everything out of my mind, I couldn't.

At 11:20 p.m., we called it a night. Denise was worn

out from her long day. As we lay in her bed, I watched her as she fell asleep. I thought about what she'd said, and it started making sense to me. The only way to help Johnson was by listening to him. Maybe there was something he needed to say to me and maybe, in the midst of all this, there was something I needed to say to him, too. I needed to sleep on it.

I woke up before sunrise while Denise was still sleeping. Between closing my eyes last night and opening them this morning, I'd made my decision on Warren Johnson. I nudged Denise to wake her.

"What time is it?"

"It's almost six. Wanna catch a sunrise?"

We got to her balcony and watched the sun as it began to illuminate the city and start a new day. It was going to be a new day for me, too. I was leaving for my house. I needed to go home before I headed back to Raleigh.

20

B y 7:00 a.m., I-85 and I were once again finding our way to Raleigh's Central Prison. I called Jason, brought him up to speed and he cleared my way back into the prison. He assured me that I wouldn't have any problems getting in.

The drive to the prison seemed to take longer, but I was there in just over three hours, faster than the previous trip. I met the same guard at the main entrance gate, gave him my name and told him whom I was there to see. He remembered me from Wednesday, or should I say he remembered me leaving Wednesday. According to him, I had left some rubber behind when I tore out of the parking lot. I'm sure he was right. Getting the hell out of there as fast as I could and not coming back were my only objectives at that time. Things in life change quickly.

He told me there was a different visiting area where Johnson would meet me. I had been placed on Johnson's visitation list, which would permit me to see him anytime during visiting hours for a period of one hour. The privilege of the death sentence. Johnson was within one week of execution. On the day of execution, he could have a maximum of three family members with him at a time. From what I gathered about Johnson, he'd be hard-pressed to put three family members together.

The same parking spot was open, waiting for me, skid marks and all. I closed my eyes for a few minutes and took several deep breaths. When my eyes were open again, I spotted T. Carter approaching me. He had the same look about him today as he'd had the other day, and tomorrow would be no different.

"Mr. Pruitt." He gave me a quick scan. "Dressing down today?"

"Not a suit and tie kind of day, T. Carter." I extended my hand to shake his, curious to see how he would respond. To my surprise, he took it but the look on his face never changed.

"Didn't think we'd see you again."

I looked at him and nodded my head. It was apparent I'd left more of an impression on this place than I had thought.

Carter got me processed in and led me to the area where Johnson was receiving his visitors. It was a much larger room, with a steel door containing a two-by-two-foot glass pane that was set at eye level so you could see what was happening in the room. There were two guards posted on the outside. I could hear voices talking inside the room, but couldn't decipher what was being said.

"He had a visitor that came in at nine-fifteen this mornin'. His time is almost up. G'on in."

Carter unlocked the door and allowed me to enter. It was unsettling to walk in on the tail end of someone else's conversation, but Carter hurried me in. Johnson sat at a table with another man. Johnson said he could hear the clock ticking on his life and then he stopped in mid-sentence.

"They sent me in," I explained to Johnson and the neatly groomed white gentleman who turned his attention to me when I spoke.

"You need some help?" he asked as he stood.

I stood my ground. Was this guy trying me? I sized him up quickly. Fairly tall, but not as tall as me. Not a hair out of place on his head or his fully bearded face. He was in pretty good shape and more tanned than a white man should be at this time of year. He also wore a couple of ostentatious pieces of jewelry on his manicured hands.

"That's him, G," Warren said.

"Little Jimmy. Shit. I'll be damned!"

I stared at the man whom I'd never laid eyes on before, listened to him call me Jimmy like it was all right.

"Pruitt, Goffrey Taylor," Johnson said, with respect to Taylor.

"Boy, I knew you when you were in diapers," Goffrey said.

"I'm sorry?" My first instinct was to ask him who he was calling boy, even if he had known me when I was in diapers. I wasn't in diapers any more.

"Smooth, I got to get out of here. I'm sure you and your brother have a lot to catch up on."

"Thanks for coming, G." Warren stood and I saw he was chained, wrist to legs.

"I had to. We aren't going to let them get you. Peters is working day and night. We'll find a way out of this. You don't have a thing to worry about."

I watched the man as he hugged my shackled brother. He was probably in his mid-to-late forties. This would prove to be an interesting connection to Johnson. There was a vibe from the guy that didn't sit well with me. I could smell trouble on him from a mile away.

"Jimmy," Taylor said to acknowledge me as he left.

He made no effort to shake my hand and I didn't mind it at all. I watched him leave. He had an air about him that said he was not to be touched. Carter opened the door for him. The CO stared coldly at him, and Taylor looked at him and smiled.

"Tom," he said.

I watched the interaction between those two and waited for the door to close before turning my attention to Johnson. The way our last conversation had gone, I kind of wished his chains could be a little tighter. He locked his eyes on me, measuring me up again.

"Welcome back," Johnson said in a calculating voice.

"I get to stay this time?"

"We'll play that by ear."

We continued to eye one another with the table between us serving as a line we would not cross.

"That your lawyer?" I knew it couldn't be, but I was going fishing anyway.

"No."

"You work for him?"

"That ain't none of your damn business."

That would be a yes. Now it was a matter of finding out in what capacity. I'd need more information on Taylor for that. That would be something I'd have to get back to later.

"Any changes in your case?"

"That ain't none of your damn business, either!"

That one touched him. Now the balance of power had shifted and I was the one in control. I walked to the table, pulled out the chair, smiled at Johnson, and sat down.

"Then do you mind telling me exactly what the fuck I'm doing here?" The smile on my face was gone and I was deathly serious. Playtime was over. Johnson's act, as short-lived as it was, had grown tiresome.

Johnson tried to conceal it, but he was definitely surprised by my little outburst. He kept his eyes on me as he positioned himself to sit down. He squatted slowly into his chair.

"Oh yeah, the lucky one's got a little heart in there."

"This some kind of a game to you? I drove three hours to hear what you have to say and this is it? *You* asked me to come here. This is bullshit. Clock's ticking on your time, homes, not mine." That was my long ball. I wanted to see where it would land. There was silence. The clock's ticking was his line. I wanted to see if it would get me home.

"I don't have much time left." He lowered his eyes as

he said that. It seemed to be difficult for him to say what he needed to. "I thought about you after you left. I wanted to know something about you before…"

He hadn't completed the sentence, although it was clear where he was headed. Like he said, there wasn't much time left.

"I didn't think you'd show." Warren was trying to regain his edge.

"Me, either." There was silence. I was looking for a rhythm, a balance between us. I'd let him do the talking. It was his show for now.

"I don't know 'bout you, but when you came in here the other day, and me bein' in here like this, I was… embarrassed. The yellin', that's what I know."

That was Johnson's version of an apology. I kept my eyes on him and waited. I wasn't going to make it easy for him. I let him keep running with the lead.

"How come I ain't never seen you before now?"

"I just found out about you a couple of days ago."

"All this time I been here and you just found out about me?"

I came here to find out about Johnson, to hear what he had to say, for my father. He wouldn't give up any info unless he got some in return. It was all about the give and take in here. It was up to me to expose myself first, but how much would it take?

"My father passed away recently, and a few skeletons fell out of the closet." I didn't look at him when I mentioned my father.

"Your father died over twenty-five years ago."

"I didn't know that man. My father, the man who raised me, he just passed."

"Weren't you raised by your grandparents?"

Where did Johnson get his information? How did he know this about me?

"Yeah, I was; only I never knew they were my grandparents." Another bone. "To me they were Mom and Dad and I was their son. Didn't know anything about my biological parents; still don't know much. How did you know who raised me?"

The room became deathly quiet as I waited for Johnson to respond.

"I used to ask about you all the time after we got separated." Johnson wasn't looking at me now. "When I was nine, one of my aunties told me you was living in Asheville with your grandparents. I figured you was okay. Nobody would tell me much else after that. After a while, I quit asking about you. So you didn't know?"

"About my birth parents?" I questioned Johnson to make sure we were on the same page. He nodded. "No, I didn't."

"You didn't want to know," Johnson said in a warning tone.

"Probably not." I was giving. Time for some taking. "Who took care of you?"

"Our mother's people, for what it was worth. They moved me around in the family whenever there was some trouble. People didn't like for me to stick around when there was trouble." Johnson paused and turned his eyes back to me. He was searching for something in me, then coldly said, "You know I killed my pops when I was six." He squinted his eyes and waited to get a rise out of me. He didn't. "When I was twelve, Goffrey took me in."

That was a chance to ask him about Taylor, but I would wait. I didn't want to lose him by getting into something too early.

"What was she like?" I asked.

"Our mother?" He looked at me to make sure that was the question I was asking. We were finding a rhythm. "She was a junkie. Used to be fine as hell, but she fell off hard. Too much of that street life beat her ass quick. She was out there and couldn't help herself."

Johnson told me what he could remember about her. Most of his memories were based on stories he'd heard about her. I'd ask a question here and there to keep him talking, but when there was an abnormally long pause, I moved the conversation in another direction.

"What can you tell me about the night when they were killed?"

"So you know about it?" Johnson said.

"Some."

"I haven't talked about that in years. It ain't nothin' I talk about."

I was losing him. Maybe it was too much to ask of him, but I had to press him.

"You had to know it would come up." I waited for the

blow up. It didn't come, so I decided to step closer to the edge. "I may not know you, but I don't think you would have called me and said you would talk to me if I was here and not be prepared for it."

"You pretty smart, huh? They teach you that in law school?"

He almost smiled, but it was gone before it appeared. I could see him thinking, lining up the events. His mood had become very somber. He looked off into the distance at the wall behind me. He appeared to be watching something as he began to speak. "Emerald Woods Trailer Park was where we lived. 1769 Emerald Point Drive. Been back there a few times. It's a shithole. You and me was watching the *Mickey Mouse Club* in the front room. Momma and Billy were in the bedroom. I heard some loud voices. Somebody else was in there. Soon as I could make out the voice, I knew who it was. My pops. There was cussing and yelling. Gunshots. You started crying. I grabbed you to get you quiet, but I couldn't. I went toward the door, quiet as I could. Then my pops was saying something, but I didn't understand him. I could hear Momma crying and she sounded muffled. Then there was another shot. I ran into the room. I saw them both, laying on that bed, in their own blood, dead. Your father was shot in the chest and slumped at the foot of the bed. Momma was destroyed. Her body was by the headboard. The back of her head was splattered against it. He shot her in the mouth, and aimed it upward. I tried to wake her up. I pulled her arm and she fell toward me. My father ran out the front door. I locked it behind him and turned off the lights. I went back to the room to try and wake 'em up, I shook 'em and shook 'em. Nothing. I put you in our room and something told me to look out the window. He was coming back. I went into the kitchen to hide. I got the butcher knife out of the drawer and I held it. I could hear him fumbling with the doorknob, trying to get it open. Another gunshot rang out. You started scream-ing and crying again. I knew he'd come after you, so I went after him first. I hit my shin on something in the dark. My recall is fuzzy, and clear at the same time. When I realized what was going on, I was sitting on his stomach sticking that knife in and out of his chest. That was the last night I saw you."

"What'd they do with you?" I went straight into pros-ecuting attorney mode. Gather the facts and separate the emotions.

"Psychological evaluations. The state locked me away in a group home for a year-and-a-half."

"Why so long?"

"Didn't talk for fifteen months. They say I wouldn't talk because I was in shock. Seeing death up close. Your daddy, my daddy, our momma. Six years old. That's what them folks came up with, shock. Emotional shutdown. When they finished with me, they sent me on to some of Mama's people. None of my father's peeps wanted to have anything to do with me. Mama's people really didn't, either. First sign of any trouble, I'd be back in my best suit and bow tie and standing on the next nearest relative's doorstep. That shit went on for five years and then I ended up with Goffrey."

"The guy that was here?" I asked, and Warren nodded. "How'd you meet him?"

Warren stopped and thought about this for a couple of seconds, then chose his words carefully.

"My pops looked out for him, and he decided to look out for me."

"And he knows what happened? That you…" I didn't get to finish the sentence.

"He knows."

Warren had opened the door to Taylor; now was my chance. But before I could pursue any questions regarding Taylor, Warren was on to something else.

"I had an appeal shot down yesterday. Called you after I found out."

I didn't know what to say or how to respond, so I just stayed quiet and waited for him to move the ship forward.

"I didn't do it," Warren said solemnly.

"Excuse me?"

"I would've never hurt her. Rape? Didn't do it. I didn't kill Sheila."

His eyes could have burned a hole through me with the intensity they were giving off.

"They barely called her an acquaintance of mine in the papers and shit. She was my lady. They ain't never put that in the papers. I loved her. We was together for over two years and nobody ever heard about that. That's real."

"Two years?"

"Two years," Warren repeated.

"You didn't rape her?" I didn't know what I would hear. I was still trying to put him together with her for two years.

"Hell, no."

"But there's DNA evidence that points the finger squarely at you."

"She was my girl. We was together that day, earlier, before she got killed. We was into some things. Rough sex, shit like that."

"Anybody know you were together?"

"It was on the low. I think some people suspected it, but nobody ever came forward to back me up."

"Why?"

"Do you know who she was? Who her father is? Congressman Louis Thurgood. That prejudiced bastard's still representing this state. Ain't nobody gonna put that mark on her family."

"What about people you knew?"

"The life I was leading, I was trying to leave. I wasn't puttin' my personal shit out to them. We was goin' to Cali, but she was killed before we broke. It was the last time I saw her. I was arrested two days later. No other suspects. They had the dead white daughter of a congressman, and a nigger to pin it on. Five-O didn't need anything else."

"No other suspects?"

"After they had me on the blocks, they didn't give a damn about anyone else. I've done some shit that could get me this same seat. I got no qualms with that if you catch me on it. But Sheila's murder, that's not me. It ain't my shit to own."

"Would you own up to it?"

"Why not? What I got to lose? I done a lot of dirt in my life, but I didn't do that. I got death coming to get..."

"Time's up," T. Carter pushed the door open and barked.

The juices in me were flowing and had just gotten cut short. I wanted to hear from Warren. I didn't necessarily believe what he was saying, but I was intrigued. I decided to stay in Raleigh for a day or two.

"I'll be back tomorrow and I'll have more questions for you."

"I'll be here."

I grabbed my stuff, nodded to him and left.

21

"Sounds like he's trying to clear his conscience. Do you believe him?" Denise finally asked after I rambled on for twenty minutes.

I was becoming the play-by-play man for my daily conversations about and, now, with Warren Johnson.

"I'm reserving judgment at this point. I've read what's in the paper, and the way the case stacks up against him is very convincing. Listening to his side has raised some questions for me. I've never seen anything written about he and Sheila being involved with each other, and he doesn't have anybody who can corroborate his story. I don't know how you can you be involved with somebody for two years and nobody knows about it. He's convinced of what he's saying, though. He wants somebody to believe him. I don't know if I do."

"When are you talking to him again?"

"Tomorrow." That was the part I hadn't gotten to yet.

"Tomorrow? Maybe you believe him more than you want to admit."

"Just want to find out more about him. I booked a room at the Sheraton on Hillsborough St. I'm staying here until Sunday. You should come up. You could bring me some clothes."

"I'll see. It would be later in the evening before I could get there. I've got the charity Fun Run event that WSTV is sponsoring. You and I were supposed to run in it."

"I forgot about that."

"Don't worry about it. With everything you've got going on, it would be too much."

She was a little disappointed. Her voice betrayed the words that were spoken. She'd issued a challenge to all of her co-workers. If any couple's combined time could beat ours, then we would take them to dinner at any restaurant of their choice. They would also have to do the same for us. At last count, there were seven people who had accepted that challenge. Now it was going to be called off.

"All that free food we're going to miss out on." Denise had already counted her winnings.

"I'll make it up to you, starting when you get here."

"I hear you. Baby, I've got to get back to work. I'll call you later. Love you."

"Love you, too," I said as I hung up.

Charity Fun Run, how could I have forgotten that? I was juggling five things at once and getting nothing done. Thoughts about Warren were beginning to take over my mind. Why did he end up like this? What did Warren mean when he said he'd done other things that could get him the same seat on the row? What about Taylor? I never did get Warren deep into a discussion about him.

Wait a minute! Something had just occurred to me. No longer was I thinking of him as Johnson, the inmate. When I thought about him now, I referred to him as Warren. Spending some time with him, listening to him, had humanized him for me. He wasn't just a name and a face in the newspaper anymore.

Thinking about Warren's situation reinforced how lucky I had been. Flip a coin and it could end up heads or tails. Our lives had gotten flipped upside down when I was a baby. I landed in what I now know to be my grandparents' home. Stable. Loving. Warren had never landed in a steady environment. Whenever things were shaky, he got flipped again. If I had seen what he had seen, been the oldest, my mom and dad not wanting me, I might be in his place and he in mine.

"Hello," Mom answered the phone.

"Hey, Ma, how you doing?" With everything swirling in my head, I had the urge to call my mom. I called her after I got home from Raleigh on Wednesday, but hadn't spoken with her since. She had no idea that I was going back to Raleigh. After my last encounter, she probably thought I'd never go back.

"Where are you? I called you a couple times at home and on your cell phone."

Something in her voice didn't sound right. She was anxious and nervous.

"I'm in Raleigh." Her silence indicated that there was some explaining to do. "Warren asked me to come back."

It wasn't the right time to go into it with her. Besides, I needed to see how she was doing. We could get to Warren later.

"What's going on, Ma?"

"It's one of those days."

This was the third time we had talked since I had left Asheville, but it was the first time there was a big drop in her spirits. Although she and Dad had been prepared for what was coming, it was finally sinking in for her. It was just one week ago that my father had gone to the hospital for the last time. She was due for a release and I had all the time in the world to listen.

She talked about the love she had shared with my father. The ups and downs and how they had survived them. She cherished the worst day with him more than the best day she could possibly have had with anyone else. She even talked about the great vacations they had taken to Atlantic Beach, S.C., just outside Myrtle Beach, during the late fifties and sixties. Back then, it was where the black folks had to go because they couldn't vacation in Myrtle. The more she reflected on their beautiful relationship, the more her spirits were lifted.

When she asked me about Warren, I didn't go into a lot of details, but let her know that we would meet again the next day. I told her I could tell her more about him after that. An offer was made for her to consider staying with me for a little while. She said she would think about it, but wouldn't make any promises; Mom's way of saying no. I promised to call her on Sunday when I got home.

North Carolina State's campus was a few miles away on Hillsborough Street. The track provided an excuse to get out of the hotel for a little while. Late Friday afternoon and springtime, I would have the track to myself if this campus was anything like Eastern State University.

Sprint work was going to be the key. I thought it would keep my mind off of everything else. I believed that while sprinting quarters, two hundreds, and hundreds, your mind didn't have the opportunity to wander. You had to force yourself to concentrate on your lane, with your brain running short of oxygen, and the lactic acid building up in your lungs and muscles. The only thing you looked for was the finish line.

At 6:30, three quarters, four two hundreds and four hundreds later, I was physically exhausted. My theory hadn't held true because my mind was still running a hundred miles an hour. The track was not able to distance me from my thoughts.

Back at the hotel, I took a shower and had dinner downstairs in the hotel restaurant. Going anywhere else to eat was out of the question. My wardrobe was down to a jogging suit, flip-flops and no underwear.

Notes kept finding their way to the napkins while I waited for my dinner. I ordered Kuna Chicken. It was chicken breast marinated in soy sauce and pineapple juice with Monterey Jack cheese melted on top of it. It was delicious, but the notes pouring out of me onto the napkins sidetracked me. I got a to-go box for the food and went back to my room.

Warren Johnson had become a tenant occupying a considerable amount of space in my mind. I made a list of questions and began formatting them on my laptop. Some things about Evelyn, his childhood, and what his life had been like. The relationship with Sheila would be a big part of the day. If he hadn't killed her, who did he think had? And what about Taylor? He was one person I kept coming back to. If he was looking out for Warren, how had my half-brother ended up on death row?

I exchanged the notepads and laptop for the remote and turned to a basketball game between the Heat and Cavaliers. I turned off the lights to watch the game, thinking that the Cavs might never recover from losing the King.

22

"You protect what's yours out there, however you have to do it," Warren said. We were back in the visiting area on The Row.

"So if that meant killing somebody…"

"C'mon, man, I ain't gonna answer no shit like that. If you found yourself in a situation where the choices were you-or-him, what would you do? I'll bet you would go with *you*." Warren looked at me. He was right. "When you played football and you fought someone for a catch, it was him-or-you. You went with you. It's the same in the dope game, only the stakes are higher and the game don't end. You cash in with your life. I was about to get out of the game, change my life. Didn't make a move soon enough."

Warren and I were sitting across from each other again. During the last hour we had talked about each other's lives growing up. Football and law in mine, slangin' and bangin' in his. He told me about Sheila and his defense attorney, Brent Peters. I told him about Denise and my career as a prosecutor.

"Who killed Sheila?"

"I don't know. I had too many enemies out there. We were on the low, but somebody knew. Muhfuckers couldn't get to me, so they went after me through her. Couple more days and they get their wish. That's all right though; she knows I didn't do it and I'll see her again." Warren paused and looked pensive. "In a way, I am responsible for her death."

He was looking for something that I wasn't sure I could give: support. My personal jury on him was still out. I listened to every word he spoke. I wasn't sure if he was innocent of this crime but his guilt was no longer a black and white issue to me.

Warren wasn't a sexual predator. Nothing in his history pointed to that type of behavior. That was his side of the story, though. I would have to do some research to get a better assessment of his background. He was a convicted drug dealer, and freely admitted as much. Murderer, yes, but I didn't like him for Sheila's.

Being convicted of rape and murder was different from being guilty of it. Denise's words; she might have a point on that one.

"Responsible how?" I asked.

"If it wasn't for me, who I was, she'd still be alive."

"You don't know that."

"I do. I'm here for a reason. I'm gonna die here for a reason. I put some bad shit out there while I was rollin'. The shit came back to get me. I don't want to die in here, but if that's how it flows, that's how it flows," Warren said as casually as if he were referring to someone else.

"Can I ask you something?"

"Might as well, you askin' everything else."

"If Taylor was looking out for you, how'd you end up in the dope game?"

"How I got there got nothin' to do wit Goffrey." Warren was becoming irritated.

"Hold up, Warren. I never said it had anything to do with Taylor. I'm just trying to understand how you got into slingin' dope." No need to rock the boat.

"Don't matter how I got into it. I got in. But I tell you this: if I ever got in trouble, he was there for me. Talk to some people, pull some strings, and reduce a conviction. He's done it for me. He's the only person that ever showed a nigger some love. Anything he ever needed me to do, I did. No questions asked."

Warren gave me the scoop on Taylor. The legitimate activities, anyway. He owned a chain of storage facilities from Virginia to Florida, had money in real estate and a popular antique store in Richmond, VA. He also owned a club named Fevers in Raleigh. Warren said it looked like an abandoned warehouse from the outside, but it was unbelievable on the inside. He said there was no telling what you might see on the inside.

Taylor certainly had a wide array of interests. I didn't think Warren had told me the complete extent of how far those interests stretched. He was extremely loyal to the man who had rescued him and given him a home when nobody else wanted him. But what kind of home was it?

"I talked to my mom last night. I told her about you."

Warren sat there, looking at nothing in particular. Then he dropped his eyes, his posture becoming less erect, a little weaker, and his body language told me what I needed to know. He was examining himself through a different pair of eyes.

"I guess you told her all about the big, bad, black man that rapes and kills."

"No. I told her about the human being that I met. There was no need to talk to her about your case. I don't know enough about it."

"What she think about me?" he asked reluctantly.

"She didn't make a judgment on you or where you're at."

"No judgment, huh? That's a first."

"That's my mom. When she told me about all this, how Billy and Evelyn were killed, she felt guilty about not being able to adopt you, too." Warren perked up a little as I talked. "The time, the circumstances weren't right. There were issues with my father."

"Like what?"

"He saw things differently; he couldn't bring a child of his son's murderer into his house."

"But I killed my own father to save me and you," he said defensively. "A year and three months I couldn't talk about that shit. A year and three months."

In front of me wasn't a massive man, but a child who was scared for his life and mine. He had done whatever was necessary to protect us. He had saved my life, but his fell apart long before he had ever known the name Sheila Thurgood. He had never felt wanted or thought he belonged until Goffrey came along.

"Thank you."

"What?" Warren looked confused.

"If you hadn't done what you did, I wouldn't be here today. Thank you."

Warren sat up a little more, contemplating what I had just said. He smiled and nodded. It was the first time he had allowed himself to smile and enjoy it in front of me.

"So your mom said she wished they could have adopted me, huh? I wish they had. Maybe it would've saved me from this muhfucker here."

Tom opened the door. "Time's up."

"Guess it's time for you to get back home."

"I'm going to hang around Raleigh until tomorrow." I put notepads, laptop and pens into my case. "Might check out Fevers and a couple of other things before I go back."

I zipped my case shut. Warren and I stood up almost in unison. Both my hands rested on the laptop case. I lifted my right hand and extended it across the table to Warren. Slowly, those chains rattled as his hands met mine. He shook my hand firmly as I did his. The solid contact reminded me that I didn't know if I would ever see him again.

"I'll call you," I said. I meant it.

"Better make it the early part of the week; the end of the week looks pretty hectic for me." He forced a laugh. "Gotta keep the spirits up."

Warren let my hand go as another CO entered. He would escort him back to his cell. I watched them leave, listening to the chains as they swayed to the rhythm of Warren's gait. As the sound faded, all that was left was T. Carter and myself.

"I'll show you out," Carter said.

"I know the way."

"Please allow me to show ya out," Carter insisted.

"It's your show, T. Carter."

"Tom."

"…Tom," I finally said. There was something this good ol' boy wanted to say. You never know; a little extra information wouldn't hurt.

There was no conversation between Tom and myself as he guided me back to the main entrance. I waited for him to initiate the conversation since he had insisted on showing me out.

"So I hear you're an attorney, a prosecutor."

"Uh-huh." I immediately became leery of Tom Carter for two reasons. One, how had he gotten that information about me? And two, we had just made a right turn into a corridor that wasn't part of the route back to the main entrance. I made a mental note of the direction we were headed, and remembered the card he had picked up.

"That's kinda odd, don't ya reckon?"

"What's odd?"

"You two boys being brothers and all."

"Who told you we were brothers?"

Carter looked over his shoulder and gave a wicked smile. We turned right into another corridor, a left and up a short flight of stairs. At the top of the landing, there was a secured door. There were no security cameras here.

"Hold up. Where are we going?"

"Out."

"This is as far as I go." I put my belongings down. If necessary, I was prepared to handle this little piece of business before going my own way. Tom looked at my case and shook his head. He looked past me to see if anyone was behind us, and he waited. He kept looking past me but I never took my eyes off of him, and I listened for any noise behind me. I watched Carter as he pulled a key out of his utility belt, and turned to open the door.

"Pick up your shit and follow me."

The door led to another landing that was six-by-six and a three-foot-wide stairwell that led to a steep walk down. We walked out and he closed the door.

"I have your card, says you was a prosecutor. Johnson's the one told me you was his brother."

"Did he?"

Carter sensed that I didn't believe him.

"Said you had no idea he existed. You know, brother and all."

"When did he tell you about this?"

"He works out every day for his hour. When I'm working, I'm wit 'im. Been like that since he been here. Some days he talks more than others. Last couple of days, he talked about you. He's on short time. Think they can save him?"

"From what I've read, it doesn't look good for him. Why do you care?" Where was he was coming from?

"I been askin' myself that for 'bout three years. You think he did it?"

"Not sure. I don't have enough knowledge about the case, either. What do you think?"

"I been here a long time." Carter leaned over the railing. "Seen a couple of people pass by the Row. A few executions, too. A lot of them people got what they deserved. I ain't no lawyer, but I got gut feelin's. Seen one die I thought was innocent. Johnson's number came up pretty fast, far as executions go. Politician's dead daughter and all. My gut's telling me I'm about to see another innocent one go."

"T. Car… I mean…" Tom and I stood there as I grasped what he was saying to me. Bottom line was that I needed to see if everything was being done that could be done to help Warren.

"I got to get back to work. Go down these steps, there's a hallway to your right with a door at the end of it. Put you out in the parking lot."

I shook Tom's hand. "I'll look into it." I handed him

another one of my cards and descended the stairs. I heard the door open as I reached the bottom.

"What do you think about Taylor?" Tom called out to me.

"Haven't made that decision." The door closed by the time I got that out. I don't know if he heard me, but there was some reason why he had left me with that thought. I was going to find out. I would get information on the businesses that Warren had told me about, where they were, how long they'd been open, anything to get an angle on this guy. Who was Goffrey Taylor?

23

"Chuck, hang out with me and Denise in Raleigh, tonight?"

"Can't do it, dog, I got plans."

Back in the hotel room less than three minutes and I finally had connected with someone on my fourth call. I'd called Jason, no answer, so I texted him. I needed to get my hands on as much information as possible about Warren and his case and Jason would be able to help me. There was no answer from Denise, either, but she was coming after the Fun Run. It was almost 3:00 p.m.; she would be here before long. The challenge would be getting Chuck out of Charlotte two weekends in a row.

"What kind of plans do you have?"

"You remember Shelly?"

"From the mall?" It surprised me to hear that name again.

"Yeah, we havin' a quiet dinner and goin' dancin'."

"You're taking her to Ballers, aren't you? Trying to hook her up with one of those poles."

"Nah, cuz, I'm diggin' her for real, no shit."

"I hate to break that up, but this is work, money."

"Loot? What time you need me there, and what are the particulars?"

"There's a club here I want to check out. The right people could be there and I want to see how they flow."

"I hate to ditch Shelly like that." Chuck was inviting his own guest.

"Don't. Bring her with you if she's up for it. Denise is on her way. We'll mix a little fun into the work."

"Cool. I'll need a room with two queen-sized beds and I'm billing everything to the room."

"What's up with the two beds?"

"Man, I told you, I'm coming at her the right way. No disrespect. Give her some space."

"Space. Did I call the right number? This is Chuck Mays, right?"

"I know, right? Something about her, man. I'm feeling it."

"Don't let Denise hear you talking like that."

"Hell, nah, I ain't gonna get caught slipping. Now who am I scoping?"

"Goffrey Taylor."

"What's up with him?"

"He raised Warren. I want to get a feel for him, check out his club. Something about him doesn't rub me right."

"Can't be half bad if he owns a club."

"Maybe. I'll fill you in on the rest when you get here."

By 9:40 p.m., the four of us were finishing up dinner in the hotel restaurant. I'd been here for two days, but this was the first time I had completed a meal at the restaurant table. It was a welcome change in the routine.

The two days I had spent with Warren became the topic of the conversation while we ate. Some of this was old-hat for Denise, but she listened intently nonetheless. Shelly and Chuck were also all ears, but Shelly wasn't the type of person who would allow you to finish a thought or statement before she had five questions for you. And Denise thought she was supposed to be the reporter.

My patience was growing thin with Chuck's guest. Denise sensed this and came to Shelly's rescue. She invited her to our room to freshen up before we left for Taylor's club. All Denise needed to do was touch up her lipstick and she would be flawless as usual, but she realized I needed a few minutes alone with Chuck and away from Shelly. I whispered a thank you to her before she got up to leave. Chuck and I watched them until they were out of earshot.

"Is she always talking like that?" I couldn't believe this was Chuck's kind of woman.

"She just nervous around you and Denise. She was excited about meetin' you two. You know you two are some intimidatin' niggas, right?" Chuck took up for her.

"What are you talking about?"

"She can read, brother, and she looks at the news."

"When you put it that way, it could be intimidating."

"She'll be cool, don't worry about her."

"What does she do, anyway?" I asked.

"Hell, I don't know." Chuck laughed at the look on my face. "She's an insurance fraud investigator."

"No wonder she asks so many questions."

"What's up with Goffrey Taylor?"

"Shady character. I met him yesterday. Hardly any words between us, but the dude was slicker than an onion. He's footing the bill for Warren's defense and Warren is extremely loyal to him. Maybe to a fault. He won't say anything bad about him."

"So, what you feelin'?"

"Things aren't adding up for me. This guy takes Warren in when he's twelve, raises him, and now Warren's on death row. All the while, Taylor's an antique dealer, real estate investor, club owner and owns storage facilities up and down the east coast. Just doesn't add up for me."

"Don't make sense looking through your eyes. Twelve is too late for the kid to be changed by somebody else. Whatever was in him that made him go bad was already there long before he was twelve years old. This might not have nothin' to do with Taylor."

"Maybe not. Maybe so. We'll never know if we don't check him out."

"I'll do whatever I can, bruh. You want me to investigate, I'll investigate. But you done what your pops wanted you to do; you met him…."

"Help him," I said, cutting Chuck off before he got started. "My father wanted me to help him."

"Okay, I feel you, but you're basin' this on a hunch. A hunch on a cat you met for a hot sec. You been under a lot, man. You might need to slow down. Warren could be full of shit."

"I got that, Chuck." Chuck was throwing things at me as a precaution, but I'd had plenty of time to think about it and I knew what I wanted to do. "I'm gathering all the info I can on Warren's case. In the meantime, there are some other avenues to be checked. Taylor's not just a hunch of mine. One of the COs at the prison asked me what I thought about Taylor. He was planting a seed. When I asked him the same thing, he just let it hang. It's worth looking into. Just check out the club, see if you can get a feel for anything that's not above board."

I gave Chuck the directions to the club. He thought it would be better if we drove separately. Chuck didn't want anyone to see us arriving in the same car. The plan was for him to stay close to Taylor. I was to give Chuck a heads-up on Taylor if he showed up. At that point, the fun would be over. We would send Denise and Shelly back to the hotel, and see if there was anything worth following up on. I was determined not to leave that club until I had an angle on getting at Mr. Taylor.

24

Warren had been right. The old dilapidated warehouse was Fevers and it sure didn't look like much to Denise and me. It was a one-level dump, but the parking lot was full of a wide range of vehicles. Everything from VW Beetles to Benzes. Cruising past the entrance allowed me to gauge the crowd. At least thirty people were waiting to get in, and the faces ranged from early twenties to forties. Chuck and Shelly's faces were among the crowd at the front of the line waiting to enter.

Once we found our place in line, it moved rather quickly. Each time the door opened, the sound of Techno Funk music erupted from the club. The short guy in front of me held a VIP card. He handed it to the cashier who swiped it like a credit card. The card was florescent pink with black writing. Under the letters VIP, the card read I GOT THE FEVER. He took his card back, walked past the cashier and bouncers, through the door into the club.

"How many?" the cashier asked.

"Two."

"One hundred dollars."

Damn! I thought to myself. *A hundred bones to get into this dump.* On the outside, I didn't flinch, but inside I was jumping through hoops. I paid the hijacker and we got our hands stamped. The cashier pointed us in and urged the next patron to come forward. There was only one way in and one way out for the general public.

"Damn, a hundred dollars?" Denise said in my ear as we neared the door.

"To get into this place," I said, as I opened the door. The hallway was dark. There were pink florescent strips at eye level to guide our way. We walked about twenty feet with the music getting louder as we approached another person looming in the shadows.

"Take this door," he said, pointing to a door on the left. "Watch your step."

Denise clutched my arm as I reached for the door. Beyond it was the source of the booming music. I looked past the figure to see what was beyond him. There were a number of doors. As we turned toward our door, I noticed the person behind us was carrying a VIP card and he continued down the hallway toward another set of doors.

"What do your think goes on down there?" Denise wasn't missing a thing either.

"Don't know. I'd love to find out, though." I pushed the door that we were relegated to open.

It was a lit stairwell that led down two levels. On the second floor down, there was a large bar area with stools and a balcony that overlooked the dance floor. The bar was rectangular-shaped, opened all the way around and operated by four frenzied bartenders.

That's odd, I thought, *where are the chairs?* There were no chairs in there, just some little tables near the wall. I looked more closely and saw benches along all the walls that met with the small tables.

The balcony was made of wrought iron. We looked out over the dance floor, which was huge. The whole bottom floor was used as dance space. There were people fully-dressed, half-dressed, and barely-dressed. The dress code appeared to be whatever was comfortable. Sweat and bodies intertwined everywhere. It was a freakfest for some.

"Look at Chuck!" Denise yelled so I could hear her over the music.

"Where?" I yelled in return, and she pointed him out.

He was already sweating with his shirt wide open. Shelly was right there with him. Both of them were bouncin' that ass. Chuck spotted me as soon as I did him and nodded. He was letting it go, but he was on point.

"When in Rome," Denise said. We went down the other set of steps and joined the action.

The club was off the hook. The music never stopped, never slowed down. I was drenched in sweat and horny as hell from rubbing up on Denise. About forty minutes had passed when I noticed Goffrey entering the second floor. He stood near the bar.

"Baby, we got to get out of here."

"What? Why?"

"Taylor just came in. Can't let him see me."

We danced through the crowd to find Chuck and Shelly. He was working a fast grind on her near the staircase. So much for taking time and showing respect.

"Taylor's here at the bar. Tan, bearded, beige shirt, brown pants." I took Chuck's keys. "I'll be in the car."

Denise and I went up the stairs and left the club. A hundred bucks to get in and we were already out of there, but it had been worth every penny of it. We walked to the car and waited for Shelly to come out.

"So what now?"

"It's Chuck's call. Maybe nothing." I tried to put her mind at ease. She knew some of the work Chuck did could get a little dangerous, and she was concerned for my safety.

"I don't like the idea of you being out here following people."

"What following people? I'm just going to wait for Chuck."

She didn't believe a word I was saying. She knew if Chuck was following anybody, I didn't have a choice but to go with him. Lucky for me Shelly came out.

"Where's Chuck's car?" I asked when she got to us.

"Over on the left side of the club, third row facing the entrance."

"You got it down, didn't you?" Denise almost laughed.

"Girl, I been practicing that all night. Chuck wanted to make sure I remembered." Shelly snickered.

"I hate to break up the party, but I've got work to do." I gave Denise a kiss. "See you later."

They both got into my car and left. I found Chuck's car, opened the door and set off the security alarm. So much for being discreet. I hit the reset button to shut it off. Shit, no wonder I didn't do this all the time. I was just supposed to sit in the car and wait, not announce myself to everyone in earshot.

Half an hour later, Taylor left the club, but he wasn't alone. Two goons accompanied him, one white and one black. They walked to the curb's edge, awaiting the arrival of the white limo headed in their direction. Where were they going, and where was Chuck? As the last goon got into the limo, there was still no sign of Chuck. Anxious, I started the car. If Chuck didn't appear at the front of the club when I drove by, he would have to find his own way back to the hotel. As I threw the car in gear, there was a knock at the passenger-side window and I almost jumped out of the seat. To my relief, it was Chuck. I unlocked the doors while trying to regain my composure.

"How the hell I miss you?"

"Took a different way out."

"There's only one way in and out."

"Not if you got one of these." Chuck held up a fluorescent pink card.

"The VIP suites? Did you get in?" I eased out of the parking space, trying to pick up the limo.

"Not yet. I was getting close to those cats." Chuck pointed in the direction of the limo.

"Good. Any clue to where they're headed?" Not knowing any better, I hit the gas to catch the limo.

"Those guys wanted to check out antiques. Slow down! You want them to know we're back here?"

"Antiques, those guys?"

"Not your average-looking antique collectors, are they? Got wind of them saying something about storage."

"Some of the storage lots he owns? Must have some antiques worth checking out in Raleigh, at night. Worth leaving a good time in a hot club to stroll around storage lots in the dark? Warren says he owns them from Florida to Virginia."

"And how many does he have here?" Chuck asked.

"One and I have the address." I slowed down and relaxed. There was no need to follow them. "Who checks out antiques at a storage lot at midnight?"

The storage lot was located on the north side of Raleigh right off of I-85. As we neared the lot, I turned off the headlights, put the car in neutral and killed the engine. We coasted to a stop about a hundred yards from the storage place. Chuck rolled down his window, turned off the radio and listened. There were faint voices in the distance. Chuck shrugged his shoulders, sat back and settled in. "This could be a while." Fifteen minutes later, a small Ryder Truck drove by and pulled up to the entrance gate of the storage lot.

"You catch that?" Chuck asked in a low tone.

"Florida tags. CZH 19725," I replied.

"Business just picked up."

Once that truck drove into the lot, Chuck was right. There was a flurry of activity. There was the sound of handtrucks and footsteps in and out of the truck as they unloaded and the voices got louder as they worked at a breakneck pace.

Within thirty minutes, the truck was off the lot, whizzing by us and heading back to the interstate. I nudged Chuck and nodded in the direction of the storage lot. He raised his hand to caution me but never took his eyes off of the entrance. The white limo and a black Ford Expedition pulled out a few seconds after that.

"Let's go take a look," I said.

"Hold up, dog. We don't need to. That's not how it's done. We don't know who else is back there."

"So what?"

"Hold up, bruh. There's definitely something going on back there; we both know that. Whatever it is back there, you ain't gonna find it, not right now. But if what you're looking for is with them, they're going the other way. That's where we need to go. This lot will still be here. Going in there, trespassing, who is that going to help? Check your balance."

I wasn't using sound judgment. I wanted to understand

Warren, believe in him. I was trying to find a way to make his situation make sense to me. My father wanted me to help him. That's what I was trying to do. If that meant listening to him for hours on end at Central Prison or sitting in a car next to a storage lot running behind the guy who'd raised him, then that's what I'd do.

"Tell me why we're doing this?" Chuck asked.

"Taylor's involved with drugs, I'm sure of it. He raised Warren, had Warren working for him. You look around today and Taylor is legit while Warren was off dealing drugs. He didn't just fall into it. Taylor's got something to do with that. I can feel it."

"How's that flow with him being on death row now?"

"I don't know. I haven't worked that out yet but that lifestyle led to him being where he is now."

Chuck agreed with me on that and spent the next ten minutes trying to convince me that there was no need for us to get over the fence into the storage lot. He asked me what it would look like if a prosecutor was in the paper one week for winning a case and was back in there two weeks later for getting arrested on trespassing charges. I conceded the point to him, exited Chuck's car, dashed the hundred yards to the fence that surrounded the storage lot and quickly scaled it. When I landed on the other side I could hear Chuck's footsteps trailing behind me.

"What the hell you doin'?" Chuck asked.

"Join me and find out," I said, looking back at him.

"Man, damn." Chuck looked at me. He rolled his eyes and then started to climb the fence. "So all that shit I said in the car didn't do you no good, did it?"

"Not really. It sounded good, though."

"Niggas," Chuck said, half-smiling as he straddled the fence. "All right, since we here, let's see if you can find anything open or left out. We might catch them slippin'. The noise was coming from the rear of the lot. You start on the other side and we'll work our way to the middle of…uh-oh."

As I turned to see what had frozen Chuck, I spotted two Rottweilers twenty-five yards away. They were quietly stalking me. They stopped as I locked eyes on them.

"Chuck," I said as quiet as I could. I hated dogs.

"Take it easy. I see 'em. If you don't make any sudden moves, they won't either."

As soon as the words had left his mouth, the dogs started barking and made a charge at me. I spun and leaped toward the fence. The impact almost caused Chuck to topple over in the direction of the dogs. I climbed as fast as I could and narrowly escaped. I was glad I hadn't ventured further into the lot. As Chuck and I landed safely on the other side, the dogs continued barking from behind the fence. The smell of their moist, hot breath was a compelling argument that convinced me that this might not have been the right time to look around. I didn't hesitate to get back to the car; neither did Chuck.

"I thought if I didn't make any sudden moves, those

dogs wouldn't either," I said as I leaned against Chuck's car.

"Hell, I don't know a damn thing about dogs," Chuck said, laughing. "I was just trying to keep you calm. I know how you are with dogs." Chuck paused, and looked back at the lot. "I think we can let that ride for the night."

"Yeah." I wouldn't offer up any more resistance.

"Know what I want to do?" Chuck asked.

"What's that?"

He held up a Fevers VIP card. "Check out the VIP section. The place was off the hook. If they was freakin' like that in the basement, imagine what it must be like in the penthouse. I might be able to bite some of that shit for my club."

"How'd you get that card anyway?"

"I lifted it off this old white dude who was coming out of the other door I found. I don't know what he got put through while he was in there, but his ass was wore out. Got to see what that was about. Let's roll."

Taylor's white limo was parked in front of Fevers when we got back there. Anyone entering or leaving the club had to pass by it. It was serving notice that the man, Goffrey Taylor, was in.

"You hold tight while I go see what they got up there in the VIP," Chuck said.

"How long you going to be?"

"Twenty, thirty minutes tops."

"Thirty minutes, cool." That would give me enough time to look for Taylor. I had to see for myself what it was that made Warren loyal to him.

I waited until Chuck was inside the club before getting out of the car. If I was lucky, I might be able to have a few words with Mr. Goffrey Taylor.

Holding my hand under an ultraviolet passed me back through my designated door. Once back inside the club, I trekked down one flight of stairs and caught sight of him standing by a balcony near the bar. He was surveying the dance floor while his two goons flanked him. I went straight for Taylor, not knowing what I'd say when I got there. There was five feet between us when the two goons turned on me fast and hemmed me up. The brother snatched up my left arm and put his elbow in my throat. The white guy jammed his forearm in my rib cage.

"What you need?" the big burly white man asked as he patted me down.

"I was just coming to speak," I stammered.

Taylor, the essence of total calm, slowly turned around and looked at me. The recognition was instantaneous. He looked from one goon to the other and with the squint of his eyes, they removed their hands from me.

"Jimmy Pruitt, welcome to Fevers."

"Thank you." I let the Jimmy slide this time, thanks to his two friends.

"Been here long?"

"A little while."

"Dice, Cat, this is Warren's little brother, James Pruitt."

I took for granted the white one was Dice and the black one was Cat because that was the order they moved when he spoke.

"You drinking?" Taylor motioned to the bartender. "Get whatever you want. Warren told you about the club?"

"Yeah, I had to see it for myself."

"You like it?"

I nodded my head. We made small talk for a few minutes, mostly about Warren, and what Taylor was doing to try to stop the execution from happening. He boasted that his personal attorney was handling Warren's defense, throwing appeals at the court left and right. He assured me that his attorney was no slouch; he was a partner at Colby and Sturgis, one of the most respected and feared firms in town. The conversation shifted to what he really wanted to know, the things Warren and I had talked about. I didn't offer many details to him, just my interest in who my birth mother was. I don't know if he believed me, but he let it go at that. Taylor didn't offer any insight as to what he and Warren had discussed regarding me.

Twenty minutes had passed since my re-entry into Fevers and I needed to get back to Chuck's car. I excused myself to use the bathroom and enjoy the club. Listening to Taylor toot his own horn about what he was doing for Warren made me sick. Were it not for Goffrey Taylor, Warren wouldn't have been in this situation in the first place. I eased out of the club and back to the car.

"What the hell were you doing? I told you to sit tight."

Chuck was already sitting in the car waiting for me when I got back to it.

"I found Taylor; talked to him, too." I got in the car.

"What for?"

"Look him in the eye and listen to him."

"So, you talked to him?"

"Yeah."

"And?"

"He's full of shit. His two bodyguards locked me down as soon as I got close to him. What's up with the VIP?"

"He got some wild shit in there, dog. Now you know I ain't no square. I run a nice, clean gentlemen's club, hear me. I got some nice, clean, respectable hoes. Lap dances, asses shakin', VIP and all, but that's it. Man, those VIP rooms are like S and M cribs. They got whips and chains and all kind of contraptions hanging off the walls. Them freaks don't mind watching each other either. At the end of one of the halls, they got a large leather romper room where these fools get together to whip and spank and torture each other. They got some shit with'em, dog. I might have to steal me a couple of ideas from this fool." Chuck rambled through this recitation all in one breath.

Listening to Chuck reminded me of something that Warren had said. He and Shelia had been into rough sex. Another life skill that he had picked up from Taylor. I had all the Goffrey Taylor and Fevers that I cared to see for the night. It was time to go back to the hotel.

"I'll have some more work for you soon."

25

At 9:00 a.m. the next morning, we were sixty miles outside of Charlotte. We were rolling three cars deep on the interstate. Chuck and Shelly were up front, Denise in the middle, and I was pulling up the rear. It was Denise's idea. Since none of us had had any sleep, she suggested a convoy would be the safest way for us to travel. It made no difference to me. I was wired, with my mind running in a hundred different directions at once. Chuck and I had gotten back to the hotel after 3:00 a.m. As I had approached my room door, there was conversation and laughter on the other side. I listened as best I could. Bet money the topic of conversation was either about Chuck, me, or some combination of the two. They confirmed my suspicion by piping down the conversation when the door opened. The phone rang and it was Chuck. I advised him that it would be in his best interest to get down here before Denise told Shelly all of his business. No sooner had I hung up the phone, than it seemed like Chuck was banging on the door.

Chuck changed the discussion to his visit to the VIP section of Fevers. He picked up a deck of cards and started shuffling them. We partnered up for a game of Spades. To make sure the heat stayed off of him, Chuck, who had always been my boy, always looked out for me, didn't hesitate to tell Denise about us following Taylor or the bonehead play I made by going back into the club and confronting Taylor. At least he left out the part about the dogs.

Just before 6 a.m., we broke up the party to take showers, get packed and be ready to check out. Shelly said that if we got out of there soon enough, she would be able to make it back to Charlotte to attend church. Denise looked at me. There was no need to put up a fight, we were going. I looked at Chuck. He looked at me, then Denise, then Shelly, and, yes, he was going, too. At 6:50, we were hitting the interstate.

At 10:14 a.m., Denise and I were changed and ready for church. We were going to meet at Friendship Park Baptist Church, on Beatties Ford Road at 11:00 a.m. It was Shelly's church home. I found that to be commendable on her part.

Friendship was a huge church with an even larger congregation. They had three services on Sunday mornings to accommodate all of the members. But it still managed to have a hometown feel to it. There was a huge bell tower that alerted all of Beatties Ford of its services.

The four of us sat in the balcony of the church. There

was no room left in the sanctuary. I was glad. I had finally hit the wall and was dropping fast. If I dozed off during the service, I didn't want too many people knowing it. Chuck sat next to me with Shelly on his left. Denise was on my right.

The organ began to play as we were called to worship. It was Chuck's first time at Friendship, so he followed the program closely. He nudged me and opened the program so I could see what he was looking at. He was pointing at the line that read Mission Offering. Then he slid his finger down the Tithes and Offerings, and rolled his eyes.

"You two boys stop playing," Denise said sharply.

For a second, I thought I was with my mom.

"What did I do?" I asked innocently.

"You sat next to him," Denise said, rolling her eyes.

I looked at Chuck and he was smiling until he turned toward Shelly. Then his smile deserted him. Shelly let him know that this was no time to play, and he straightened right up. There was something about Shelly that he really liked. Any other woman, he would have gone about his business like he hadn't seen her.

Shelly insisted that we stand when they called for visitors. Chuck was reluctant to do so. Fortunately, there were quite a few visitors in the large church, so they didn't have time to ask everyone his or her name and church home. That helped put Chuck at ease. Denise and I had visited a lot of churches in Charlotte, including

Friendship, but we hadn't found one that we wanted to join yet. I still considered myself a member of Mt. Olive in Asheville. Denise's church home was the one she was baptized at back home in Richmond. I don't know what Chuck would call his church home. He wasn't exactly a big fan of organized religion. We sat back down after all the visitors were sufficiently welcomed.

The choir's last selection before the preacher gave his sermon was "His Eye is on the Sparrow." I hadn't noticed it in the program earlier. My father's favorite song. My eyes welled up as the song took me back to my father's funeral. Nine days. It had only been nine days. It seemed like forever and, simultaneously, like no time at all. It still didn't seem real.

Denise grabbed my hand and held it firm. She always knew when I needed her and when there was a need for some space. I listened to that song, holding her steady hand and got through it. Maybe no one else would pick up on the moment I was having. It would definitely take some time to work through my feelings.

The pastor gave a wonderful sermon. The great thing about the Word is you may not always get what you want, but you pay attention and you'll get what you need. The pastor told us how God watched over Moses and Noah, the Israelites, and the sparrow. He said, if God can watch over all of that, then you, all that's come before you, and all that will come after you, are well taken care of. You get what you need. I needed to know that my father was taken care of.

"You okay?" Denise asked after the service was over.

"Yeah, I am." I had a long way to go to make sense of what was going on in my life, but I did feel better.

"You feel like eatin'?" Chuck said. "Man, I was sittin' up in that joint thinkin' about floatin' down the street to McDonald's Cafeteria until I remembered it was closed."

McDonald's Cafeteria was a staple of Charlotte's West Side, specializing in soul food. The restaurant had been opened in the early seventies by John McDonald. It was a gathering place for people of all races, promoting community and diversity. Black entrepreneurship at its finest.

Too bad it was closed. I could still smell the baked chicken. Denise and I decided to pass on anything that would prevent us from going back to my house, unpacking, and getting some rest.

I parked in the garage next to Denise's car to make it easier to unpack them both. I checked the mail and picked up my Saturday and Sunday papers from the yard. After rummaging through the junk mail, I opened the Sunday paper. I didn't look at the Sports page first today. The front page of the *Observer* had an article about Warren Johnson. With four days left until the execution, it was story number one. There was a triptych picture of Warren, Sheila Thurgood, and Congressman Louis Thurgood above it.

The article focused on the Senator's desire to have his nightmare end. He thanked his fellow politicians and constituents for their support, and said how it had helped him and his family deal with their loss.

There was no mention of a possible relationship between Sheila and Warren. No out-cry of support for Warren. There was no mention of Warren's defense team or his attorney. The article did state, however, that his appeals had been exhausted and there was ironclad proof that, thanks to DNA testing, they had the right man scheduled for execution.

"What are you reading?" Denise asked as she came into the den.

"Check this out." I handed her the article.

She read the article and shook her head. "It doesn't look like anything is going to change for him."

"Nobody's going to touch him either. That's what's sad. A politician's daughter and his DNA was clearly identified. In Texas and Florida, African-American males are being executed on evidence that is suspect at best. Vague descriptions, nearsighted witnesses identifying suspects they saw at night sixty yards away, coerced confessions. Did you know an illiterate man in Detroit was beaten so badly he signed a confession he couldn't read so the police would stop beating on his head? He was functionally retarded. They had no murder weapon, no witnesses, not one person who could place him at the scene of the crime and he was executed. No, it doesn't look good at all for Warren. He says he didn't do it. Two weeks ago, a week ago, even three days ago, I would have been right there with them. DNA matches burn him. But now, I'm not sure of it. My judgment might be a little off because of everything that's happened, but after talking to Warren, I want to believe him."

"For somebody who was dead set against him, you have certainly changed your mind."

"I know, right? I don't know what it was I was looking for in Raleigh or why we even followed Taylor. If he's dealing drugs, and he got Warren involved in it, it still doesn't have anything to do with the rape and murder of Sheila. I want to blame Taylor for how Warren's life turned out. He never had a shot, you know. From the time he was six years old. Never had a chance. He killed his father, got shipped from home to home. Always felt like no-body wanted him. He never had a legitimate opportunity at life. If it wasn't for my mom and dad, that could have been me."

I was tired and couldn't stand to read any more. It was after 2:00 p.m. and neither of us had had any sleep over the last thirty hours. We went upstairs, talked for a little bit, had some fun with each other and fell asleep.

"Help him," I heard my father's voice say and it jarred me awake. It couldn't have been any clearer if he and I were standing face to face. Why he still wanted me to help, and how, I didn't know. But my father's presence was so strong in the room that I had to. There was something here that I needed to do, that I had to do, but the question was, what?

26

onday morning, it was time to get back to work. I beat the sun into my office. A ton of work would be waiting on my desk, but it could wait. Jason would meet me at 6:15 a.m. in the law library. It was after 10:00 the night before when we had finally connected with each other. He and Beverly had gone to the beach Friday night without the kids, and they were just getting in. We didn't have much time to talk, but I quickly brought him up to speed on Warren.

I was knee-deep in research, vigorously poring over case studies, scanning appeals in capital murder cases. The three years since I had passed the bar exam were dedicated to the prosecution of drug traffickers and racketeers. My experience with capital murder ranged from slim to none.

"Dude, this is almost too early for me," Jason said as he entered the library.

"I know you better than that. You miss having this place to yourself," I said, as I looked up from the books. I stood to shake his hand.

"How are you?"

The tone of his voice implied more than a greeting.

Jason was concerned about how I was dealing with the death of my father.

"I'm okay, dealing…but I'm okay."

"Yeah?" Jason dug for a little more.

"I'm still off balance sometimes; can't find my rhythm."

"Rhythm?"

"I'm not functioning the way I normally would."

"You will. It takes a little time."

"Been hearing a lot of that. You and Beverly have a good time?" I needed to move the subject away from me.

"Oh yeah. Hilton Head, two days, no kids and we didn't have to keep quiet for anybody. We were loving life."

"Sounds like it."

"How's Denise?"

"She's good. She came to Raleigh Saturday while I was there. She got a little heavy on me last night, though."

"Why?"

"Like I said, I've been a little out of rhythm. Chuck and a friend of his met us in Raleigh."

"One of his dancers?" Jason was grinning like a kid in the candy store.

"No. Believe it or not, it was somebody he's interested in." This bit of information removed Jason's grin. "Yeah, that same Chuck. To make a long story short, I wanted Chuck to get some information on somebody and I decided to help him. Denise thinks that kind of thing is too risky for me."

"Sounds like a wife. Bev gets on me all the time about

doing this or not doing that. So who were you following?"

"Goffrey Taylor. White male, mid-forties. He owns a club called Fevers in Raleigh."

"Goffrey Taylor?" He was trying to place that name. "Why were you following him?"

I told Jason that this was the man who had raised Warren. I gave Jason a rundown of the two days I had spent with Warren, his unsubstantiated relationship with Shelia, his drug dealing, and his fierce loyalty to Taylor. Warren said that Taylor had been there at every turn for him whenever he had gotten into trouble. Jason agreed with me that it was odd that a legitimate businessman, who owned an antique store, a chain of storage lots, and was heavily invested in real estate, would continue to associate with someone who was involved in dealing drugs. Finally, there was someone who agreed with me. "Taylor's also paying for his defense."

"Goffrey Taylor. Why do I know that name?" Jason continued to ponder it. "Where's he stand with appeals?"

I shook my head. "Everything to this point has been denied. There isn't much left for him, unless the governor grants it or he gets a conditional pardon. In order for that to happen, though, there would have to be some new evidence that could clear him or at least raise a strong argument on his behalf. All he's got is four days. One minute after midnight Thursday and it's over for him."

"You got anything else on this Taylor?"

"Not anything solid yet. Picked up on something at

his storage lot, though. Could be nothing; could be something. Chuck's going to do some more checking into Taylor, some unconventional sources. See what comes up."

"I've got a contact at the Circuit Court of Appeals. Went to law school with him at Berkeley."

I didn't give Jason a chance to finish. "Be interesting to see what these appeals look like, huh? His attorney's name is Brent Peters. He's with Colby and Sturgis in Raleigh. It's a real moneymaking firm."

"I know them. Peters is a partner. Let me see if I can do something to get my hands on those appeals. I'll get back to you." Jason left the office with a new mission charted for him.

"Mr. Pruitt, Mr. Mays is here to see you," the voice on the intercom said.

"Send him to my office, please." That was odd. Gwen never referred to Chuck as Mr. Mays. Gwen was an attractive, twenty-three-year-old, African-American receptionist who had arrived in the prosecutor's office three years ago. She had been hired not long after me. She attended college at night and was majoring in Advertising.

"What did you do to Gwen?" I asked Chuck as soon as he opened the door.

"I see they still got you stuck in the supply closet. How many more cases you got to win before you get out of here?" Chuck exaggerated his efforts to get into my office.

"You keep eating like you have been and one day you won't be clowning when you come in here; that's going to be for real." I glanced at his stomach as he sat down. "Well, what's up with Gwen? She's never referred to you as Mr. Mays before. She used to giggle and call you Chuck. So what up?"

"You know how it is. We hung out for a little bit and I tapped it about three weeks ago and I ain't talk to her since. Now she trippin'. Man, them skirts be..."

"Yeah, she's trippin'," I said to Chuck. "You ain't crazy; you know how that goes."

"Shit, I apologized to her. That's more than I'm willing to give to any of them women."

"Apologized?" That was a departure from the Chuck I knew. My man could get with a honey one day, hit it, look her dead in the face the next day and swear to her that he'd never seen her before in his life. "What brought that on?"

Chuck was dumbfounded. "I don't know. Seemed like the right thing to do. Damn, I almost sounded like a grownup, didn't I?"

"Yeah, I was about to ask you who you were?" It was time to do a little fishing. "What did you and Shelly do after we left?"

"We ate at Sylvia's on Graham and then hooked up with some of her friends and went bowling."

"Bowling? Did you get any sleep?"

"I bowled a couple of games and then I was out. I told her I had some work to do. But yo, dog, you gonna trip off of this. It was four couples right, all of them married. Two of them niggas knew me. I get money from them about three or four times a month."

"No, they don't." Was this really coming next?

"Them niggas be up in Baller's on Friday night like they got nowhere else to be. Buck wild, hear me. I ain't never seen no rings on not one of their fingers."

"C'mon, Chuck, you sure?"

"If them cats wasn't making so much noise and droppin' loot like they do, I wouldn't know 'em. If you would have seen the looks on their faces when I showed up, you wouldn't have any doubt, either. They kept cuttin' their eyes at me, lookin' like, please don't tell, please don't tell. Hell, I was sayin' to myself, I hope these niggas don't tell Shelly that's my club.

"You still haven't told her you own that club?" My telephone rang. It was almost 11:00 a.m.

"Hell, nah," Chuck said.

"Hold up a second, Chuck." I picked up the phone. "James Pruitt."

"I just got an email with some confidential information. You need to see this." It was Jason. "I'll be right over."

"Chuck's with me. We'd better come to you." The office was cramped enough with two people. I couldn't imagine it accommodating three.

"Did he get anything on Taylor?"

"I'm sure he did. He just got here; we haven't gotten into that yet. We'll be right there." I hung up the phone. "You do have something on Taylor, don't you?" I asked Chuck.

"You know I wouldn't be here unless I did. Once I'm on it, dog, you don't see me until I got what you need."

On our way to Jason's office, we ran into Gwen in the hall. She wanted to turn the other way.

"Gwen, send any of my calls to voicemail. Chuck and I are going to be in Jason's office." Business as usual, as if Chuck had never mentioned a thing about her.

"Yes, sir," she said.

Gwen never looked at Chuck or acknowledged his presence as she continued past us.

"Boy, you know how to keep them happy, don't you?" I said to Chuck when we turned the corner.

"I'm good like that."

Jason met us at the door to his office and hustled us in. He immediately handed me a folder full of documents. They were the appeals filed on behalf of Warren Johnson.

"Take a look at those."

I started scanning through the appeals. They were filled with legal jargon that said virtually nothing. They were standard boilerplate appeals that hadn't required much effort on the part of the attorney who had filed them. You could change the name and the circumstance and file the same appeals for seventy percent of the inmates on death row. Page after page, it was the same thing.

"This is bullshit," I said.

"Those are the kind of appeals his defense has been submitting. Not the type of work you'd expect from a prestigious law firm like Colby and Sturgis."

"Not at all."

"What's up with it?" Chuck asked.

"It's cookie-cutter defense. No effort. They put a stamp on it and let it go," I said.

"Chuck, what do you have on Taylor?" Jason inquired.

"Ya'll gonna love this." Chuck loved to set up the show. "He's been in and out of courts for the last twenty years: bribery, extortion, money laundering and aggravated assault. Never convicted on any of that. Spent two years at Butler prison on a stalking charge. They popped him for bullshit, not the good shit. Here's the kicker: he's been under investigation for the last six years. Drug trafficking. They just can't pin the right shit on him. Whenever they get close to him, people either end up missing or shit gets fixed."

"How did you get all that?" Jason asked.

"Don't worry about it, it's reliable," Chuck said with a smile.

"What are the chances that a legitimate businessman, who raises a kid, introduces him to a drug lifestyle, is paying for his defense, which is shady at best, might have something to do with him being in prison in the first place?" I asked.

"It's a theory. After seeing those appeals and listening to Chuck, I'd say it's a theory worth looking into," Jason said.

"Chuck, get any and everything you can on Peters and Taylor. I now have somewhere to start. Thanks, fellas. This isn't just a hunch anymore."

Chuck promised to get back to me with anything he came up with. Jason would do the same. For now, it was time to get back to work.

"Hello?" I quickly answered my cell phone. It was a Raleigh area code. Hopefully, it was the return call from Brent Peters. I had called the law offices of Colby and Sturgis nonstop every fifteen minutes since leaving Jason's office at 11:36 a.m. So much for work. It was now 3:53 p.m. Eight minutes since my last call and seven minutes until call number fourteen. "Hello," I said again.

Then I heard the voice recording. "You have a collect call. Caller, please state your name."

"Warren Johnson," the voice on the other end responded. I accepted the call immediately.

"Jimmy, I hope you don't mind."

"No, don't worry about that. How are you?"

"Makin' it."

His voice told another story. I didn't know him very well, but I knew this wasn't the same person I had sat with two days ago. I needed to get his motor running, make him think about something else.

"How was your workout today?"

"Didn't work out today. Wasn't wit' it."

"What did you do with your hour?"

"Nothing. Sat there. Thought."

"About?"

"Anything…everything…skipped the workout. That was the only thing I had left to hold on to. Don't make no sense now. Three days left. So I just sat there. Looked at the sky; smelled the air. Funny how you pay attention to shit when you don't have it no more."

"You got time. Your lawyers are still filing appeals, aren't they?"

"I don't know. Don't matter no way. Ain't seen none of them muhfuckers for five days. Fuckers call me every couple of days to tell me what else got denied."

Peters was avoiding everybody. I couldn't bring myself to tell Warren that the appeals that Peters had been filing for him wouldn't do him any good. I wanted to tell him that I had a theory about Taylor being connected to his case, but it wasn't time yet. Knowing how loyal Warren was to him, I'd have to connect some more dots before I let him know what I was doing.

"Has Goffrey been back to see you?"

"Not since Friday."

"Uh-huh."

"Uh-huh what? He'll be back. He don't like being in here, that's all. He's like anybody else. You wouldn't trade places with me, would you?"

"No, I wouldn't."

"Neither would he. It's all good, though. I'll flow these three more days." Warren was despondent. "I'm a see

Sheila again; be together with her. She'll tell me what happened and welcome me. That's what I look forward to. It's all I got left."

I was stunned. I didn't know how to respond to that, but I needed to keep the conversation moving. "How did you meet Sheila?"

"What?"

"Sheila, where did you meet her?"

"You ever seen an execution?" Warren asked.

Now he was almost happy. His emotions were bouncing up and down like a yo-yo.

"They used to have the electric chair, but they stopped that a long time ago. Up 'til 1998, an inmate could choose the gas chamber or lethal injection. Now it's just the injection. They stopped usin' the gas chamber cause back in '94, this cat was in there fightin' against his restraints yellin', 'I'm human; I am a human being.' Politicians got wind of all that beggin' and couldn't stomach that shit so they went to lethal injections. They prepare you in a small room next to that fuckin' execution chamber. They put you on the gurney and tie you down, across the arms and chest. Then they stick them tubes in you. Once you layin' there like a stuck pig, they push that gurney into the execution chamber. When everythin's set, they open the curtains for the show. The first injection is Thiopental Sodium. It puts ya in a deep sleep. The second injection is Pavulon. That's a muscle relaxer; make you stop breathing; stops your heart."

He was giving me a step-by-step guided tour of his

own impending execution. Emotionally, he was cut off from the brutal reality that would overtake him in only a few more days.

"Two more days and I'm done. I'm gonna get to see her again."

"Warren, you don't know what could happen between now and then."

"Don't matter. I'm straight out here. You reap what you sow."

"What?" Reap what you sow. What the hell? Had he done it? "What do you mean? Did you…"

"Hell no," Warren cut me off. "Them enemies, they the ones that got me. All that bullshit I put out there, them rotten seeds. This how they came back to me and I gotta eat 'em." Warren paused. "Look…I'm glad we got together again. Glad you turned out okay."

"Hold up, Warren, it's not time for all that yet."

"Yeah, it is. I'm done. You take care." He hung up.

I had been calling Brent Peters every fifteen minutes; now it would be every ten minutes. He had to provide some answers. I wanted to confront the hack of an attorney. If nobody else would fight for Warren, then it would be all up to me—his brother.

"And he never called back?" Denise asked in disbelief.

"Never; not one time. I called him six times between four and five p.m. and he never called me back. Warren hasn't heard a word from him, either!"

"James, keep it down," Denise said. We were in her office. The 5:30 and 6:30 p.m. newscasts were over, but at 7:40 p.m., there were still plenty of people around. She wanted to make sure my relationship with Warren was kept quiet for the time being. "You know it doesn't take much for anything to get out around here."

"That may not be a bad idea."

My theory about Taylor and Peters was coming together. It was up to me to expose them and I would do whatever was necessary to make that happen.

"Baby, slow down. You've got a theory, but nothing to back it up. You start throwing accusations around too soon and you won't help Warren at all. Instead you'll find yourself in some mess you can't easily get out of. You're the one who was talking about the DNA evidence they had against him. Now you believe his story, so you're changing sides, but you don't have anything tangible to fight with."

Not yet. I didn't have anything tangible—yet. What she was saying made perfect, logical sense, but I wasn't a big fan of logic at the moment. There wasn't a lot of time to find a way to help Warren and if that meant revealing he was my brother to do it, if it meant putting myself in harm's way, then that's what I would do.

"How did Warren react to your theory?"

"He didn't. I haven't shared it with him yet. He was all over the place, jumping from one thing to the other. He quit. He thinks he's getting what he deserves."

"Do *you* think he's getting what he deserves?"

How should I respond to that? If, as I believed, he hadn't committed the crime, no, he didn't deserve to die. But by his own admission, he'd done things so vile, so reprehensible that he would be in prison anyway if he'd gotten caught doing them. Morally, this might have been the right thing to happen, but I wasn't prepared to make that call. The life he had presented him little in the way of options. He had killed his own father. Nobody had wanted him. And when Taylor finally took him in, he didn't alter the path Warren was on. Instead, he enabled his negative lifestyle, led him further down that path. Taught him to flourish in it. That is where it took him.

"Warren's had a lot of things go down with him, most of it bad. At some point, we all have to take responsibility for our own shit. Warren was trying to do that. He wanted to leave his old ways behind him when he got caught up. He doesn't deserve to die for that crime if he didn't kill Sheila. Everything we do, will do, or have done has an effect on what happens next. That's karma."

"So, what he's getting is karmic justice?" Denise said.

"Seems like it," I said.

"Seems like it? You're not getting too close to this, are you?"

"What do you mean? No, it's not that. I'm just not sure if the best efforts have been made on his behalf."

"You don't have to worry about that. You have to leave that for someone else to handle."

"Someone else handling stuff for him is what has him this close to an execution."

"Baby, don't be so defensive," Denise said.

"Defensive?"

"Wait a minute. Look, a lot of things are happening real fast. You haven't had time to put things in order, to deal with your father's death. I know your father wanted you to help Warren, even thought you should see him. But, you're overcompensating. Instead of dealing with your father, you're focusing your time and energy on Warren."

"That's bullshit! I'm determining if the right thing is being done here, and you think I'm overcompensating for my father." The discussion, for me, was over.

"Look at some of the rash decisions you've made lately. You haven't been yourself, and that's understandable, but you can't put yourself at risk for Warren."

I didn't know how she had meant this, but to me, it sounded like she thought she was talking to a child.

"Okay, whatever, Denise. I wanted to share what was going on with me, but apparently, it would be better for me to work these things out for myself." I stood, gathered my things and headed for the door. When I was sure that I had succeeded in ticking Denise off, I walked out.

27

"Good morning. Brent Peters, please," I said into the phone.

"Who's calling?" the voice on the other end asked.

"This is James Pruitt." I looked at Chuck, sitting across the desk from me. He had arrived shortly before 9:00 a.m.—two full days before Warren's execution.

"Hold please."

It was 9:01 a.m. on Tuesday morning. At 6:15, I had been at my desk, dressed and ready. It was my second day back at work and my goal was to get something done today. Yesterday I had been consumed with trying to get information on Taylor. I would have been better served not being here. As soon as 9:00 rolled around, I was on the phone to Peters. There was no way I would let today pass without us speaking with one another.

"I'm sorry, Mr. Pruitt, Mr. Peters asked me to take a message," the voice finally said.

"Tell him Warren Johnson's brother called." I hung up. Who was I kidding? He wasn't going to call me back. The man was leaving me with no choice.

"Gwen, clear my schedule, I'm going to be out the rest of the day," I said into the intercom.

Chuck smiled and looked at me. "Raleigh?"

"Raleigh," I replied.

"Let me go with you?" Although posed as a question, Chuck wasn't requesting, he was letting me know he was coming.

This would be another one of those rash decisions that Denise had cautioned me about. The split-second decision to leave for Raleigh wasn't going to help anything between the two of us.

Gwen was given specific instructions to let only Jason know where I was going; he would know how to contact me. If anyone else called, she was to cover for me. She still wasn't talking to Chuck.

The road to Raleigh was quickly becoming a routine drive. Chuck followed me; we could get around better if we both had transportation. Chuck had told me his leads on Taylor had run their course in Charlotte. He thought he might do better in Raleigh.

It was 12:35 p.m. when we arrived at the law offices of Colby and Sturgis. It was located in the heart of downtown Raleigh. There was several news trucks parked in front of the building, but nothing like the media circus I was expecting. It should have been crawling with reporters. Warren's lawyers should have had every piece of print and television news media within a three hundred-mile radius honing in on what was happening with Warren. Trying to find some validity to his argument that he hadn't raped or killed Sheila Thurgood. Human rights groups

outraged over the miscarriage of justice his case represented. Someone concerned about the life of an innocent
black man! Instead, there were just a few reporters waiting
for the inevitable. They were there to hear the typical
"nothing has changed" line and to learn that the execution
was still on schedule for one minute after midnight on
Thursday.

"Do you know where the office is?" Chuck asked.

"Not really. I need to get by the reception desk. You
got a plan?"

"I've got an idea. Give me a few minutes to work something out. Then it's on you to get where you need to go."

We were parked on the third level of the parking garage.
Chuck got on the elevator to go down to the first floor.
I waited for the doors to close before going to the stairs.
There was no hurry to get down them. Chuck needed
enough of a window to create an opening for me.

As I approached the lobby of Colby and Sturgis, loud
voices and arguing could be heard. I opened the door
and there was Chuck in the center of the commotion,
yelling about his money and the fact that that rat bastard
Sturgis was holding out on him. Two elderly black security
guards were barely containing him. Chuck was allowing
himself to be contained by them. I'm sure he didn't want
the responsibility of causing either of them a heart attack.
Two cameramen were filming the excitement. A TV
reporter, trying to stick her earpiece back in, was pointing
a microphone towards Chuck. Someone was scribbling

on a notepad and people were coming out of offices to see what was going on. I rushed over to the receptionist, who was trying to regain her composure.

"James Pruitt, with Adams, Harris and Hodge. I had a 12:30 with Brent Peters. Which way?" I blurted.

"Second floor, turn right off the elevator and go all the way to the back. Stop at Elaine's desk." She was so flustered she didn't take her eyes off Chuck to notice me.

Scurrying by, I looked back at Chuck as he continued to demand his money. He gave a slight wink as I slipped into the elevator. Following the receptionist's directions, Peters' office was easy to find. In front of his office sat a heavyset white woman with a nameplate on her desk that read Elaine Faulkner. She had gray hair and the face of a bulldog. She looked like a gatekeeper guarding the door to hell.

"Can I help you?" she said in a pleasant voice. It didn't match her appearance at all.

"I'm here to see Brent Peters."

"Mr. Peters doesn't have any appointments today."

"Ma'am, I assure you, this is an urgent matter concerning Warren Johnson."

"Reporter! You'll try anything." The pleasant voice was gone and the growl in her voice now matched her face. "I'm calling security."

"I'm not a reporter. I'm his client's brother! My name is James Pruitt and I wouldn't be here right now if Peters would have given me a call back!" I wanted to make enough noise so Peters could hear me inside his office. "Since I can't get him to call me back, I'm paying him a visit."

Elaine was punching numbers on the phone when Peters stuck his head out of his office door. There was no doubt he had heard everything I'd just said. He stepped out of the office. He was five-foot-eight, bald on the top of his head, wearing horn-rimmed glasses on a narrow nose that was reddened at the tip. He was slight of build, and he appeared to be a bundle of nerves—all of them bad.

"What can I do for you?" Peters said, making a feeble attempt at bravado.

No wonder he wouldn't speak to me. Six words out of his mouth and it was evident where the weak link was in the chain.

"I want to know what you're doing for my brother, Warren Johnson?"

"Your brother?"

Peters tried to act shocked, which only served as an accelerant for the fire burning in me. "Yeah, his brother! The same brother who's been calling you the last two days. Don't act like you don't know my name. I'm sure Goffrey Taylor has mentioned it to you." I was fishing again. Judging by the look on his face, I had just hooked him.

"Come to think of it now, he did mention you." He paused for a second, and then became defensive. "I'm his attorney and I'm trying to prevent his execution."

"Really? Then you can answer some questions for me. First, can you tell me why there was never another suspect?"

"The District Attorney had DNA evidence that identified Warren. They had no need to find another suspect."

"And you didn't find any reason to look for anybody else, make them go in another direction? Just groom him for death?" I pulled out the copies of the appeals and slammed them on Elaine's desk. "See this. You filed this mess on behalf of Warren Johnson. This is bullshit. A second year law student could wipe his ass and come up with better stuff than this.'

"Appeals?" Peters was stunned at the sight of them. "How'd you get these?"

I didn't acknowledge the question. He was reeling. There was no time to waste, so I continued to press him. "This firm is making money hand-over-fist and I know it can't come from substandard work like this. You and your firm are either hiding something or incompetent. Take your pick. Either one can get you disbarred."

"Mr. Pruitt, I will not have myself or the integrity of this firm impugned in that manner!"

"Get used to it! I'm just getting started."

Coming up behind me were the two elderly security guards fresh from trying to restrain Chuck. They looked worn out as they dragged themselves toward me. Elaine stood and pointed at me.

"I thank you for leaving." Peters tried to sound like he was in control when he realized he had some backup.

"Found you a set," I whispered to Peters. "Have a nice day. Gentlemen, there's no problem here," I said to the security guards. They already had had a tough enough time with Chuck. I didn't want to add to their stress. I picked up the appeals and left.

"He's the weak one. We get something on him, he'll crack. He'll be the one who gives us what we need," I told Chuck. He was waiting at my car.

"Maybe, but I hope it's somethin' we want. There ain't a whole lot of time to work with; can't waste any."

"True. I'm going to the prison. It's time for me to let Warren in on my theory, see if he can help me. You want to tag along?"

"No doubt."

Turning to Chuck as I unlocked my car, I said, "Tell me something. How in the hell did you get out of that mess?"

"I told them I wasn't going nowhere till I met with Brian Sturgis and I got my money."

"Brian Sturgis? The partner's name is Raymond Sturgis."

"No shit. I know what the fool's name is. If I had used the right name, do you think I'd be standing here right now?" Chuck was on point. "I'll follow you."

"Who's that?" Warren pointed at Chuck. His speech was slurred. The man I had sat with three days ago was gone.

Chuck and I watched him being led into the visiting area by two guards whom I hadn't seen before. His feet were unsteady; his speech and movements were sluggish;

and his chains rattled as he moved. The guards propped him up in the chair and left us.

"This is my partner, Chuck… You all right?" I asked. Warren's eyes were clear and cloudy at the same time. They weren't bloodshot, but he wasn't able to focus on us. He appeared to be detached from reality.

"All right. Shit. I'm more than all right. Nigga, I'm flyin'."

"What did you take?"

"Yo, kid, like he blunted," Chuck said to me.

"Yeah, but there ain't no wood like this. They got some shit up in here," Warren said. "Yo, hold up; you the nigga Jimmy played ball wit, right? Shit, I got some loot off your ass." He reached out to shake Chuck's hand, the chains rattling as he barely made contact. "My bad, this shit I'm on got a brother twisted."

"I feel you. What you hittin'?"

"Don't know. Valium and some other shit. They bring it; I take it. Calm my nerves. Calm enough to let these people kill me. Ain't that somethin'?"

"Warren, don't take anything else that they give you," I demanded.

"Huh?" He was fading. "Man, I ain't blowin' my buzz." His words were barely understandable.

"Warren, listen to me and focus. Peters is not helping you. Taylor is paying for a defense that is letting you fall. Taylor is letting you fall. There's something missing here and I need your help to find it."

"No, Goffrey pays the bills…raised me…good white man…took…took me…nobody wanted…"

"They're both dirty, Warren. The only way for me to help you…Warren?…Warren?!" I shouted but it failed to rouse him. "Warren! Shit!"

"That brother's callin' hogs," Chuck said flatly.

"Guards!" The guards rushed in like there was something to break up.

"Take him back to his cell; he can't do me any good like this. Who's giving him the pills?" The guards exchanged looks and shrugged their shoulders. "Get me Tom Carter!"

Minutes later, Chuck and I sat face-to-face with Tom. His loyalty was still in question, but at the moment, he was the best shot that Warren had.

"Who gave him the drugs?" I asked.

"He got them from the infirmary. He don't sleep at night; can't blame him. Kind of the norm when an inmate is as close as he is." There was genuine concern in Tom's eyes. I could tell he'd seen the process many times before.

"I need his head clear. I'm trying to make sure he doesn't get on that gurney."

"That's his lawyer's job," Tom said.

"That's the problem. His lawyer's doing a half-assed job," Chuck said.

"You know anything about Peters?" I asked.

"That greedy sonofabitch would sell his mama for a dime if the heifer was worth it. That weasel ain't worth shit; got no conscience."

"Tell me about Taylor. Did you know he did some time at Butler?"

"I was there 'bout eleven years ago. He was there for six months on a stalking charge; ended up doing another eighteen months 'cause he shanked an inmate. I helped break up that fight, and caught the shank in my back. Always thought that was a set-up, but couldn't prove it. After that, I came to Central. Only a matter of time 'fore he's back in here, or some place like it."

"He's under investigation." Chuck was cutting to the chase.

"Drug trafficking," Tom added.

"What's the connection with them?" Chuck pressed.

"I don't know where it started, but Peters is by his side on everything. Peters, and that firm of his, got some real deep political connections. Always seems to keep Taylor clean. Look, gotta get back. Johnson won't get any more dope. You got my word on that." Tom stood to leave.

"Thanks, Tom," I said.

"Have you found anything on the girl Taylor was stalking?" Tom asked.

"No. Couldn't find anything," Chuck said.

"Figures. Crooks and politicians is cut from the same cloth. The way I heard it up at Butler, her name was Sheila Thurgood." Tom dropped his bomb and left without realizing its impact.

Neither Chuck nor I could believe what we'd just heard. My theory was gaining weight. I had a direction to go in and it wasn't shooting blindly in the dark.

28

"What are you talking about?"

"There's nothing else you can do, Chuck. Go back to Charlotte." I said.

"Just like that, after all this shit. You got to be out your damn mind!"

"Listen to me. What else do we need? Taylor's under investigation for drug trafficking; you know this. It's only a matter of time until they close him out. This situation with Warren, I'll take care of that myself. All I needed was a solid link to tie Taylor in to this, and now I got it."

"What link?"

"Come on, Chuck. Taylor's got a thing for Sheila. He's stalking her, does time behind her. Dude gets out two years later and the woman's with somebody else. But it's not just anybody. She's with Warren Johnson, the kid he raised. The black kid whom he took under his wing and raised. Bet money that put him over the edge."

"Okay, I give you that. It's probably your missing piece. But if that's true, then this shit's about to get real."

"I know it's real."

"You keep pokin' around on this level and you gonna get hurt."

"Then that's on me. This is something that I've got to do. I got to take this to Warren, let him know what's going on."

"Fine. I'll stay here with you."

"No need. I got it."

"In case anything else pops off, I got your back."

Now he was starting to irritate me. "Chuck, this ain't business no more. I'm not paying for your time. I got it."

"No, this ain't just business, and no, it ain't about you payin' me."

There was something Chuck wanted to say, but he was hesitant. I waited for him to speak. He looked down, shuffled his feet a couple of times and then raised his head as he started.

"I talked to Denise and your mom last night."

"You what?"

"Shut up!" he snapped at me. "Denise was upset after the fallin' out ya'll had. She called your mom and they called me. Bruh, you ain't been yourself lately and you don't see it. You doin' irrational shit. You sittin' up here fightin' for a brother you hardly know so you don't have to deal with your family shit. I get that, but they worried you gonna get into somethin' you shouldn't 'cause you ain't thinking straight. They thought it might be best if I kept close tabs on you." Chuck paused. "I agreed with them."

Now I was pissed! Not only did my mom and my girl think I couldn't handle myself, but neither did my best friend.

"How much you charge to baby-sit now?"

"Dog, that ain't what this is about."

"Fuck that! I'm trying to do what my father wanted me to do. Everybody thought I should talk to Warren. I did. Came back here a second time when I didn't want to. Now that I believe he didn't do it, everybody wants me to back up, slow down, think it through. Too late; can't do it. Now I'm respectfully asking you to go back to Charlotte because I got this shit. I don't need a fucking babysitter!" Out of anger, I shoved Chuck away from me, causing me to lose my grip on my laptop case. The impact of it hitting the pavement didn't sound good.

"People are just trying to look out for you!" Chuck shoved back.

I stared at Chuck, but didn't respond. The conversation was over. I'd said all I had to say.

"Nobody wants anything to happen to you." Chuck paused and waited for me to respond. "You willing to put your life on hold for this?"

My response was a continued stare. I was prepared to speak to him with my hands if it came to that.

"You don't want me to stay?"

"I'm straight, Chuck. What part of this don't you understand? This isn't college anymore. I don't need you holding my hand. Not you, or my mom, and for damn sure, not Denise."

"Bruh, ease up. We all family here, right?"

"No, we're not all family. My mom is family. Warren is my family." I let that statement hang in the air. My exclusion of him and Denise had drawn the line. He and Denise weren't family. This time, it was Chuck's turn to stare. I could see his jaw tightening and his body becoming rigid.

"Fuck you!" Chuck said through clenched teeth. He turned, walked to his car, got in, and drove away.

My fear was confirmed: the laptop had been damaged during its fall. Without having the benefit of the laptop, my next stop would be the public library in downtown Raleigh. I needed to check out Tom's story about Sheila. The periodicals would be kept on microfiche. Surely, there would be something on Taylor's arrest and conviction for stalking Sheila.

After getting turned around a couple of times, I found the library that was located downtown on Seventh Street right next to the police station.

It never entered my mind that the woman Warren was in love with could have possibly been the same woman that Taylor had done time for. I could kick myself for having missed that. I had lost half a day following the wrong trail. I needed to confirm that Sheila was the woman Taylor once did time for. The quickest way would be through Warren. He would know, but because of the condition he was in, I wouldn't be able to get anything from him right now. The library and the Internet were my next best options.

The Internet search didn't return anything on Goffrey Taylor or Sheila Thurgood. Multiple combination searches led to one dead end after another. A search through the periodicals would be a painstaking, but necessary process.

I set up camp in front of a desktop near the microfiche machine the librarian guided me to. She was a spry young lady of seventy and didn't mind telling anyone how old she was. She sprang to her feet when I told her I was looking for the periodicals on fiche for the *Raleigh News and Observer*. She was more than happy to help.

"Recent?" she asked.

"No, ma'am, I'm looking for information that goes back to 2000."

"Just one minute." She was on her way to get the fiche that held that information.

2000 would be a good place to start. I wasn't sure when Taylor did his time for the stalking, but Tom said it had been eleven years ago when Taylor shanked him. I could start there and work my way back.

"Here you go, sweetie."

She moved twice as fast as a woman half her age. She handed me a stack of microfiche film in chronological order.

"My name's Mildred. Just holler if you need anything else."

"Yes, ma'am. I sure will."

I began the slow process of scrolling back through one fiche after another to locate any article that had Taylor's name attached to stalking charges. Forty minutes after my search began, I was no further along toward the information I needed. Miss Mildred was back at my side.

"Have you found what you were looking for?" she asked.

"Not yet, but I will." I was getting frustrated. All of the fiche was beginning to look alike. "How long have you been working here, Miss Mildred?" A little chatter might make the process easier.

"It's been forty-eight years this past March," she said with pride.

"Really?"

"Oh, yes. I've been here all my life. Elementary to Meredith College, all right here in Raleigh."

"You don't say. Well, I guess you keep up with these periodicals then."

"Lordy, yes, I try to. They're my favorite. Seems there isn't a day goes by I don't read or hear about somebody I know. I might not be as young as I used to be, and my hair's a lot more gray, but my mind still works a lot faster than any computer in here. So why don't you tell me what you're looking for? Put Miss Mildred to the test."

"Okay. I was trying to find some information on a stalking case, probably eleven or twelve years ago."

"What's the name?" She was already flipping through the periodicals in her head.

"Taylor, Gof—"

"Goffrey Taylor?" she said before I had finished. "Fall of ninety-nine." She closed her eyes for a brief second. "October…October twenty-eighth. Check the fiche."

I fumbled through and found the fiche containing October twenty-eighth. I loaded it and scrolled through to find the edition for that date.

"The Local section."

I couldn't believe my eyes. There it was. She had called it down to the day. It was an article detailing the arrest of one Goffrey Taylor. I scanned the article but didn't find the name I was looking for, Sheila Thurgood. The article listed the victim as one Marie Hairston.

"Says here the victim's name is Marie Hairston. I was looking for the name Sheila Thurgood?"

"That's her. They used her middle name and her mother's maiden name, but that's her.

"How in the world did you know where to find this?"

"I love periodicals." She smiled. "And I have a photographic memory."

"Thank you, Miss Mildred. You don't know how much of a help you've been. You just saved me three hours' worth of work."

Miss Mildred may have been seventy, but she was right: her mind was sharp as a tack. She wasn't letting age slow her down. She told me about the shock that people had been in when the news about Taylor broke. He had been a boy from the wrong side of the tracks who had made good anyway.

"Oh, but when he got in trouble, people turned against him. Some people were leery of him anyway. People who had never talked bad about him before, didn't hesitate to start. Said they knew something wasn't right about him."

"Any truth to that?"

"Not that I know of. That isn't any of my business." She smiled again. "Some people are just envious. He didn't have the degrees some of those people did, but he had a lot more money than they did. He was a scrapper."

As much as I enjoyed listening to Miss Mildred, and she could probably talk for days, I'd spent enough time at the library. I thanked her again for her time and help before I left.

"What the hell are you doing? Ruck's been looking for you," Jason said to me over the phone. "How come you haven't returned my calls? You okay?"

"I didn't know my battery was dead." I had my cell phone plugged into the car charger. I was so consumed with my work, I hadn't heard the phone go dead.

"Hell, I even tried Chuck. Gwen said he was with you."

"Not any more. Chuck should be on his way back to Charlotte. What did Ruck want?"

"The Salerno files. He wanted to poll the information on the RICO case that they're building against him. I covered it; he's all right. Why's Chuck headed back here? Trail still cold?"

"No, but I got what I needed. Told him that I'd be fine from here. The prison guard, Tom Carter, he put some weight on my theory. I have the name of the woman that Taylor did time for stalking?"

"Who?"

"Sheila Thurgood."

"No shit."

"Seems so simple now, doesn't it?"

"Have you told Warren what you're doing?"

"No, he's so jacked up on pills he doesn't know who he is. You got anything for me?"

"Yeah. Peters is very interesting. His work was topnotch, impeccable. He became a partner in less than seven years with Colby and Sturgis, but the last five or six, he's been sinking. Losing cases that should have been easy wins."

"I met him. Doesn't surprise me; he's real shaky."

"Came across some other info you might also find interesting. He got into some trouble back in eighty-seven. He was pushing acid and LSD, small time stuff in college, before he went to law school. Guess who he ran with back then?"

"Goffrey Taylor. This shit is getting too easy. It's all falling into place."

"I wouldn't go that far; it's still an uphill climb. These two go as far back as junior high. Taylor's about two years older than Peters from what I gather. They lived in Emerald Woods Trailer Park. Both of them are from dirt poor beginnings."

"That's the trailer park Warren said we lived in. Taylor used to run with his father."

"I'll be damned. It does get easier when you make a few connections. Anyway, Taylor took the heat off of Peters for that one when he was in college. Peters goes on to graduate from law school, top ten percent, goes to work for Colby and Sturgis and his life is good. Works hard, but he's always been connected to Taylor."

"Bet they've been covering each other's asses ever since. Peters is the weak link. I think he's ready to pop. I'll take this to Warren. Once he sees what's going on here, he'll help me fight this, and Peters is going to crack. Good work, Jason. I'll talk to you later."

"Wait, I've got one other thing for you. Have you talked to Denise?"

"No." That question didn't sound good.

"She came by here looking for you."

"You didn't tell her I was here, did you?"

"Didn't have to. When she realized you weren't here, she knew. She's worried sick about you. She called you here, at home, on your cell phone, and you haven't called her back."

"We had an argument about this stuff last night. She thinks I'm in over my head. That's why I didn't tell her what I was doing today. I'll call her later. If you talk to her again, tell her everything is okay."

"Done. Hey, look, be careful. Taylor's no lightweight. His attorney might be soft, but his law firm isn't. They've been able to keep this low-key up to this point. There's a blind eye on this one. That DNA evidence hurts. It's staring Warren in the face; it's going to be hard to get your theory to stick."

"It's all I've got."

At 5:40 p.m., I was settled into my room. I had checked back into the Sheraton in the late afternoon. The channel for news was on as I waited for the 6:00 p.m. newscast to begin. The lead story was about Warren, and they switched to a live broadcast outside the prison. A blonde-haired, blue-eyed female reporter said Warren was resting. She stood among rivaling protesters carrying picket signs. The consensus of the protesters was that the death penalty was cruel and inhumane. Other signs were adamant that the right decision had been made. I didn't detect any signs that claimed Warren's innocence. Nobody had a clue that there was the possibility that Warren was innocent. His fate had already been sealed. It was not a coincidence that the reporter placed in the middle of the controversy among the two groups painted an image of Sheila Thurgood.

When the piece ended, I called the prison to leave a message for Tom. To my surprise, he took the call. I wondered if the guy ever went home. He confirmed that Warren was resting. In fact, he hadn't been awake since Chuck and I had left earlier in the day. I told Tom I was going to be there in the morning and asked him to get word to Warren that I'd be there to help him. Tom suspected I had something, but knew we couldn't discuss it on the phone. He assured me that Warren would know. He told me Warren wouldn't be able to have visitors until 10:30 a.m., but there were no limitations on the number of visitors or the length of time they could stay for the remainder of the day.

It was time to stop ducking the issue. At 7:40 p.m., I called Denise at home. After the fourth ring, the answering machine picked up. I thought to myself, *Good. I'll just leave a message.*

"Denise, it's me. Look, I'm sorry about last night. I—"

"Hello." Denise picked up the line.

"Hey, baby, you okay?" Hell, I had thought she wasn't there.

"Yes, I am." There was irritation in her voice. "I've been calling you everywhere. Where are you!?"

Denise wasn't just irritated; she was pissed. I couldn't blame her, but I wasn't going to be talked to and treated like I was ten years old either.

"I'm in Raleigh."

"Raleigh?" she said.

I could hear that slight sucking of her teeth. This had the potential of being a lot more than a heated discussion. She had known I was in Raleigh before she'd asked. I'm sure she suspected it the first time she called me at work and I wasn't there.

"We agreed that you weren't going to get involved in anything dangerous," she chastised.

"I don't know what *you* agreed to before you left, but I didn't agree to anything."

"You know that kind of work is out of your league. You've got no business being involved in it."

She had just challenged my manhood. What kind of shit was that to say? *Out of my league.*

"Hold up. I ain't out of my league. I'm the only one here trying to do something about Warren, and I don't need any babysitter."

"What's that supposed to mean?"

"You know what it means. I don't need you calling my mom to tell on me, or you two getting Chuck to hold my hand when I do something."

"Chuck told… The only reason why we asked him to be with you is because we were concerned. We don't want you to get hurt."

"I'm not going to get hurt! Damn. I'm just trying to do what my father wanted me to do! Why is that so hard for people to understand?"

We both sat silent for a minute. I hoped that now she heard what I was saying. I had taken it upon myself to do what my father couldn't. My father couldn't take Warren in and treat him like family; I was doing that. Denise finally broke the silence, but she didn't say anything close to what I wanted to hear.

"James. It won't bring him back."

"What? Is that what you think I'm doing? I don't bel… I have to go."

"James, baby, wait."

"I can't. Don't call, I'll call you later. Bye." I hung up the phone and I shut down. My emotions would not be up for discussion tonight.

Hearing that statement, "It won't bring him back," hurt. I'd never been hit that hard before. That's not what I was trying to do. What in the hell was wrong with these people? They didn't get it. I was done with it. There were too many things I needed to get done before tomorrow. I would be damned if I was going to wallow in this bullshit. I pulled out my notes and articles. It was time to map out a game plan for tomorrow. No need to stress over what Denise had said. It was time to refocus my energy, think only about tomorrow and the limited time I had. Peters would be there. I could only imagine the look on his face when I looked him eye to eye and laid this out in front of him. Peters would break. I would see to it.

29

Sleep hadn't been an easy commodity to come by. I had gone through my theory, line by line, until midnight. Warren would have a full understanding of where I was coming from. If I could make him see the case through my eyes, then he'd know my theory wasn't a shot in the dark. It was something worth pursuing.

When I lay down for some shuteye, my theory kept replaying in my head. Taylor stalks Sheila and Warren ends up with her. Taylor finds out about it, has her killed in the place she shared with Warren. Warren's DNA is pulled from the seminal fluid they find in her. Ironclad case. Taylor's attorney defends Warren. Taylor pays for the defense. A defensive team that never aggressively seeks any other suspects. They merely search for loopholes that don't exist, essentially running out the clock and waiting for the time to pass by until the execution date.

At 7:14 a.m., it was less than seventeen hours until the execution. I was showered, dressed and ready for checkout with nowhere to go. I went to the lobby of the hotel and proceeded to pace it. The continental breakfast was inviting, but I had no desire to eat. I was anxious to get to the prison. Ten-thirty a.m. might as well have been a light year away. I needed to find something to do to pass the time. Then it came to me. There was a place that would help me to pass the time.

"Can I help you, sir?" the hotel clerk asked, smiling. She was much too chipper for this time of morning.

"I hope so. Have you ever heard of Emerald Hills?"

"Emerald Woods?" she corrected me warily. "Yes, sir."

"Yeah, Emerald Woods; can you tell me how to get there?"

"The trailer park?" she said in a tone that suggested I might not want to go there.

"Yes, the trailer park."

She reluctantly gave me the directions. I thanked her and left to see the place that was my first home. It was a place that held no memories for me.

The drive took less than a half-hour. I followed the hotel clerk's directions to Emerald Woods. Warren had told me the place was rundown, a shithole. But nothing he had said could have prepared me for the reality. Emerald Woods was not the right name for this place. Emerald Woods sounded like some place you would want to be. It wasn't. Broken beer and wine bottles littered the sides of the road. Broken windows on some trailers that I was sure housed some broken spirits. Some of the trailers appeared to be condemned, while others should have been or were soon to be.

The entrance sign hung on a small wooden post with barely visible paint that read Emerald Woods Trailer Park. I turned into the park and began to look for 1769 Emerald Point Drive. It never entered my mind that a trailer park could be so big; it was a mini-city. Every street was Emerald something. I passed Emerald Love Drive, Emerald Sky Drive, Emerald Dawn Drive, Emerald Run Drive, before I came upon Emerald Point Drive.

I parked in front of what I thought was 1769. It was hard to tell because the single-wide trailer was partially burned out and its numbers were barely legible. I got out to take a closer look and confirmed it was 1769. The whole trailer couldn't have been more than forty feet long. There was no underpinning and you could see that they'd used cinder blocks to try to balance it. I walked up the three shaky wooden steeps and tried the door. It was open. *What good would a locked door be on this place?*

Against my better judgment, I went in. The floors were unsteady beneath my feet and the stench from the burn-out still lingered, stinging my nostrils. I was standing in what Warren had described as the front room. It was where they had found him stabbing his father. I followed the narrow hallway to the back of the trailer, passing two doors on the left. The back room was where my bio-logical parents would have been killed. The door, barely hanging on its hinges, was open. You could hear the sound of flies buzzing and smell a musty odor. I stared in, imagining what the scene that fateful night must have looked like.

Back up the hallway, I paused to look in the first door on my right. It opened into a bathroom that was smaller than my pantry at home. The next door led to another bedroom. It had to be the room that Warren and I had once shared.

There were no memories here for me. I thought that seeing the place would spark some kind of connection for me, but it didn't. In the front room, I stepped on a board that creaked. There was something about that sound that made me recall the *Mickey Mouse Club* theme song. For an instant, I could picture a black and white TV. I could see the silhouette of three people, perhaps Warren, Evelyn, and Billy, but the image didn't last. I stepped on the board two or three more times to see if the noise would trigger any other long buried memories, but it didn't work. The images hadn't lasted long enough to make the place real to me. I walked out the door, down the shaky wooden steps and back toward my Jeep.

I looked around at the other trailers surrounding 1769 Emerald Point Drive. Some were more rundown than others, but nothing was as bad as the gutted single-wide behind me, and I thanked God I hadn't grown up here.

I hated thinking like that, making a judgment on people and a life I didn't know. I would never meet or know these people, had no idea what their goals and aspirations were. If I had grown up here, would I be the same person I was today? I honestly didn't think so.

At 10:18 a.m., I was at Central Prison waiting for Warren to arrive. I had killed time at Emerald Woods by walking around the dirt roads to see if any other memories came back to me. There were none to be had. Judging by the number of rebel flags I had seen on different trailers, it was a good thing it was daytime. The qualifications for living in Emerald Woods in the seventies must have been different from today. Today, you couldn't just be poor; you had to be a poor, rebel-flag-waving redneck.

The door opened behind me. A guard led Warren in. I looked in his eyes; they were clear and focused. He was glad to have someone here. The chains shook as he entered. The guard unhooked his bindings and he came to sit in the chair beside me instead of the chair across from me where he would normally have sat. It was the closest we'd been to each other. Even when we shook hands, we had always been at arm's length.

"You don't mind if I sit here?" Warren asked.

"No." Truth be told, I was a little nervous at first. "How are you doing?" We never looked at each other.

"I'm here. Tom told me you wanted them to stop my buzz, that you was on some kind of kick. Why you do that?"

"I needed your head clear so we could talk about something."

"Talk? Shit, Jimmy, I'm 'bout to die," Warren said solemnly. "Ain't much for me to talk about."

"I'm trying to save your life." I looked at him; he still

wasn't looking at me. "Have you talked to your lawyer today?" I watched Warren as his head dropped a little.

"No, can't find him," Warren said through clenched teeth. Then he changed the subject. "Them muhfuckers asked me what I wanted to be buried in. I told them to bury me butt ass naked."

"Warren!" I snapped. That got his attention. I was going to run the show today. "How'd you meet Sheila?"

"What?"

"You never told me how you met Sheila. You told me about her, but you never told me how you two met."

"I met her because of Goffrey."

Warren waited for me to say something, but I didn't. It was his turn. I'd let him do the talking, but I was going to control where we went with it.

"Goffrey had a thing for her, and he got in some trouble behind it."

"Stalking," I said. That froze Warren.

"You checked him out?"

"I wanted to know who had raised you; that's all. Please, go on."

"He wanted me to keep an eye on her, and I did. Peters got me to meet her after Goffrey got in trouble. One thing led to another and the next thing you know, we was flowing."

"Why would he ask you to do that and not anybody else?"

"He wasn't raisin' anybody else. I was the only one he trusted."

"It must have hurt him pretty bad when he found out about you two."

"He didn't know anything 'bout us till she was killed."

"You kept that from him for three years? What did he say?"

"He backed me up. He's paying for my defense. I came clean to him, told him everything. He was glad I told him and he said he'd do whatever he could to help me. He was done with her after he'd done that time."

"Warren, I've got a theory that might save your life. Some of it, you're not going to like."

"I ain't got time for no more pipe dreams."

"It's not a pipe dream. Taylor knew you were involved with Sheila long before you told him. My gut tells me he and Peters are involved in this."

"C'mon, man, you're fucking crazy. He wouldn't do anything like that, not to me."

"Yeah, he would. He was stalking her and he didn't just turn that off after he got in trouble for it."

"He told me he was straight with it. He's all I got left. He…" There was nothing for Warren to say.

"Where is he? You're scheduled to die at one minute after midnight, and where is he? Where's your lawyer? He's filed bullshit appeals and your friend is paying for it." I opened my case and pulled out every document, every newspaper article, everything I'd done since I had met him. Line by line, I explained my theory to him. "They are letting you die and nobody cares because the state thinks that a black man raped and killed a white woman.

If there's anything you can tell me, I can use it to help you. We can go after Taylor and Peters and save you." I was pleading with him.

"Goffrey wouldn't…" He sat there in stunned silence, looking at everything I had given him. It was a lot to absorb at the last minute. "If everything you said is true, then I really don't have anything left," he said. He was hollow and empty. He pushed the information I'd laid out for him back to me. "This ain't gonna do me no good."

"Warren, if you don't let me help you, you're going to die tonight." Warren was unfazed by what I'd just said. "Did you hear me? You are going to die."

"Jimmy, leave it alone."

"You've got a chance here, man. Reach out and take it."

"I'm already dead!" Warren exploded.

The guards started to come into the room. I got up to stop them. It took some convincing, but they relented and left us alone. I sat back down, but this time in front of Warren. I looked at him and he looked at me. Neither of us spoke for a few minutes.

"What do you mean, you're dead already?" I gave in.

"I am. Been here eight years, waitin' for somethin' to change, getting' my hopes up. Every time I thought I had a shot, I'd get knocked down. Eight years countin' one day after another after another. Rememberin' everything about Sheila—the last time I saw her, how she wore her hair, the way she laughed, even the way she cried. Eight years thinkin' 'bout how we held each other. That beat on me, Jimmy. Every day I was losin' a little bit more. You know what else I been thinkin' 'bout? I been thinkin' 'bout them people who ain't here because of me. Four of 'em. Dead. And nobody will ever find them. I took 'em away from somebody else. I never thought much about 'em till Sheila was gone." Warren's eyes filled. "This is the last day that I go through it. There ain't nothin' for me out there. It's been eight years. What am I gonna do? I can't fuck with this life no more. It's over. I'm gettin' off this ride."

I took in what Warren had to say, but refused to believe he was willing to go down without a fight. If he wasn't going to do it for himself, then his younger brother would do it for him.

"It's not time to get off yet. It ain't over. I'll be back in a little while." It was time for me to leave.

"You're not listenin', man. I can't do it no more."

"Warren, I feel you, but I'm in too deep." Warren looked up at me and shook his head. "Believe me, Taylor isn't all you got."

Warren nodded. "Can you be here tonight?"

"Bet on it." I replied immediately. If I wasn't there, nobody else would be.

It was time to take the fight straight to Peters and Taylor. I cornered Tom on my way out. Brought him up to speed and told him I needed to get to Taylor and Peters. He didn't know how to get to Peters' house, but within minutes, he produced the address to Taylor's house and had a route mapped out to get me there.

Peters was the link that would break first. Colby and Sturgis would be my first stop. Taylor was the last resort; hopefully it wouldn't come down to that.

I headed back toward downtown Raleigh. At 11:19 a.m., I was stuck in traffic. I turned on the AM band to search for a traffic report, and I soon found out there was an overturned eighteen-wheeler on I-40. After the traffic report, I picked up on what the hot topic of the day was. The execution of Warren Johnson.

The co-hosts talked back and forth about how the Thurgood family had suffered through the awful tragedy and how justice was being served. There was not a favorable or defensive comment made on behalf of Warren. Not by either co-host or any of the callers.

At noon, the radio station cut to a live feed from the governor. He was preparing to make a statement regarding Warren Johnson. The accident was moved off the road to the median and traffic was moving slowly in the right lane. I listened intently for the voice of Governor Davidson.

"Ladies and gentlemen, briefly I would just like to say that no stay of execution has been or will be granted to Warren Johnson. His latest appeals have been rejected, and there is no new evidence that has been presented that could alter that position. I am at peace with my decision to execute. Our state enforces the death penalty and this vicious crime will be punished. Thank you," Governor Davidson concluded.

I turned off the radio. There was nothing else for me to hear. I needed to get something concrete, something on paper, not just a theory, if I wanted to help Warren. It was now within twelve hours of the execution. The need to work quickly was an understatement.

Colby and Sturgis was a madhouse when I arrived. Reporters were in front of the office doors, circling and hounding, trying to gain entrance to the office. Apparently they were anxious to get something from Peters or his firm in response to the statement made by the governor. Colby and Sturgis security guards as well as police officers who were brought in to help protect the firm were holding them at bay.

It was 12:27 p.m. and I had no idea how to get to Peters in all the chaos. Unfortunately, this time, there was no Chuck to run interference for me. I doubt he could have helped me get through the frantic wave of people anyway.

As I turned to leave there stood Elaine, Peter's secretary. She must have just gotten off of the other elevator. She was looking at the sea of media in disbelief. My luck was changing.

"Elaine."

"Oh, my God," she said slowly as she continued to look at the crowd.

"Elaine!" That got her attention; we made eye contact

with one another. "I'm Warren's brother. Do you remember me?"

"You were here yesterday. I'm getting security." She was nervous, not the bully she'd been yesterday.

"Please, don't." I looked at the size of the crowd that she would have to fight just to get to the security guards. "It's not worth the trouble. I'll be gone by the time they get here. Elaine, I need your help."

She hesitated. There was definitely something on her mind.

"I'm trying to help save Warren's life. Things about his case don't add up. I don't believe he committed the crime. Maybe some other people have some doubts." I was trying to plant some seeds to see where I'd get. "Please, help me."

"How?"

"Can you get me to Peters' office? I've got some information that might help Warren."

"It won't do any good. Mr. Peters isn't here."

"What? Let's move." I didn't want anyone to hear what we were saying. I put her arm in mine and led her further down the hall. "Where is he?"

"Nobody knows. He left right after you did yesterday. Nobody's seen or heard from him since."

"Maybe he's with Taylor?" Judging from the shakiness in her voice, she wasn't lying.

"Mr. Taylor called here looking for him this morning. Nobody can find him."

"Nobody outside this office knows that, do they?"

"I don't think so. This morning we were forbidden to inform anybody about it," she said, in a hushed tone.

"Here." I pulled out a business card and jotted down my cell number. "Let me know if you hear from him." She took the card, but didn't respond positively or negatively. "I'm going to get in touch with Taylor."

"Start with his home. According to Mr. Peters, he's hardly ever awake before noon."

"I'll check on him and see. He'll want to keep up with what's going on." There was no need to let her know what my intentions were. She needed to believe I was on their side for now. I wanted to shake up Peters, get him to roll over on Taylor, but nobody knew where he was. I was the one shaken up. It was down to the last resort. Now was the time to test Taylor.

30

Lunchtime traffic in Raleigh was as time-consuming as Charlotte's. It had been an hour since I'd left Colby and Sturgis and I still wasn't at Taylor's. The long drive forced me to reconsider my approach to Taylor. Chuck would have had it all figured out without any reservations, but I didn't have that crutch to lean on. If I had gotten to Warren or Peters, I sure as hell wouldn't be doing this.

What I wanted was to get my hands on Taylor and beat the truth out of him, but that wouldn't happen, nor would it do any good for anybody. I was going to step on his toes, but be cool about it. With any luck, Peters would be there. His behavior in Taylor's presence would be telling.

Churchill Downs subdivision was a golf club community. The houses were brick, stucco, and stone, with perfect lawns. The landscaping was professionally done with impeccably manicured hedges. The houses easily went for seven hundred grand or more. Taylor had come a long way from the Emerald Woods Trailer Park. The distance could not be measured in mileage.

Tom's directions took me to 13790 Avondale Court. The house was tucked behind a twelve-foot-high, wrought-iron gate. The driveway sloped down toward the house. The colossal gray stucco compound stood out among the other elaborate homes.

There was an intercom to the left side of the drive-way. I pulled close to it, pushed the button and waited for a response. There wasn't one. I pushed the button again. Still no answer. There was no time for this. If it required jumping the fence to get in, that's what I was going to do.

"Who is it?" the voice growled through the intercom.

"It's James Pruitt. I'm here to see Mr. Taylor." There was more silence. I waited for a reply.

"Who'd you say you were?" This new voice was less gruff.

"James Pruitt, Warren's brother."

The gate opened. Apparently that was my invitation to enter. The driveway made its long descent and circled in front of the house. I parked right in front of the house and studied it for a minute. Not a hedge or a brick or a blade of grass out of place on the immaculate, contem-porary home. Real estate, antiques, and storage lots apparently paid well.

Goffrey met me as I approached the door. He was wear-ing a white, full-length caftan. Not a hair out of place, and cologne so thick it seemed like he'd swum a couple of laps in it. He stuck his hand out to shake mine. My first instinct was to spit on it, but I resisted the urge to do so. I shook his hand instead.

"Please come in. Forgive the intercom. Cat's a little harsh when he answers it."

The main entrance led into a marble foyer. It opened up to a circular staircase. At the top of the staircase was a walkway overlooking the area.

"You heard the governor's announcement?" Taylor asked.

He put his hand on my shoulder as he led me into a large gathering room. The large windows allowed me to see the deck and the pool out back. Two guys occupied the pool; it was the two who were with Taylor Saturday night, Cat and Dice. They were enjoying the company of six women. The ladies were in and around the pool in various stages of undress; they would fit right in at Fevers. Taylor loved to have him some freaks around. One was a leather-wearing dominatrix who had Dice on his hands and knees tied to a piece of patio furniture submerged in the shallow end of the pool, spanking him. Why Taylor wanted me to see this, I didn't know, but he was too preoccupied at the moment to be the least bit concerned with Warren.

"I couldn't believe the governor's statement; they won't give him a stay," Taylor repeated.

I was supposed to believe that he was concerned? He was standing there in Mediterranean pajamas, showing me his freak party and he was trying to front like he was concerned.

"I heard it. Where's your lawyer?" I didn't have time for him to play games with me.

"I've been trying to find him all day."

I looked at him, then to his pool. "In a fucking bathrobe, lounging with those hoes." So much for keeping my cool.

"Don't disrespect my house!" That got the full attention of his thugs by the pool.

Now I realized he'd put me in a visible position just in case anything jumped off. He knew that once I saw what was going on here, it was only a matter of time before the fireworks began.

"Disrespect? Warren is going to die tonight. It's almost two o'clock. He's got a little more than ten hours. He hasn't seen his attorney in two days, and you ain't doing shit. This is fucked up and you're talking about disrespecting your house?"

"Look, you little cocksucker, I raised Smooth. He's my family." Taylor grabbed me by the collar. "So don't roll up in my camp telling me what's fucked up."

Out of the corner of my eye, I saw Cat heading my way. Dice would have been right beside him, except he was still struggling to free himself from bondage in the pool. I snatched Taylor's hands off of me.

"Don't you ever put your fucking hands on me." I backed up a few steps so I could keep an eye on his boys when they made their way into the house. Cat was in first.

"It's okay," Taylor said. "Just a little concern about Smooth."

"Warren was set up and I have an idea who it was that did it. He had some enemies in places that he never knew existed. I'm going to get the motherfucker that did it." I looked Taylor dead in his eyes when I said it. He wasn't giving anything away.

"I hope so; we're running out of time."

That cold, calculating son of a bitch had said the words without flinching.

"Warren's running out of time," I responded just as coldly. We both stuck our chests out. Somebody's would get caved in. "I'll show myself out."

I turned and walked toward the door and hoped there wouldn't be anything catching me in my back. I had just bitten off something that I wasn't ready to chew. Out the door and back into my vehicle and I couldn't get to it soon enough. I'd laid out the bait; now it was on Taylor to take it. I only hoped, for Warren's sake, to be ready when he did.

31

"Is Rucker still cool?" I was talking to Jason on my cell phone.

"No. You getting anywhere?" Jason spoke quickly.

"Yeah, in trouble. I was at Taylor's house."

"Taylor's house?" You're supposed to be working Peters. What were you doing there?"

"Nobody can find Peters. Not his firm, not Warren; hell, his secretary said Taylor had been looking for him. Taylor was my last option."

"A dangerous one."

"I had to put him in play. It's two-thirty and I got zip from anybody."

"What did Warren think of your theory?"

"He was devastated. I laid it all out for him, but he doesn't want to fight it. He's ready to let it all end."

"So, what are you doing?"

"Finishing what I started."

"If he's not fighting it, why should you?"

"Where's that coming from?"

"Dude, if he's willing to let it go, you should too."

"Jason, you knew what I was doing… You talk to Denise again?" I waited for his response. "Did you talk to Denise?"

"She was in tears. James, you've done all you can. You're chasing something you don't need to."

"Who's that talking? You or her?"

"It's not just that. We got a call from Colby and Sturgis. They are turning up the heat. They let Ruck in on your unofficial investigation. They are putting the pressure on him to make you drop it or lose your job."

"The hell with that job! If Ruck is going to turn tail because of their pressure, I'll tell that man what he can do with his job. You never talked to me."

"Jimmy, if Warren's giving up in spite of what you laid out for him, maybe you need to reconsider some things. If he can let it go, does it make sense for you to put your life and career in jeopardy messing around with these people? I don't think that's what your father had in mind."

"This isn't just about my father anymore." I couldn't believe it. Denise had convinced someone else it was all about my father. "It may have started there, but this is about justice. I believe Warren when he says he didn't do it. If I believe that and I don't do anything to help him, how am I supposed to sleep when this is over? I've got a little more than nine hours to make something happen, and I'll spend the next forty minutes getting back to the prison. If there's nothing you can add to help me, thank you for your time." I hung up before Jason could say anything.

Everyone who had encouraged me to speak to Warren, people who were more curious about him than I was, now wanted me to back off because they thought it was getting too dangerous. Denise, Mom. I hadn't even bothered to speak to them since I had come back to Raleigh. Chuck, and now Jason. Jason had been the last one on my side. Now Denise and threats about my job had gotten in his ear.

There was no time to concern myself with those thoughts; it was time to get back to the prison. Maybe Peters would be there, but I wasn't holding out hope for that. Some of the pressure I'd brought to Taylor was bound to make something happen.

It was 3:35 p.m. when I got back to the visiting area. Time wasn't slowing down for Warren or me. Tom was the first person I came in contact with. He was waiting on me when I got there.

"They ain't grantin' no stay," Tom said, pulling me to the side.

"I heard. How's he doing?"

"Hard to say. He 'bout to die, but he's talking to people like it's okay."

"He's tired of fighting a losing battle. Peters show up?"

"No. You didn't find him?"

I shook my head. My head hung a little lower, disappointed that I had yet to deliver something.

"Sombitch!" Tom tried to keep his voice down, but didn't manage too well. "Did you find anybody else?" He was suddenly much quieter, looking around to see if anybody was in earshot.

I knew what he was asking. "I did. I didn't make a new friend, though."

"What happened?"

"He knows I think Warren was set up by someone who knows him."

"You accused him."

"Not directly, but I'm sure he's got a clear understanding of where I'm coming from."

"Son, you got more balls than I gave ya credit for. I didn't think you'd see this thing out. Stay on your toes. He ain't nothin' to play with."

"Me neither. It was my last shot. I'll have to sit tight for a little while and see if it goes anywhere."

"At least you're trying. It's better than what Johnson got anywhere else."

"Thanks, Tom." Here was somebody who understood what I had been doing.

"Better get in there to see him."

"You'll be here tonight?" Funny that the only people standing up for Warren would be a corrections officer and me—a half brother who hadn't remembered Warren until a week ago.

"Probably. I get off at eleven, but I'll stick around tonight."

Warren was talking to one of the corrections officers when I walked in. He was relaxed, maybe relieved, as I entered. What was someone supposed to act like before an execution? I'm sure it was different for different people, but it was eerie for me.

The conversation quickly came to an end as Warren turned his attention to me. I wanted to tell Warren I'd found him a way out of this, that his people broke down and confessed. But none of that had happened. At this point, there was no way to tell if what I'd done would help him. I stood there, mouth open, preparing to speak, but having nothing to say. I'd run around trying to find some way to help him and now, looking at him, it had begun to sink in. That was a dead man in front of me. He now had less than eight hours to live.

"I… I never been through anything like this before."

"Same here." Warren gave a half-smile.

It was a futile attempt at humor. Another time, another place, maybe it would have been funny. Not here and definitely not now.

"Lighten up, little bro. It's okay." He put his hand on my shoulder to reassure me. There were no chains rattling. For the first time since I had met him, Warren wasn't cuffed. "This is the way it's supposed to end."

"I don't believe that."

"Got to. I do. Could you excuse us?" Warren said to the guard.

We waited for the guard to leave and post himself outside the door. Warren motioned to the seats and we sat down facing one another. I forced myself to believed it wasn't over. That he was ready to give me something; something to help nail Taylor and save himself.

"I didn't find Peters, but I got to Taylor. I'm—" Warren put his hands up, motioning me to stop.

"I'm not interested in that."

"What?"

"Jimmy, there ain't no mistake 'bout what I said. That ain't why I wanted to talk to you." He paused to make sure he had my undivided attention. "While you was gone, I started thinkin' about what you said. It could be true, but I ain't fightin' this no more. Now I know you didn't just roll over and land on that shit. It took you some work to do all that. 'Specially when you didn't have to for a nigga like me. The way I did you when you first came here, I didn't deserve your help. Regardless of what supposed to happen here tonight, I wanted you to know I appreciate what you tried to do. I'm glad you're goin' to be here tonight. You mighta come late, but at least you came. When this is all over, I know that you did what you could. Leave the rest of that bullshit here."

Warren was giving me my release. He wanted to make sure I didn't carry around any *what ifs* with me.

"I'll try to remember that."

"Don't try, do it. Let's get off that deep shit. What's up with your girl? You ain't said nothin about her or your moms lately."

"I thought you wanted to get off the deep shit."

"Homefront ain't tight?"

"Just needs some fine-tuning. They think I'm too wrapped up in this. Putting myself in danger."

"They probably right. But you know Denise like that because she got them feelings wrapped up in you. She the one?"

"She was last week. I hope she still is. I was about to propose to her the night my father died."

"Damn. That's fucked up. You ain't asked her?"

"Haven't had a chance with everything that's been going on."

"Let me tell you somethin': if she the one and you know it, you need to make that happen. I been sittin' here for eight years wonderin' why I didn't make a move a year earlier, a month, even a day. I waited too long and it all got away from me. Fix it as best you can and get on with it. That's what I'm doin', gettin' on with it."

I took note of the advice. I was going to have to fix it and move on. We spent the next two hours talking about whatever came to our minds. I shared countless stories about my mother and father, a family Warren admitted he would have loved to have been a part of.

We talked nonstop until Warren's dinner arrived at six-thirty. I was surprised to find another dinner for me. The amount of food they had for us would have put a Thanksgiving dinner to shame. Turkey, stuffing, green beans, squash, macaroni and cheese, deviled eggs, corn, cornbread, and cranberry sauce.

The whole time Warren and I talked, I still kept hope

out there. Maybe Peters would show or Taylor would break. With each hour that passed, it was less likely that Taylor would make a move. He didn't have to; he was too cool for it. He'd let things play out unless he was in any real danger of being exposed. Without Warren or anything to substantiate my theory, and no time left, there was nothing left to be done. I hoped that Warren would change his mind and give me something, but he wouldn't. However, like he said, I had tried. I might not stop his execution, but I vowed to myself that sooner or later I would get Taylor. I would clear Warren's name of the rape and murder and the state of North Carolina would be forced to admit they had sentenced and executed the wrong man.

The pace of the conversation between us slowed as we continued to work through our meal. At 7:20 p.m., Warren finally stopped eating. I was surprisingly hungry and ate my share, but Warren was unbelievable. He pounded the food down like it was a sport. Joey Chesnut would have been proud. He devoured all of his food and what I didn't finish of mine.

"You gotta be full," I said.

"Yeah," Warren grunted. "Might as well eat. Shit, I ain't countin' calories no more." He ate until he was tired, not full.

"Like you ever counted calories?" I tried my hand at joking.

Warren slowly smiled. "Look at me. Hell, no. I wish I

could remember countin' calories. I ain't never had no need to."

We both looked toward the door as we heard it being opened again. The guards were letting a pastor into the room. At least that was my assumption. He had on the black shirt with the collar, and he was carrying the Bible. It stunned me for a second. I hadn't expected to see a white chaplain, or any chaplain for that matter.

"Father Doyle." Warren stood to walk over and shake his hand. "How you doin', Rev?"

"Fine, and you, my son?" Doyle replied.

Warren shrugged his shoulders. "I'm good. Rev, this is my brother, James." He motioned toward me.

I stood to shake his hand.

"This here's Father Doyle. He a Catholic, but he all right anyway." They laughed. I could see there was a genuine rapport between them. He was someone Warren felt comfortable with. "He's the prison chaplain; always got a minute for you."

"Good to meet you, James," Father Doyle said.

"You too, sir." Funny how people always stood a little straighter, talked a little cleaner, and threw out a couple of sirs or ma'ams whenever a minister came into the room. It didn't matter what their religious background was.

Once the formalities were over, Father Doyle wasted no time getting down to business. Warren wanted me to stay close, so I didn't leave the two of them alone. Warren knew what Doyle was looking for. In Doyle's eyes, it was a chance for Warren to confess to this crime, but he held steadfast to his position. He was not guilty of the crime. He told Father Doyle that everything he'd ever done, anything that he needed to confess, they had already discussed. Doyle told Warren that God always knows the truth and that he alone would pass the final judgment. Warren smiled at him and said he was ready.

Father Doyle read from the Bible to Warren. The 23rd Psalm was what Warren wanted to hear, over and over again. The three of us talked about the promises God had for all men. Eventually, the conversation moved from religious topics to three men just having a conversation. Mostly, I just listened.

My cell phone rang. I looked at my watch. 9:19 p.m. I was so engrossed in the conversation that I hadn't paid much attention to the time. We were within two hours and forty minutes of the execution. It was also surprising that my cell phone hadn't rung before then. I must have really pissed everybody off. Nobody had fooled with me in awhile.

"Hello?"

"Mr. Pruitt?"

There was a female voice on the other end, but it wasn't one that was familiar to me.

"Yes?"

"It's Elaine Faulkner. Brent Peters' secretary."

"Yes!" I stepped away from the conversation with Warren and Father Doyle. My heart began to race.

"You wanted me to call you if I heard from Mr. Peters."

"Did you?" My heart was pounding, the adrenaline starting to race through my veins.

"Yes. He wanted me to go by the office and pick up some documents he wants delivered to you."

"Did he say what they were?" I contained my enthusiasm. I didn't want Warren to pick up on what I was talking about.

"No, but he wanted me to get it to you ASAP."

"I'll meet you at your office. I'll park in front of the building." I hung up. "Warren, I'll be back," I said, turning my attention to him and Father Doyle. I moved out before either could utter a word.

I asked one of the guards to get in touch with Tom and have him meet me in front of the prison. Colby and Sturgis was a good thirty-five minutes away. I was going to have to shave ten minutes off of that time.

"What's going on?" Tom asked when he met me.

"Peters' secretary has got something for me. I'm going to pick it up. It could be what I need. Can you meet me at the front gate in an hour? I want to make sure I can get back in here."

"Yeah, I'll do it. But you watch yourself while you're out there."

"Already ahead of you. I'm meeting her in the front of her office building. Can I borrow your car? I don't want to be out there driving mine."

I kept one eye on the road and one on the rearview mirror, and at 9:58 p.m., I was in front of Colby and Sturgis. Within seconds, Elaine was scurrying toward Tom's car.

"Did you talk to him anymore?"

"No, this was left on my desk." She handed me a letter-sized envelope. I could feel something in the bottom. It felt like flash drives. I started opening the package to see what I had.

"Thanks, Elaine." I said, indicating the thick envelope. "Thanks for calling. I've got to get back to the prison."

"Be careful, Mr. Pruitt."

"I will."

I thought better of trying to read the information while I was idle in one spot. I would read as much of it as I could while I drove.

Once I was back on the interstate, I turned on the interior light and unsealed the envelope. I reached to the bottom of the envelope. My guess was right. There were two flash drives. Those I placed in the passenger seat. I didn't have any way to access the information right then, thanks to the cracked laptop. I fumbled through the envelope and pulled out a group of documents that contained twenty pages or more. Scanning over a number of pages, I realized I was looking at documentation of wire transfers, drops and pickups, and brief recounts of how money was laundered. The documents weren't in any particular order; they were just pages picked at random that linked Taylor to his illegal activities. The full history of his illegal involvement was likely to be on those flash drives.

Flipping through the rest of the pages, I knew I had Taylor nailed, but I was looking for something else. Something that would implicate Taylor in Sheila's murder and free Warren. There was nothing. The flash drives might have what I was looking for, but unless I could make time stand still so I could check them out, the drives wouldn't do me any good. I was pissed. I turned the light off and stuffed everything back into the envelope, and then hit the gas. There was no time left to waste, I had something on Taylor, just not what I needed to clear Warren.

Ten thirty-one, and outside of the prison had become chaotic. It wasn't a group divided. There were a few anti-death penalty protesters. But that number was dwarfed by the hoards of death penalty supporters who were eager and waiting for Warren's execution. I weaved through the crowd of people gathered near the entrance gates. There were no problems re-entering. Driving Tom's car had been a major advantage, I thought. Tom emerged from the guard station.

"Any trouble?" Tom asked as he jumped in.

"None. Look at that envelope." The envelope was now lying on the floorboard of the passenger seat.

"This is what she gave you?"

"I got Taylor by the balls, but I got nothing for Warren unless it's on those two flash drives in there."

Tom turned on the interior light and pulled everything out of the envelope. I glanced at what he had and noticed a letter that I hadn't seen before.

"What's that?"

"What?"

"That sheet of paper. That letter. I didn't see it the first time I went through the envelope. What is it? What's it say?"

"It's from Peters."

"What does it say? How did I miss that?" I was thinking to myself and talking out loud at the same time.

"Mr. Pruitt," Tom began to read in his Southern drawl, "I am providing you with evidence that links Goffrey Taylor to his illegal activities. Providing this information is a breach of the attorney/client privilege and I know I would be disbarred, if anybody ever found out. I have allowed greed and immorality to cloud my judgment. For that, I am sorry. As I'm sure you're aware, Goffrey is under federal investigation. This is all you'll need to put him in prison for the rest of his life. For Goffrey, prison would be worse than death."

"Fuck that, he doesn't say anything about Warren."

"Hold ya horses, I'm gettin' there," Tom mumbled as he skipped down a couple of lines. "Says here Warren Johnson is innocent in the death of Sheila Thurgood."

"It does." I slammed the brakes and snatched the letter from Tom. "Where's it at?!"

"Start right there." Tom put his finger on the spot.

"In the death of Sheila Thurgood," I picked up the reading, "I withheld this information because I am partially to blame for Miss Thurgood's death. I witnessed firsthand the abuse and vicious beating she received, and, God help me, I could not stop it. I could only leave her there to suffer and die. Goffrey Taylor is responsible for her not being here. Goffrey used my knowledge of the situation as leverage against me, and manipulated me into allowing the situation with Mr. Warren Johnson to happen. By the time you have this information, I will be long gone. Again, I am sorry." I looked at the typewritten confession. I finally had something, but I was angry because it might be too late in the game.

"Told ya that sombitch wasn't no good, him or that ass-wipe Taylor."

"Has the governor gotten here yet?" I asked.

"Not yet. The boys down at the gate were expecting him any minute."

Tom took over the driving duties. He knew where the governor's limo would be parked, so we went there to intercept him. Tom gave a quick rundown of what was going on and who I was to the guards who were on duty. Reluctantly, they let us stay there in the entranceway. Tom had gone all out for me. He realized, like I did, this was likely my last shot.

At 10:53 p.m., a convoy of three Lincoln Town Cars carefully made their way into the parking lot. The middle car was a stretch limousine. Tom and I watched from the entranceway as the two Town Cars parked on either side of the limo. Eight men emerged from the two cars that flanked the limo and started to secure the perimeter. Then the limo driver got out, went to the rear of the car and opened the door for the governor.

Two aides and another guard from the governor's security team got out before Governor Davidson did. The rest of the security team formed a human barricade around the sharply dressed, fifty-eight-year-old governor. They all moved in unison as the governor neared the entranceway.

The governor and his entourage would have to stop in the entranceway before going through the security checkpoint into the prison. This would be the only time to approach him, my moment of truth. I waited as three members of his security team made their way in. That's when I made my move. I was within four feet of the governor.

"Governor, can I talk to you for two minutes, sir?" I spoke fast and low. The words were barely out of my mouth before his security attacked me. The ones who didn't attack were reaching inside their jackets as all hell was breaking lose. Maybe it hadn't been the ideal way to approach him after all. But as they always say, hindsight is twenty/twenty.

"Let him go, he's clean!" I could hear Tom's voice ring out over all the other voices. He'd gotten close to the action.

It took a few seconds for the situation to sort itself out

and everything to calm back down but it seemed like a lot longer than that to me. Time can seem like forever when you're locked down in a corner with four or five semi-automatic weapons pointed at you.

"Governor, this is James Pruitt. He is the brother of Warren Johnson," Tom said, interceding on my behalf. "He just got some information that could help Johnson."

Governor Davidson looked at me and the manila envelope that one of his men had taken from me. "I'm sorry, son. I can't talk to you." His manner was very condescending, and he started to continue on his way.

"Can't or won't," I said.

"Get rid of that man!" one of his security men ordered.

"Damn it, Governor. You're about to execute an innocent man and I can't get two minutes from you?"

That stopped the governor dead in his tracks. "All right, you've got one minute."

His guards let me go. I grabbed the envelope back from the guard who had it. I pulled out the letter from Peters, and noticed the envelope felt different. The flash drives were missing and the envelope was torn. I was about to question the governor's security man when I caught sight of Tom out of the corner of my eye. He was patting his pocket. The governor came back toward me and I gave him the letter. He began to examine it quickly.

"And you would like me to do what?" the governor said when he was finished.

"Stop the execution. Re-open the case."

"Why? For what reason?"

"This letter is from Peters. That's Warren Johnson's attorney."

"It's typed, not even signed. It could be from anybody. It could even be from you. It might be from Peters. And if that's the case, it has less credibility than if it came from you and I have no idea who you are. This is nothing more than an eleventh-hour scam cooked up by a defense attorney who didn't have the courtesy to show up for our meeting this morning. Now he's blaming himself and Goffrey Taylor, a man I know and respect. He's attempting to implicate him in some murder…"

"This isn't a scam, sir. It's for real. Peters has provided documentation of Taylor's illegal activities. If he's not fabricating stories about that, then he's not lying about Warren, either."

"That's not good enough, son. Mr. Johnson has had eight years. Eight years of appeals. Eight years to prove himself innocent. To discredit the DNA tests. And now I'm supposed to spare his life based on that piece of paper?" He took the envelope from me. "We'll have someone look into these other allegations." The governor handed the envelope to one of his flunkies and continued into the prison.

"He didn't do it. It's the wrong man! Governor, it's the wrong man! Read those documents!" I shouted after him, but my words fell on deaf ears.

Tom grabbed my arm and led me back out of the

entranceway as some of Governor Davidson's security staff looked on.

"It's over, Pruitt. He's not going to help you. You need to get back over to the holding area."

"He just took the shit and left. He won't do anything to stop this. Just took the letter and the documents. That motherfucker!"

"I got them flash drives. I told you, crooks and politicians." Tom tried to reason with me. "You might not stop this, but if these files are good, you can take care of Taylor."

"Didn't think you'd make it back," Warren said calmly as I entered.

It was 11:17 p.m. He was sitting on the gurney. Father Doyle was still there. The medical technicians were preparing Warren's veins for his intravenous drip.

"Told you I'd be here." I struggled to keep my composure. I walked over to be closer to him. I wanted to tell him what I'd tried to do. There wasn't any reason to. Despite all my efforts, it didn't change a thing.

Warren stood as I neared him. The large, brooding man whom I hadn't known existed as my brother two weeks ago, who'd had nothing but disdain for me the first time we met, extended his arms to me and I hugged the big brother who rescued me all those years ago.

"Thanks for letting me know you," Warren said. "Take care of yourself and that woman."

"I will. Warren, I tried—" I intended to tell him what happened, but he cut me off.

"I know you did. Thank you."

There was nothing else to be said. Warren sat back down on the gurney and let the technicians finish their work. They laid him down and put the retention straps on him, connected him to an EKG monitor, put a rubber tie on his arm and once they found a suitable vein, inserted the needle for his IV.

At 11:45 p.m., I was removed from the holding area and escorted to the viewing gallery of the execution chamber. There were two sections of the viewing gallery separated by a concrete wall. I sat to the right of the chamber, alone, with no one joining me on Warren's family side. Congressman Thurgood and his wife were likely gathered on the other side of the concrete wall with the governor of the great state of North Carolina. I sat down quietly and waited.

There was a clock on the wall. My eyes locked on it until it hit midnight. There was no need to let my eyes wander around the room; they would not find compassion in the empty room. The curtain to the chamber was pulled back and there lay Warren on the gurney. He lifted his head and searched the room until he found the only pair of eyes that supported his. He winked at me and then laid his head back down. As the clock struck 12:01, a green light went on inside the chamber; the process had begun. The Thiopental Sodium was now entering his veins. This would induce a deep sleep. I looked at his eyes. They were clear, but within seconds, they had lost their focus, rolled back into his head and then closed. After that drip finished, the Pavulon was started. The muscle relaxer would cause him to stop breathing and his heart to fail. I watched his chest as it rose and fell slowly until it stopped. I looked at the concrete wall, picturing the governor on the other side, and heard the EKG ping down to a flat-line. My brother was gone. Everything I had tried to do, what my father wanted me to do, it was over. I stared at the concrete wall, picturing the governor. There was a rage in my stomach that I could feel growing inside of me. I stood there feeling helpless and infuriated at the same time. Tears formed in my eyes and began to fall. Despite Warren acknowledging my efforts, I had failed him and I had also failed to do the last thing my father asked of me.

There was one thing I could do though, to make things right. I was going to confront Taylor one more time. This time there would be no dancing around what I thought, no innuendos. It would be him and me face-to-face. Not through anybody else, not in the morning, but right now.

32

"Leave that alone, son. Ya got everything ya need to lock 'em up on these flash drives." Tom was stopping me from closing the door to my vehicle.

"Fuck that! I want to know. I want to hear it from him!" I said.

"If I got to have the police arrest you to stop you from getting killed, I will."

"That's not enough to stop me, Tom, not tonight. This is something I got to do."

There was nothing Tom could say or do that would get me to change my mind. He shook his head. "You know this is your neck you playin' with now, don't you?" He was slowly moving out of the way.

"I know. Make copies of those drives and take the copies to the D.A.'s office and the FBI, first thing in the morning."

As I pulled out of the parking lot, Peters' letter raced through my mind. The would-have, should-have, could-have game battled against that letter in my head.

This time I could see myself losing balance. Not my physical balance, but my mental balance. Although I recognized what was happening, I didn't give a damn about controlling it. Warren's execution had pushed me further off center than I had been before. Somewhere in the back of my mind, my excuses had come to an end. In the last few days, I'd pushed everyone close to me away. My woman, my mom, best friend and colleagues. I was making this walk alone. I had put everything I had into Warren and still had come up empty. Bottom line was, he had become my focus because I wanted to help him. I believed he was innocent in Sheila's case. But it also allowed me to put my pain over the loss of my father aside for a minute. Now it was back on top of everything else. The perfect place for me to release everything was going to be on Taylor's head.

Driving down the long isolated highway was giving me a chance to think about my father. Then I heard his voice—*Always do the best you can with what you have to work with.* Dad had said that I should help Warren and I had done the best I could with what I had to work with. There hadn't been a whole lot for me to work with.

Being so caught up in my thoughts, I didn't notice the headlights that were gaining on me until it was almost too late. I couldn't make out the car. Tom had probably called the police anyway, but now I was glad that he had. As the car got near me, it slowed and stayed behind me. I waited for the blue lights to come on. They didn't.

Instead, the car banged my back end. No cop would do that. I glanced up and down the dark road and there were no other headlights in sight. I floored it, but before I could put any distance between us, the car rammed my back end on the left side and caused me to skid across the two-lane highway. I fought for control of the wheel, but couldn't get it back. The vehicle skidded out of control and landed in a rut on the opposite side of the road, but it was still running. I hit the gas and went nowhere. Put it in reverse; still nothing.

In the distance, I could hear brakes squeal. Whoever had knocked me off the road wasn't done and this wasn't an accident. The door wouldn't open; it was jammed shut. Rolling down the window and climbing out would be the quickest escape route. I didn't want whoever it was following me to know that I was no longer in the vehicle. I went left and made my way into the nearby trees and foliage lining the roadway. I was about thirty yards into the woods when three gunshots rang out. I could hear the shots striking metal. Even though they were shooting at my Jeep, it didn't stop me from hitting the deck.

As I lay on the ground, breathing heavily, I turned back to see what was happening. The headlights from both vehicles were on. There were two figures that had taken target practice at my Jeep. They carefully approached from both sides, waiting to see if I would be coming out. They reached for the doors in unison.

It was a black male and a white male. As the headlights

illuminated them, it was easy to recognize them. Cat and Dice. My greetings were courtesy of Goffrey Taylor.

Remaining crouched on the ground, I removed the white shirt I was wearing. There wasn't a full moon out and not a lot of light but the white shirt would still give me away. I hung the shirt on a small tree. I moved quietly among the trees and brush, keeping my eyes on the two thugs.

"Pruitt, come on out of there and make it easy on yourself!" Dice yelled.

I was now about fifty yards into the treeline and waiting. I'd have to get to them one at a time. All I needed was enough distance between the two to make a move.

"Let's get him, Cat," Dice ordered.

"Man, I ain't gettin shit."

"Go get him!" Dice said again.

As they stood near the cars, I could see the silhouettes of the two. Dice turned his gun on Cat. That persuasive argument convinced Cat that he should be the one to go first. "I'm going in the other direction. We can cover more ground that way."

Precisely what I needed. It would be easier to handle them separately. They were handing themselves over on a platter. Cat headed in my direction, but was reluctant to venture too far into the dark woods. I watched both of them as best I could, but soon lost sight of Dice. Cat finally started moving deeper into the woods, slowly and methodically. When he stepped, I stepped.

Cars could be heard approaching on the highway in the distance. With any luck, someone might see the headlights and the wreck and call for help before something went down. But that wasn't something I could count on. Time had already run short.

Cat was within five yards of my shirt when he spotted it. He made a charge and attacked it. He fell clumsily into the brush. My footsteps were soundproofed by the ruckus he made; I was able to close within feet of him. Before he could recover his footing and realize what was going on, I kicked his face as hard as I could. I tried to kick his teeth out of the back of his head.

Cat squealed in pain; his reflex action caused him to fire off a wild shot before he fell on his face and dropped the gun out of his hand. I thought the fight had been knocked out of him, but he tried to reach out for the gun. I stepped down hard on his hand and dropped my left knee into his back, turned his head to the right and gave him a hard open hand slap to his right ear. If he survived tonight, his equilibrium would be shot for the next week. The big boy wouldn't stay down, though. I let him rise unsteadily to his feet. He was already leaning to the right. He took a wild swing and fell completely off balance. I caught him from behind and rammed his head into the biggest tree trunk I could find. I had to work fast. I knew Dice would be closing in.

"Hold it, nigger!" Dice's voice rang out.

I let the unconscious body of Cat fall. I could hear

Dice as he inched closer behind me. He walked slowly, allowing me to hear his every step.

"How smart do you feel now, Mr. Prosecutor?" He was getting closer. "You fucked with the wrong one. Goffrey's not bush league. He's the big time and you wasn't ready for this." Dice was right behind me with the gun barrel jammed against my head. "A little something from Goffrey," Dice whispered.

This was it; this was how it ended. And then I heard a shot fired.

"Next one's in the back of your head, you don't put that gun down," I heard a familiar voice say. I didn't know where he had come from or how he had gotten there and I sure didn't care. I thanked God for his arrival.

"You all right?" Tom asked, and waited for Dice to move. "I'm not playin' with you, boy. Give me an excuse."

Dice put his gun down and backed up. When I mustered enough nerve to turn around, I saw Tom as he whacked Dice across the back of the head with the butt end of his weapon. Dice started to fall and Tom caught him with another blow to the head before he hit the ground. While Tom dealt with Dice, I picked up Cat's gun to make sure he would not have another chance to get his hands on it.

"This might be your lucky night, huh?" Tom said. "I told you these guys play for real."

I was standing there in stunned silence. I was seconds away from what was sure to be my death. I didn't want to think about what would have happened if Tom hadn't found me.

"Tom, thank you. I thought I was done. You saved my life."

"Don't worry about it." Tom was kicking at Dice's limp body. "You were doing pretty good for yourself until Dice got the drop on you. Wasted too much time on that other fella. Got any rope in that Jeep of yours?"

"I don't think so."

"You got a SUV and no rope? That ain't gonna get it, son. Look here, my car's too far away. We gonna have to pull these big boys outta here and put them in the trunk of their car."

We dragged them out as fast as we could. They started coming to a couple of times. When they did, we would stop, and Tom would smack them upside the head once or twice with his gun, like it was nothing. Then we'd keep right on moving. I was impressed by Tom's strength and stamina. He was not a big guy, but he was able to pull Dice with relative ease. We dragged the unconscious bodies close to the treeline. Tom guarded the bodies while I moved the car closer to where the two were laid out. Tom smacked their heads a couple more times before we loaded them into the trunk. I'm not sure if they needed it, but Tom sure enjoyed the additional punishment he was able to distribute.

"We need to take these fellas to a police station."

Tom was right. That's what we needed to do. But it wasn't what I was going to do. A few minutes ago, with a gun pointed at the back of my head, I had changed my mind. Somebody else could handle the dirty work. Not now. Taylor had sent the two punks after me, and now I wanted them returned to sender, by me.

"You're right, Tom. I'll get them there," I said.

"I'll handle it from here. You're liable to find yourself in some more trouble."

"I've had enough of this, Tom. It's not the kind of work I do. I swear to you, man, I'm getting my hands out the pot. I'll get them there." Tom was leery of what I was saying, and he had a right to be. Hell, I was a lawyer. "You saved my life, man. I owe you. I'll get them there."

"Take me to my car. I'll lead you there."

I took Tom to his car. I needed to find a way to distract him. I convinced him to call a tow truck. I told Tom that he knew the roads better than I did and he'd be able to describe the location of my Jeep better than I would. We stood outside of Tom's car. As he talked with the towing company, it provided the distraction needed. I slowly pulled Cat's gun on him and waited for him as he hung up.

"You gonna use that?" Tom knew, without looking, that the gun was drawn on him.

"I'm sorry, Tom." I snatched his gun from him. "I'm going to take these two, along with Taylor, to the police station. Now, if you don't mind, would you open your trunk and take that rope out?"

Once he took the rope out, I quickly struck him on the temple the same way I had seen him do to Taylor's two thugs. I hog-tied him and stuck him in the back seat of his car.

Before I left, I stopped at my Jeep. I got a black shirt and some tennis shoes out of my gym bag. I was trading in the wing tips. Once I was back in the car, I pulled out, ready to confront Taylor.

"Who is it?" a voice asked over the intercom.

"Cat," I said, masking my voice.

"What's the matter with you?" The voice belonged to Taylor.

"Hurt," I replied.

The gate began to open.

"Where's Dice?"

"Didn't make it."

Once I was inside the gate and making the descent toward the house, I positioned a cinderblock down on the gas pedal and jumped out of the car. As I hit the ground, I rolled a couple of times, and wondered what the hell I was thinking. When I got to my feet and realized I was okay, the rage inside me took over again. Taylor might as well have stuck Warren on the gurney himself and now he was coming after me. This shit was going to be finished tonight.

The car went straight through the circular driveway and smashed into the front of Taylor's house. If the fellas in the trunk came to, the bump would be enough to put them back out again. I had to move fast. There was about fifty yards to cover before anybody got to the door. The boys in the trunk had been the only ones I'd seen close to Taylor, but that didn't mean he had no one else working for him. I made it to the side of the house as someone started struggling with the door.

"I can't get it opened," a voice said as he continued to fight with the door. It definitely wasn't Taylor. "I got it."

"Is he all right?" Taylor asked from inside the house.

I moved alongside the hedges to get closer. I didn't pick up any other voices. I squatted down and waited for someone to appear.

"I can't tell," the voice said.

"Go look at the fucking car!" Taylor ordered.

A stocky, five-foot-ten white male rushed to the hood of the car.

"I don't see nobody."

"What?"

"Ain't nobody in there." Then he spotted the open door and made a move toward it.

"What're you doing?"

"Door's open. Maybe he fell out."

"Something's not right." Taylor was slinking back into the house.

As the stocky guy climbed over the hood to the driver's side of the car I made my move toward him. His awkward movements covered mine. By the time he realized there was somebody else with him, I'd delivered a right to his kidney and plowed his head through the window's glass. Like Tom had said, get it over quick.

I sprang to the hood of the car and leapt inside the doorway. There was Goffrey Taylor, waiting. Whatever shock the car crashing into the house had had, it had worn off. Taylor was settled and ready, almost anticipating the confrontation as much as me.

"Told you I'd find the motherfucker who set my brother up! You want to do me, do it yourself!"

"Won't be the first time." He glared at me with those cold blue eyes. "Not even the first time tonight," Taylor said, and we both knew exactly what he meant.

I lost control, lashed out and swung wildly at him. Taylor surprised me with his swiftness. He ducked under my swing and jammed his shoulder into my ribcage, knocking the wind out of me and driving me backward. The lights in the house were very dim and it was hard for me to gain my bearings. I dropped my weight on Taylor hoping to drive his head into the marble floor. He pulled up before his head hit. I was younger and stronger, but he was extremely cagey. Taylor lunged at me. I caught him by his shirt, stuck my foot in his chest and flipped him. We were back on our feet quickly, but Taylor made a break for the stairwell. I pursued him. Taylor hit two steps and I stumbled on them in the near darkness. He caught me with a foot to my chest. The force of it knocked me backwards. I tumbled down the stairs, landing on my back at the bottom. I only saw the first punch he threw. He hit me two or three more times at least. That's how many flashes of light I could vaguely recall before falling into unconsciousness.

As I faded back into consciousness, the first thing I heard was the sniveling of someone next to me. My eyes were unfocused as things were still hazy, but sitting next to me was Brent Peters. He looked to have been roughed up pretty good. He was tied to a heavy piece of iron patio furniture by Taylor's pool. The pool was lit at night and I could see the bottom, but couldn't gauge how deep it was. When I tried to move, I realized that I was bound to the same patio furniture.

"Good to have you back with us," Taylor said.

The stocky guy, whose forehead was now bloodied, walked up to me and struck a vicious blow to the side of my head. I struggled to maintain my faculties while Taylor expressed his enjoyment by laughing at the shot I'd taken. He was wielding a brass fireplace poker in his right hand.

"Peters! Stop crying. Fucking sissy." Taylor looked at me. "You got balls. You're stupid as hell. You're gonna die; but you got some balls. Unlike that coward over there. Heat gets to him and he freaks. By the way, I don't appreciate how you treated my boys locked in the trunk of their car. Neither one of them can stand up. Where are my files?"

"What files?"

"Don't play dumb. This sniveling bastard told me all about it. Didn't you?" he said to Peters. Peters just put his head down. "Where are the flash drives?"

"I never had any flash drives."

"Uh-huh." He turned his attention to Peters. "Brent, you wouldn't lie to me, would you?" He pointed the poker at him.

"No, Goffrey, I wouldn't lie to you. I never have," the ever-obedient child said, looking up at Taylor.

"No. No, you wouldn't, but you would give me up and try to run away. Everything I am on a flash drive. You even told him I was responsible for Sheila's death. C'mon, Petey, you know we…"

"I never touched her," Peters whimpered.

"You might as well have; you were right there with me." Taylor watched Peters put his head down again. "You knocked on the door and got her to open it. I reached through, cracked her in the temple and she went out like a light. When she woke up, she found herself tied up, much like you two are right now. I had on rubber gloves and this poker in my hand. She smelled so good even though she was fucking that monkey. I tried to kiss her gagged mouth, but she wouldn't let me. I whacked her in the head a few times. It was what she wanted so I gave it to her. And you tried to convince me to stop. I wasn't stopping. It was too late by then. I told you to get out of there and you didn't waste any time leaving. Fucking sissy. When we were alone, I tried to kiss her again. The bitch tried to bite me through the gag in her mouth. That fucking whore wanted to be with Warren instead of me. I started smashing her face and head with this poker. Just like this." Taylor unleashed a series of brutal blows to Peters' head.

I couldn't bear to watch and turned my head. I heard the sound of the poker slicing through the air and landing against flesh and bone. There were at least nine swings of the poker before Taylor relented. If Peters was still alive, he wouldn't be for much longer. Without any warning, Taylor kicked his chair. The sound of iron skidding against concrete before the chair fell into the pool. I turned back and helplessly watched Peters' limp body topple headfirst into the water and hit bottom. It was about five feet deep where he went in. Then Taylor came up behind me. Coming here was a bad idea that had progressively gotten worse.

"That's my best friend. Imagine what I have in store for you."

"You killed her yourself; nobody did it for you. Then you let Warren die for that, because you couldn't have her." I was trying to buy a few more minutes of life while I was trying to grasp what he had just said about Sheila and what he'd done to Peters. He'd admitted his own hands had Sheila's blood on them and I had witnessed for myself what he was capable of.

"Fuck Warren. If you think that's something, you're going to love this. It's a great story for you. It takes place at Emerald Woods. A man and woman are killed. A jealous ex-lover kills her and her man. The ex-lover is a drug-dealing pimp. Hell, he used to pimp his old lady out. I know. Your mama was my first piece of ass when I was fourteen. It was some good shit and she kept lettin' me come back for more. Now, I ain't gonna tell you I'm your daddy or no shit like that. See, I was in the car outside the trailer when I heard them gunshots. I was scared. I got out of the car and started to run and hide, but then I doubled back to the trailer. I went through the window in the kitchen. The whole place was dark. I pulled a butcher knife from one of the drawers and I heard another gunshot. You were in the bedroom, crying and Warren was curled up on the floor like a baby. He was completely out of it, in a daze. The gunshot shattered the lock on the door. I waited and as soon as that door opened and Warren's daddy stepped inside, I stuck that fucker in his heart. He fell back instantly. I couldn't stand the way that bastard treated Evelyn. I stabbed him a couple more times just for that. I picked Warren up, put him on top of his daddy, and put the knife in his hand. All his life, that stupid son of a bitch thought he did it."

Taylor started laughing. "Two set-ups in one lifetime."

"You motherfucker!"

"You got that right. Now tell me where the fucking flash drives are and we can be finished with this."

"I don't have them. They're out of my hands. Kill me, so what? That's it for me, but you'll spend the rest of your life in prison no matter what."

Taylor started to wind up that poker, but something stopped him. Things started to move in slow motion. In the midst of the chaos, I could hear a whistling noise and the sudden meaty sound of flesh being pierced. I looked over and the stocky guy was clutching at his throat and blood was rushing out of his neck in spurts. He dropped to the ground next to us, still clutching his neck.

"Back up off my dog before you get some of this hot shit."

Chuck? There was no mistaking that voice. I couldn't pinpoint the direction, but I knew it was Chuck. I thought for a second that everything was going to be okay until I felt myself being thrust forward into the pool. Goffrey was pushing me in. I took a last gasp of air before I hit the water. I was lurching headfirst into the pool. If I cracked my head on that cement bottom, that was going to be it for me. I tucked my head into my chest and tried to force myself into a spin that would land me on my back. I succeeded and hit bottom back first. The impact forced some air out of my lungs and I fought to keep what I had left in. I struggled with the ropes on my arms and legs in an attempt to free myself and I heard another splash, maybe it was Chuck. I looked to see who or what it was. Even though the pool was lit, it was difficult to make out who it was until the body sank down a few inches from me. It was Taylor, his eyes were wide open, but there wasn't any movement from him.

I was running out of oxygen fast. Hitting the bottom of the pool knocked more air out of me than I had realized. My lungs were beginning to burn. I could feel my concentration drifting. I could see Denise and my mom. My mind started racing, a succession of memories flashing by: Chuck and Jason; winning my first big case; being sworn in after I passed the bar. Denise watching me with pride. When I played ball in college, when I was hurt, Denise was there, too. My mind raced back to childhood. Everything was gray and beginning to dim to black. That's when I saw my father. He didn't open his arms to me.

He stuck out his right hand to me, palm out, signifying to me that he would let me go no further.

"Hold on, Boy!" my daddy said to me.

I barely heard the splash, but I felt myself being lifted up. At least I was moving in the right direction. Couldn't tell if it was reality or if it was what I was feeling as I made my exit from this life. But then my head broke the water.

"Breathe, Jimmy! Breathe, damnit!" Chuck barked in my ear.

I took a deep breath, coughed and gagged as some water came up with the breath. I hadn't been down there long enough to get water in my lungs, but the water told me I wasn't far from it.

"I got you, man. You all right?"

I couldn't speak. Chuck lifted me to keep my head out of the water. He held me by the chair and all. I just nodded my head to respond to him. Chuck started walking me to the shallow end of the pool where the water was only three feet deep.

"See if you can keep your head up." Chuck eased me back down. The water was up to my neck, but I was okay. "I got him, but I need to make sure he's done."

Chuck walked back down to the deep end and stood there for two minutes, staring at one spot. He slowly started backing away. It had been almost three minutes since Taylor had hit the water and Chuck was satisfied that he was dead.

Untying the ropes from around my hands was a little

difficult for Chuck. I thought it might be due to the rope's immersion in the water, but when I got a good look at him, I realized he was shaken and unnerved by what he'd just done. I was so glad to be alive, that I hadn't thought that Chuck had been forced to kill two people to save me.

"You straight?" I asked him.

"Yeah." Chuck took a deep breath. "Shit, ain't nothin like the shooting range." Then he dismissed the thoughts.

"I owe you everything, Chuck."

"No shit." He gave me a smile. "Ain't gonna be no more of this for you."

"I was going to say the same thing."

Chuck finally freed my hands. The sounds of sirens could be heard in the background and getting louder. He started working on the ropes around my chest.

"Police got great timing, don't they?"

Once my arms and chest were free, I stood with my legs still tied to the chair. I got to the edge of the pool and started to climb out. Chuck lifted the chair for me to help me out of the pool.

"They put some knots on your dome, didn't they?" Chuck said, looking me over.

"Yeah, they did. I thought you had gone back to Charlotte."

"Never did. I knew better than to listen to you. Been staying close to you since you told me to get lost."

"And you waited until I was at the bottom of that pool to do something."

"Shit, I got here in just enough time to do that. I got held up at the prison when the execution was over. I ran up on your Jeep. Tow truck was gettin ready to pull it out, but there was no sign of you. I asked the tow truck driver about you and he didn't know who had made the call; he just had a pick up. That's when I decided to make my move here."

"You didn't see Tom?"

"Never saw him."

"He was tied up in his car about half a mile away. You had to pass by it."

"Never saw it. I had one thing on my mind—getting here."

The sirens got louder and louder until I could see the reflection of blue lights off the front of the house. We got my legs free and Chuck pulled up a chair and sat down.

"You know we in trouble, right?" Chuck said, shaking his head.

"What are you talking about?"

"Look around, dog. You got three men dead. One tied to a chair in the pool, another one in the pool with three holes in him."

"Three?"

"If I didn't miss. And a third one lying poolside with a bullet hole in his throat. All of them white. You got two men alive, soaking wet, sittin' poolside, chillin'. They black. What you think?"

I contemplated. "We're in trouble."

The police cuffed us and led us out, and we were happy to comply. We walked out of the front of the house and were promptly read our Miranda Rights. The police cautiously entered the house and began to secure the area. I warned them about Dice and Cat being in there somewhere. Tom stepped out of one of the squad cars accompanied by the police captain.

"Pruitt, you two all right?"

"If we could get these cuffs off?" Chuck said.

Tom nudged the officer next to him and he ordered two cops to remove our cuffs.

"This here is Captain Owles. That's James Pruitt, Johnson's brother and Chuck Mays," Tom said, pointing us out. "Pruitt's the one I got the flash drives from."

"What's it look like in there?" Owles asked.

"Three dead. Two in the pool; one beside it," Chuck said.

"One of 'em Taylor?" Owles asked.

"Yes, sir," Chuck replied.

"Well. We're going to evaluate the situation and we'll have to ask you some questions, so just sit tight."

"Yes, sir," Chuck and I said together as Captain Owles went to join the investigation.

We leaned up against the squad car. He looked at me, and I knew there was an *"I told you so"* coming, but it never came. We were confident there would be no charges brought against us.

"I should'a let him take you downtown," Tom said. "You

know how I looked when that tow truck driver found me with my ass up in the air?"

"Sorry about that, Tom. Your head all right?" I didn't know what else to say.

"Don't worry about it," he said, rubbing his temple. "I understand. Let me get you fellas some blankets. After what you two survived, it'd be a damn shame to die of pneumonia." He smiled at us. Then and there, I decided that for a redneck, Tom Carter wasn't too bad a guy at all. And if there was ever anything that he needed from me—he had it.

33

The police finished questioning us at 6:15 a.m. They informed us that no charges would be brought against us and we were free to go. Tom waited with us until we were released.

He had made three copies of the flash drives. He was leaving one set with the police, taking one set to the FBI, giving me the two original drives and keeping one for himself. That was fine by me. As far as I was concerned, the point was moot. Putting Taylor away wasn't an issue anymore. He was dead. I would clear Warren's name of Sheila's death and everything else would sort itself out. It was time for me to go home. There was unfinished business for me there.

Tom extended his sympathy to me before I left. He told me if there was anything that he could do for me, to let him know. I assured him I would hold him to that and if there was anything he needed from me, I would be there for him, too. I owed my life to him and Chuck. You only have so many mistakes you can make in your life before you pay the ultimate price. Last night I had used up two of them. We shook hands and left. I hoped he understood how grateful I was. My respect for him was immeasurable.

Tom told me where I could find my Jeep. He was going to see to it that the windshield was fixed and have it checked for additional damage. He'd give me a call when it was ready. Chuck and I stopped at the body shop so I could get everything I needed out of it before we hit the interstate back to Charlotte.

"That Tom's straight, ain't he?" Chuck said.

"True. Sometimes you never know about people."

"How's that?"

"Tom. When I first met him, I never would have taken him to be the kind of man he is."

"I feel you."

"C., I had him pegged as a card-carrying member of the KKK, wearing Klan T-shirts and waving the rebel flag. That was based on the way he looked, the way he talked. Should've known better, as many times as people have made assumptions about me. That wasn't him at all. He took it upon himself to look out for me when he didn't have to."

"Somebody had to. You was loose, dog."

I took my time before responding to Chuck. "You're right. So was Denise, and my mom…even Jason. When I was lying flat on my back, at the bottom of the pool tied to that wrought-iron chair, that realization became crystal clear. I should've listened, but couldn't hear anybody at the time."

"If it was me, I don't know if I'd'a heard you, either."

"Hey, man, I'm sorry about that family thing."

"I know where we at." Chuck hesitated before his next question. "You gonna call Denise?"

"Man, I want to, but she's not feeling me right now. We got into it pretty heavy."

"Trust me, dog, she'll talk to you. She was worried about you. Didn't want nothin' to happen to you. Wasn't that nobody thought you couldn't handle yourself; you were just goin' about it all wrong. These cats was blood raw." He smiled. "You just couldn't really see what you was fucking with. You was just trying to do right by Warren. We know that; Warren knew that. You fought the good fight and I'm saying it if nobody else don't, we're all proud. Your father would be, too. The glory ain't always in the winning; sometimes it's in the battle."

"My dad used to say that."

"I know. Where'd you think I got it? I was with you a couple of times when he said it." He reached over, opened the glove compartment and pulled out his cell phone. "Call Denise. That's a battle you can win."

I called Denise. The phone rang once and she picked up. Usually she was in deep sleep at that time, but she was very much awake. I told her I was on my way home.

She asked me, "What happened? Are you okay?"

I looked at myself in the mirror and felt some of my

knots and bruises. "I'm a little scuffed up, but I'm fine, mostly. I'll tell you everything you want to know when I get there."

"Have you talked to Chuck?"

"Yeah. Actually, I'm riding with him."

"Why?" Her concern was already starting to grow.

"I needed to leave my Jeep to get some work done, but everything's fine."

"You sure?"

"Yeah. Baby I...I love you."

"I love you, too," she replied.

"Yo, dog! You can go through all that when you get there," Chuck said loudly enough for Denise to hear.

"Tell Chuck to go to hell!" Denise fired back. "And tell him thank you for being there."

"I will." She would soon find out how much she had to thank him for.

I hung the phone up with the promise that I would see her as soon as I got home.

"Denise wanted to make sure I told you thank you," I said.

"Sheeiit, she could tell me that her damn self." Chuck laughed. "You a lucky man. You know that woman's down for you. You need to handle that business, man, for real. You know I always got your back, and I know you don't need me to say this, but she got your back and every-thing else. You came through this for a reason. You saw it all the way to the end and that's good, but it's time for you to get back to your life. Leave them streets to me. Okay?"

"You don't have to worry about me. I've had enough to hold me for a good long while."

Chuck dropped me off at my house just after 9:30 in the morning. It was the happiest I'd been to see my house in a long time. True to my word, I called Denise and asked her to come over. She agreed, but I could tell she had had enough time to stop worrying and was working on being mad. There was some explaining to do.

I took a long, hot shower to help myself relax. I was trying to work the soreness out. The beatings I had gotten playing ball didn't compare to the way I was feeling now.

The doorbell rang while I was getting dressed. Looking out the window, I could see Denise's car in the driveway. She's pissed, I thought. Usually she pulled into the garage and came into the house. I grabbed the Friedman's box that I had set on my dresser and put it in my pocket. Regardless of what had happened, today would be the day. I rushed down the steps and opened the door.

"Hey, baby." I couldn't wait to hug her. Put my arms around her and pull her close to me, feel that rhythm and know we were still connected.

"Hello," she said matter-of-factly. She walked right past me and never looked for a second.

I closed the door and turned to face her. She stopped in the foyer. Her back was to me.

"Are you okay?" I asked. What had I done that for?

"No, I'm not. Do you know what I've been going through the last two days? I wasn't able to eat or sleep, or concentrate on work. If it wasn't for Chuck and Jason letting me know you were okay, I don't know what I would have done." She still had her back to me. "I was scared something was going to happen to you, and when I tried to talk to you about what was going on with you, you shut me out. You wouldn't let me help you work through it. You've never done that before, and that hurt."

"I'm sorry, Denise."

"You're damn right you're sorry!" She turned to face me. She was seeing my face for the first time in a couple of days. "Oh, my God!" She was horrified.

My left eye was already turning black and some of the abrasions were scabbing up. And if my jaw wasn't swollen, it sure felt like it. Tears flooded Denise's eyes and I could see the pain I had caused her. What I was feeling physically didn't amount to a tenth of what she was feeling emotionally. She reached her hands out and put them gently on my face, pulled me to her and kissed my left eye. I felt her teardrops as they struck my cheek.

"Are you okay?"

"I'm fine. I'm sorry I hurt you."

"What happened to you?"

I told Denise everything I could remember, starting

with yesterday morning in the trailer park at Emerald Woods. The time I had spent with Warren, thinking I would save his life, and the execution. I told her about Cat and Dice, and how Tom saved my butt. Then finally, there was Taylor's house. That was where the bulk of my injuries had occurred, and I gave her every detail, refusing to be vague about any of them. I told her that three people had been left dead at Taylor's house. Taylor, Peters, and another guy whose identity I didn't know. Chuck helped me out and was responsible for me being here today. I told her the details of Sheila's death. It blew her mind to find out that Taylor had killed Warren's dad and let Warren believe all of his life that he was responsible for his father's death. That fact disgusted Denise to no end. She detested Taylor as much as I did.

"Warren spent his whole life and died thinking he had killed his father?" Denise said.

"That's what Taylor wanted him to think. Warren never got over that and he never spent too much time talking about it when I was with him."

"Had to be hard for him." Denise paused. She was a reporter. "Wait a minute, let me back up for a second. You said that Taylor, Peters and some other guy were dead, and that Chuck saved you. Where were you when Chuck saved you?"

That was the only detail I had been hoping to avoid. "I was at the bottom of the pool, tied to a chair like Peters was." I could see that this made Denise uncomfortable, but she was developing an enormous gratitude for Chuck. "When I was trapped under there, wondering if I'd survive, I saw my life flashing by, just like I've always heard people say. I saw my dad and mom, I saw Chuck, Jason, even Warren. I saw college, football, everything. And through all of it, I saw you with me. I should've never shut you out. You were right. Everybody was right. I needed to handle the situation in a smarter way. I wasn't ready to deal with my father's death, but I am glad I tried to do what my father wanted. My approach was off balance. That became clear to me as I started blacking out at the bottom of that pool. Then my father came to me; he was the only thing I could see. He stuck his hand out to stop me and he said hold on and that's what I did. I see you and I know why I'm here. With you, I have balance. I needed to go through some of this by myself to find that out. My soul is anchored by your love." We were still standing in the foyer. I led her into my living room. I wanted to propose to her in the same type of room that my dad had proposed to my mom.

I bent down on my right knee and took a deep breath. Anticipation was building for Denise. She knew where this was headed.

I pulled the box from my pocket. "This is something I intended to do two weeks ago, before everything got turned upside down." I opened the box so she could see the ring. I saw her lip quiver, and I took the ring out.

"This isn't fair," she said. Her eyes filled with tears again, but these were tears of joy.

"It's not fair, but it's right." I put her left hand in my left hand, and held the ring in my right. "Last night, I was lucky, but if you take this ring, I'll know I'm the luckiest man on Earth. Denise, I love you. Please marry me."

Tears ran down Denise's face as she looked at me. Slowly, she kneeled down in front of me. When we were face-to-face, she raised her ring finger and held it out for me.

"Yes."

I carefully slipped the ring on her finger, looked into her beautiful face, wiped the tears from her cheeks, kissed her, and held her in my arms. I could feel her heartbeat, her rhythm helping me find my balance. That, no doubt was right. Anything I ever did, any move I'd ever make, she would be the first to know about it.

34

It was Sunday. Three days after Warren's execution and I was back in Asheville. Some very good friends and family surrounded me. Most of the friends were old ones. One was new. That was Tom Carter.

Over the last couple of days, I had apologized to anyone and everyone I might have slighted when I was shutting people out. Everybody was more forgiving than I would have hoped for and sympathized with me.

Word of my engagement to Denise spread quickly among all the people closest to us. Congratulations were bombarding us from everywhere. It even preceded our arrival in Asheville. We came here this weekend to share our engagement with my mom and friends but that wasn't the only reason. I was starting to move on and I needed to finish some business at home.

I contacted Tom late Thursday. I wanted to know what the state was going to do with Warren's remains. He informed me that since Warren had no next of kin, they would bury him at a graveyard reserved for members of the penal institution. I let Tom know I had a place for him. It was a place that my mother had suggested.

I sat in a chair between my mom and Denise. We were at a gravesite. It was our family plot. Chuck, Shelly, Jason, Beverly, Mr. Otis, Mrs. Bernice, Uncle Johnny and Aunt Sarah surrounded us. Even Aunt Martha made it. Tom volunteered to escort Warren's body from Raleigh to Asheville.

Sitting next to my father's grave, it was difficult listening to the eulogy the preacher gave but mom believed it needed to be done. No one here, with the exception of Tom, Chuck and myself, had ever spoken to Warren at all. But the people that were here, they were here out of love and support for my mom and me.

Everybody watched as they lowered Warren to his final resting place beside my father. Nobody moved.

"Thanks for letting him rest here, Mom."

"It's only right. He's family. He didn't have anywhere else to go. Nobody else to take him. I regret that he never had a place with us in life. At least now he can rest with us and know that he is loved and will be missed."

Listening to my mom, the strength and compassion she had never ceased to amaze me. Denise held my arm a little tighter after hearing that. The qualities that I admired and respected in my mom were the same ones that had made me fall in love with Denise.

I inhaled that spring mountain air. I looked at Warren's plot, and my father's grave. I knew some days would be better than others and some days would be worse, but with the friends I had and the two women that I loved, all who'd helped me find balance, I would be just fine.

ABOUT THE AUTHOR

J. Leon Pridgen II is originally from Aberdeen, Maryland and makes his home in North Carolina, with his wife and two children. His journey in life so far has taken him from the jungles of Panama with the 82nd Airborne Division, to Hollywood film sets starring opposite Halle Berry and Omar Epps in the college football film, *The Program*. He has performed in numerous theatrical productions. One of his best and most challenging experiences was working with Director Larry Leon Hamlin on the August Wilson play, *Fences*. He continues to work as an actor, writes screenplays and performs as a voice talent.

Leon hopes readers of his first published novel, *Hidden Secrets, Hidden Lives*, will enjoy his sophomore foray into the literary world with *Color of Justice*. You may visit the author at Facebook.com/jleonpridgenii.

DISCUSSION QUESTIONS

1. After reading *Color of Justice*, what is your feeling about capital punishment?

2. Have you or anyone you know ever been wrongly convicted of a crime? If so, what was the outcome of that situation?

3. Have you ever been placed in a situation that has caused you to behave erratically and out of your normal character the way that James does in *Color of Justice*? How did you find your way back?

4. If you were Denise, in what different ways would you have handled the situation with James? Would you be willing to deal with a man that you witnessed emotionally shutting down?

5. Have you ever discovered secrets within your own family? Would you agree that the more you attempt to hide a situation, the more power you are giving to it?

6. Do you have a family member that is like Aunt Martha or are there people in your family that would consider you to be like Aunt Martha?

7. Is Warren a sympathetic character or did he deserve the outcome of his situation?

8. Do you believe that the lives of James Pruitt and Warren Johnson would have been altered if they were raised in a different environment? Is it safe to assume that the environment we live in can shape our character?

9. Have you ever found yourself judging a book by its cover, as is the case with James and his initial impression of Tom Carter?

10. Do you believe the energy that we put out into the universe, whether it is positive or negative, comes back to us?

11. If you were to rewrite the end of this novel, how would it end?

IF YOU ENJOYED "COLOR OF JUSTICE," BE SURE TO CHECK OUT

HIDDEN SECRETS, HIDDEN LIVES

BY J. LEON PRIDGEN II
AVAILABLE FROM STREBOR BOOKS

CHAPTER 1

A secret past was the fuel to Travis Moore's fire. It woke him up in the morning and daily, he put more distance between it and himself. It had driven him to the success that he now enjoyed as the internal auditor for Home Supply Emporium, a large hardware firm. His past also had led him to where he was now driving, the Garrison Addictive Disease Center.

Travis had volunteered a few hours a week at the center and its adolescent treatment program. The last two months at work hadn't allowed him to stop by Garrison. Home Supply was on the verge of going public, and Travis recently had uncovered an embezzlement scandal that could threaten its initial public offering. Today, he had to make an exception. Jarquis Love, "Baby Jar," was in trouble.

Baby Jar had completed Garrison's treatment and recovery program two months ago. Travis had heard that Baby Jar didn't last a month back home before he was deep into the street life again. Travis wanted to find out what had gone wrong.

He followed South Boulevard from downtown until he came to Fremount Road and made the right turn leading to Garrison Center. Its appearance had changed over the last three years since Travis had started volunteering his time there.

Garrison used to strictly be a treatment center for adults with alcohol and drug abuse. Gradually, it increased its emphasis on drugs, as the problem exploded among teens. Two years ago, Garrison applied for, and was granted a government license to operate a federal halfway house. So, in came the barbed-wire fences, wooden gates, and the division of the Garrison campus to separate federal inmates from adults in treatment. Adults were separated from the adolescents.

Garrison was lucky so far. There hadn't been any incidents among the federal inmates or the residents of the treatment center. Having teen males in close proximity to federal inmates begged for something to happen. If young men had observed what happened in a federal halfway house, they might have gotten the impression that doing time wasn't so bad.

Travis parked his brand-new black Volvo in a nearby empty lot. The administrative staff and the counselors called it a day between 4:30 and 5:00 p.m. It was a few minutes after seven o'clock. Travis wasn't able to get away from work as early as he wanted. The evening counselors were the only staff remaining at the facility. He had considered not going; he would be interrupting Group. Travis was compelled to find out about Baby Jar.

Group was when all adolescents gathered in a circle for a joint therapy session monitored by two or three counselors. A teen would read the story of a recovering addict and relate his personal issues to the story as best he could. Then the counselors encouraged everyone to share their thoughts if they wanted. If anyone had an issue they wanted to discuss, the floor was open to them. Other peers offered advice to help that individual develop coping skills for various problems.

Travis removed his tie, loosened his collar, and tossed the tie into the passenger's seat before stepping out the car and feeling the cold January night. He cinched up his black cashmere overcoat as he watched his breath escape into the night air.

Slim heard the bell ring. He nodded to his co-worker to inform him that he would answer. He then excused himself from the group meeting and entered the staff office.

Slim opened the door for Travis. He looked over his shoulder through the glass; he knew most, if not all, of the teens would have their eyes in the office instead of their circle. Slim glared at them and this did the trick; all eyes went back to the group. Not one of them dared to cross Slim. He was a dark-skinned, well-defined, two hundred forty-pound man that moved with the grace of a panther. He was hard on the teens because of their experiences and potential outcome. Clarke "Slim" Duncan would do anything he could to help them.

"Come on in the house, Travis." After the kids were admonished with his eyes, he turned his attention back to Travis.

"What up with you, man? Face all tore up, chest all swoll. Little cold weather didn't make you that hot, did it?" There was silence and they stared at each other. Travis was looking up at the six-foot-seven imposing figure in front of him. Slim was looking down at his five-foot-ten frame. It was a game of Chicken to see who would be the first to flinch. "What? C'mon, you ain't mad for real?"

Slowly, the corners of Travis' mouth began to arch upward and gave way to a devilish grin. "Gotcha!" He extended his hand.

"Ah, bulls…" Slim glanced over his shoulder again. "No, you didn't." He took Travis' hand and shook it. "I was scared, though." His voice was much lower.

"Damn straight, you scared." Travis dropped his voice as well, to be mindful of the teens.

"Scared I was going to have to mop up this floor."

The new linoleum tile was laid last week and the floor was spotless. Travis was confused.

"Mop the floor?"

"Yeah, from the blood you were about to spill 'cause of me bouncin' yo' butt off this floor." The two laughed.

"Don't let the height difference or this suit fool you." Travis unbuttoned the coat and took it off. He held it out for Slim.

"That's nice. What is that, cashmere?" Travis nodded. "That thing will be on the floor if you're waiting on me to hang it up." Slim moved his head in the direction of the coat rack. "There you go, playa."

"Had to try it." Hedging past Slim to hang up his coat, he caught a glimpse of the group in session. "Got another half-hour?"

"Nah, I think they're going to finish pretty soon. Running a short one tonight; they had a long day."

Travis spotted a few new faces since the last time he was at Garrison. "What you got? Twelve, thirteen?"

"Fifteen. Two of them are missing."

The group started to get up. "Group's about to end. You want to hit this Serenity Prayer?"

"Most def'."

The two walked out the office and joined the group. The seats were in the middle of the floor in a circle. The teens stood in place and draped their arms over one another's shoulders. The enclosed circle represented unity; when one couldn't stand on his own, there was a shoulder to lean on. Donny, one of the co-workers, and the two absent teens came in the main entrance in time to join in. The circle opened for them and welcomed their return. The group always welcomed anyone; the only requirement was a desire to stop drinking or using drugs.

In unison, the group began to recite, "God, grant me the serenity to accept the things I cannot change, the courage to change the things I can, and the wisdom to know the difference." The group disbanded and proceeded to take the chairs from the circle and stack them in the room that contained vending machines.

When Group was over, Donny and Rob, two of the counselors, divided them into smaller groups of six teens each to take to a Narcotics Anonymous meeting. Three of the newest teens had to remain at the center to complete their individual study. They weren't eligible for outside meetings yet. They were doing book work on drug and alcohol addiction.

Slim sat in the office, keeping a watchful eye. He filled Travis in on Jarquis Love. Slim could tell that Travis was unusually disturbed.

"You all right?" he asked. Travis nodded his head. "You know the drill, man; it happens."

"I thought that kid was ready to change his life. I mean, I spent a lot of time with him."

Slim was analyzing his answer. He was trying to get a handle on where Travis was coming from, and why this was hitting him so hard. He'd hung out with Travis. He'd even been over to his house. He knew what kind of work had brought him to Charlotte. But he was unaware about his past. Sometimes, he felt like he didn't know Travis at all. This was one of those times. If Travis didn't volunteer information, Slim didn't ask. He felt they were fortunate to have someone like Travis come by on a volunteer basis. They didn't want to make him feel unappreciated.

"What was it about him?"

"Don't know. Guess I saw a lot of myself in him."

"How's that? He's from the hood. He didn't come from Ballantyne Country Club."

"Neither did I," Travis responded flatly. The silence echoed in the room. "I grew up in a neighborhood like his. Neighborhood…a housing project. I was smart like he is; hell, he's a lot smarter than I was. I saw education as my way out. I thought he would, too."

"Some people need a bigger push than others."

"I thought I was pushing."

"Did you share your story with him, Trav?"

"Yeah…some."

"Some?" Slim's voice was full of skepticism. "Let me guess, you left the past vague. You showed him the big picture, but you didn't let him see the fine print."

"What?" The question was simply habit. Travis knew what he meant.

"You don't give it up, man. Your past. You're wide open about your life now, what you do, and who you are. But you keep that other life to yourself. I heard you talk about school at N.C. State, living in Raleigh, the job that brought you here three years ago. Telling him you lived in a project doesn't mean shit to him. In his mind, you don't see the same stuff he sees, unless you give it to him. If you don't, it's cool. I respect that. Some things might be better kept secret. You can make that choice. You're an example; shit, probably the exception. I'm saying all this because we want to keep you coming around here. We appreciate it and, sooner or later, some of these cats will, too. Just don't be disappointed when one of them doesn't."

"I feel you." Travis was pensive, pondering his next question. "So, how did he get himself out there so fast?"

"Donny said he was down with a hitter. Cat named Kwame Brown, but they call him Bone."

Travis was staring at the floor listening to Slim, but his body became rigid at the mention of the name Kwame "Bone" Brown…a name he'd hoped he never hear again.